By ELIANA WEST

Be the Match
Dreidel Date

Published by DREAMSPINNER PRESS
www.dreamspinnerpress.com

BE THE
Match

ELIANA WEST

DREAMSPINNER
PRESS

Published by
DREAMSPINNER PRESS

5032 Capital Circle SW, Suite 2, PMB# 279, Tallahassee, FL 32305-7886 USA
www.dreamspinnerpress.com

Be the Match
© 2024 Eliana West

Cover Art
© 2019 L.C. Chase
http://www.lcchase.com
Cover content is for illustrative purposes only and any person depicted on the cover is a model.

Trade Paperback ISBN: 978-1-64108-745-2
Digital ISBN: 978-1-64108-744-5
Trade Paperback published May 2024
v. 1.0

To Be the Match and their lifesaving work pairing mixed-race donors with patients in need. www.https://bethematch.org

Acknowledgments

This book would not be possible if it weren't for the Dreamspinner team. Thank you for your encouragement, kindness, and support. I am so grateful to have found such a warm and caring place I can bring my characters home to.

To Carmen Cook: You are truly one of the strongest and bravest people I know.

To Damon Suede: Thank you for always keeping me motivated. I am so happy to have you in my life professionally and as a trusted friend.

CHAPTER ONE

"I'M SORRY, Mr. Blackstone, I know this is hard to hear so soon after losing your wife," the pediatric oncologist said in a sympathetic and yet emotionless tone. Ryan figured when you'd given the news enough times, it became easier to say—but not easier to hear. "I concur with my colleagues that have reviewed your son's case. Leo has leukemia."

What was it about that word that sounded like a snake wrapping itself around his son's tiny body? Ryan gripped the arms of the chair and tried to slow his heartbeat.

"What happens now?"

The doctor steepled his hands. "We'll begin a course of chemotherapy. The first round will be aggressive. You need to be prepared for that."

"When will we know if it's working?"

"Months. Or longer. We can't predict how a body will respond."

Ryan walked out of the doctor's office in a daze. His wife's passing in a car accident three weeks ago was terrible. Now the same accident that spared his son led to a horrible diagnosis. It was an unspeakable thought, but it was a slight consolation that he could give up the role of grieving husband and focus on Leo.

A widower for three weeks and he was already sick of the sad looks and words of comfort everyone around him wanted to offer. He couldn't stand another person telling him how perfect he and Lindsay were together and what a wonderful life they'd shared. Ryan didn't know what wonderful was supposed to be, but it wasn't what he shared with Lindsay. His sister Stephanie had introduced them. Lindsay and Stephanie were sorority sisters at Florida A&M. Lindsay McKenzie was vivacious and driven. His parents thought she was the perfect partner for him. His sister insisted they were right for each other. He proposed to get people to stop asking him when he was going to rather than as a declaration of love. At first it was convenient that Lindsay took over their homelife so he could manage the rapid success and growth of Blackstone Financial Technologies. As time went on, her insistence on living a lifestyle that matched her vision and goals strained their relationship.

Seattle Children's Hospital was only three miles from his home but separated by Lake Washington. Thankfully, the traffic on the 405 bridge wasn't heavy in the late morning, and he pulled up to his home on the other side of the lake in less than twenty minutes. He looked up at the white façade, and the usual feeling of gloom settled over him. Ryan hated the house Lindsay insisted they had to have. The white stucco exterior with massive columns, arched windows, and terra-cotta roof belonged in California, not in the Pacific Northwest. He'd wanted a midcentury home or maybe a classic Craftsman. Lindsay insisted they needed something grander where they could entertain clients and her society friends. The right home, the right friends, belonging to the right country club, those were the things that mattered to Lindsay. It made her a better fit with his family than he was. His parents and sister adored Lindsay, their values all aligning: money, social status, and conservative views.

Ryan parked in the three-car garage next to the house, his gaze flickering to the empty spot where Lindsay's Mercedes had been. She had insisted a $150,000 SUV was necessary when she became pregnant. Not because it was supposed to be safer, but because it's what her friends with kids drove. *That* car still sat at the far end of the garage. No, it was her other Mercedes, the one she insisted she needed for her "fun" car, that couldn't withstand a head-on collision with a street racer who lost control.

His sister pounced on him as soon as he walked in the door. "What did the doctor say?"

He took a moment to steady his voice. "He confirmed the diagnosis. Leo will need to start chemotherapy. We have an intake appointment with oncology at Children's tomorrow."

Blue eyes the color of the lake outside the window, a match to his own, became bright with unshed tears. "Oh no. Have you told mom and dad yet? Lindsay's parents?"

"No, I'm still trying to process the diagnosis myself. Where's Leo?"

"He's upstairs in his room with Mrs. Lieu." Stephanie's mouth turned down. "I think now it's even more important to hire a proper nanny for him. Mrs. Lieu is hardly qualified for the special care Leo is going to need."

"Stephanie, I'm not going to have this argument with you again. Mrs. Lieu has worked for me since before I married Lindsay. She's a part of this family and an excellent caregiver for Leo."

Stephanie's mouth pressed into a thin line. This wasn't over. He could see the fight in her eyes. Most of the time it was easier to give in than argue, but Mrs. Lieu's presence in his life was nonnegotiable.

His sister never warmed up to the Vietnamese woman he'd hired as a housekeeper. When he first started his company, he bought a building in Seattle's Belltown neighborhood and used the lower floors for office space. Ryan turned the top floor into an apartment. Mrs. Lieu kept him fed and the condo from turning into a pigsty while he worked a grueling schedule at his financial tech company. It was the one thing he put his foot down with Lindsay. Whatever home they moved to, Mrs. Lieu came with it. Lindsay realized with Mrs. Lieu around she had more time for her friends and hobbies, so she let go of any complaints. The two women weren't friends, but as long as Lindsay stayed out of Mrs. Lieu's way, and as long as Mrs. Lieu kept the refrigerator stocked with salads, there was peace in the land.

Ryan ran his hand through his hair and heaved a sigh. "Look, Steph, I have a lot to take care of before tomorrow. I've got to rearrange my schedule, and I'll be working remotely from now on."

"I've got it. I'll take care of work for you. Don't worry about that."

"I didn't mean to snap at you before. It would be good for Leo to have a nurse. I can't ask Mrs. Lieu to care for Leo and manage the house. That would be too much for her."

Ryan never intended for Mrs. Lieu to help care for Leo and handle everything else she did: cooking, cleaning, and managing scheduling for the gardener and other services. He knew she would if he asked. Mrs. Lieu was more of a grandmother figure to Leo than Ryan's own mother was. She loved Leo as if he were her own grandchild, and Ryan loved her for it, but it was too much to ask of her. He'd been putting off hiring a nanny. At first he thought he could manage everything on his own, but he was already overwhelmed trying to keep up with work and Leo's care. His sister was right; as usual she was looking out for him, and he needed to remember to appreciate it.

His sister's expression brightened. "I'll call an agency tomorrow."

He should take care of it himself, but he already had so much to deal with, it would make it easier to let Stephanie take care of it.

"Thanks, sis."

Between Mrs. Lieu and his sister, Ryan could focus on what he loved, writing algorithms and studying numbers. He'd always had a natural affinity for math. He happily spent hours analyzing data. Before he received his degree in data science and his master's in business and technology, he sold the first banking program he'd written. A year after college he created an investment algorithm that every investment firm in the country was clamoring to buy. Instead of selling the program, his parents encouraged him to start his own firm, and Blackstone Financial Technologies was born. With his family's involvement and Stephanie's leadership in sales, they grew the company to nearly a billion dollars in revenue last year. He started life in a well-to-do family; now they had wealth that meant anything they wanted or needed was always within reach. Ryan didn't care about the money, but he enjoyed the convenience it brought to his life and happily shared it with his family and Lindsay's parents. Being able to use work he enjoyed to take care of his loved ones reassured Ryan he was fulfilling his role in the family. Oldest son, big brother, responsible husband and father. All the roles he'd been taught a man was supposed to fulfill. For a long time, he'd believed it was enough to make him happy. Since Lindsay's death and Leo's diagnosis, he'd started questioning what brought him happiness and a sense of fulfillment.

"We'll talk tomorrow. Don't worry, Ryan, everything's going to be okay." Stephanie gave him a quick peck on the cheek and said goodbye. Thankfully, she didn't mention prayer, as Lindsay's parents constantly preached. Their answer to everything was faith, sometimes putting prayer before common sense.

Ryan went upstairs to Leo's room. His heart stuttered the same way it had every day since the accident. The dark shadows under Leo's eyes, against his pale skin, seemed to get worse with each passing day. He was going to lose his light brown curls, the fine strands a mixture of his parents'. Every day Ryan got to look at bright blue eyes that matched his own and brought him more joy than he'd ever thought possible.

"Daddy!" Leo pushed himself out of Mrs. Lieu's arms and threw himself into Ryan's arms.

Ryan's little boy wasn't as energetic as he used to be, and the bruises he'd gotten in the accident still stood out against his skin. Ryan picked him up, Leo's small body clinging to him like a spider monkey.

"Did you have a good day, buddy?"

Leo's face fell. "I didn't get to go to school again, Daddy."

Ryan rubbed his back, sharing a worried look with Mrs. Lieu over Leo's shoulder. "I know. But you know what? Summer is almost here. What do you think about starting summer early and not going back to school?"

"Because I'm sick?"

"Yeah." Ryan's voice became thick. "You're going to have to spend some time at the hospital, but I'll be there with you the whole time."

"But Mommy won't be there, will she? Because she's still dead."

A child's wisdom could bring great joy or break your heart. There wasn't a parenting book in the world that could prepare you for that. Ryan decided early on that honesty was best when it came to what happened to Lindsay. Her parents could weave fairy tales about how she was an angel in heaven, but Ryan didn't want to create a narrative that would give his son false hope.

"You're right. Mommy won't be there. But I'll be there, and Mrs. Lieu will be there, and your Aunt Stephanie. Maybe Grandma and Grandpa McKenzie will come for a visit, and grandma and grandpa Blackstone too."

"Grandpa McKenzie only wants to talk about football." Leo pouted while he fastened and unfastened the top button on Ryan's shirt.

"I think Grandpa McKenzie likes to share about his job with you."

"I don't want to play football or be a football coach."

"And you don't have to. You can be whatever you want to be when you grow up."

Leo wiggled out of his arms. Ryan put him down gently, and he went to play with his Legos.

Mrs. Lieu gestured for Ryan to follow her out to the hall.

"What did the doctor say?"

"The same as all the others: leukemia. He's going to have to start chemo right away."

The diminutive woman's face fell. After a few moments, she nodded. "Okay, then. I'm going to cancel my trip home."

"I can't ask you to do that. You've been looking forward to visiting your family in Vietnam for months."

"You aren't asking. I'm telling. You send me every six months. Missing one trip won't be a sacrifice. Besides—" She tilted her head, gazing up at him, her dark eyes beginning to brim with tears. "—you are my family too. You were there for me when I lost my beloved Danh nine years ago, and I'm going to be here for you now."

He'd argue, but once Mrs. Lieu made up her mind about something, she became a heavy stone that would not be moved without a significant amount of effort. It was a different kind of stubbornness than his sister's. Mrs. Lieu always listened, and her determination came with motherly love. Knowing she would be with them for the tough days ahead was a relief.

"Thank you, Su." He rarely used her first name. Calling her Mrs. Lieu seemed to fit. It might have seemed more formal, but it was always said with genuine affection.

She patted his cheek. "We'll get through this one day at a time. It's not going to be easy, Ryan, but I'll be here."

SLEEP ELUDED him again that night. Sleepless nights had become a constant after Leo's diagnosis. Ryan would need every moment of rest he could get to make it through the tough days ahead. Fear kept his eyes open. Staring at the ceiling, Ryan couldn't stop replaying the meeting with the doctor in his head. At the first signs of the sky lightening to a dull purple-blue, Ryan left his bed. It would be another rainy spring day in Seattle. The gray reflected his mood. He walked into his home office and sat down at his desk with a heavy sigh as he made preparations for what was to come. As weary and heavy as he felt now, Ryan wasn't prepared for the brutal days, weeks, and months ahead fighting to keep his son alive.

CHAPTER TWO

"MR. MCKENZIE, can we read *How to Catch a Unicorn* for story time tomorrow?"

Dylan looked down at the little girl wearing a sparkly unicorn T-shirt. Emily was going through a serious unicorn phase right now and requested the same book every day.

One of the boys slapped his forehead with an exaggerated moan and grumbled, "Again."

Dylan sympathized. They'd already read *How to Catch a Unicorn* several times. If he didn't navigate the situation carefully, an all-out war was going to break out between the pro-unicorn kids and the rest of the class.

"Do you remember what we talked about yesterday?" he asked.

Emily nodded with a solemn expression.

"It's nice to give new things a try, right?" he asked, and his class all nodded. "We're going to read other unicorn books and dinosaur books. I've got books picked out that I think each one of you will enjoy, and you might even discover something new that you didn't know you liked." He leaned forward and said in a loud whisper directed at Emily, "There might even be a book with a unicorn that's friends with a dinosaur and a shark." Two of his other students sat up, their eyes sparkling with excitement. Dylan stood up and clapped his hands. "Okay, everyone, it's cleanup time. We have ten minutes before the bell rings."

Ten minutes passed in a flurry of desks being cleaned, lunch boxes collected, and backpacks packed.

He ushered his students out the door to their buses and waiting parents, sending each student off with high fives, hugs, and waves.

Alexis, his fellow second-grade teacher, sidled up next to him, waving to her departing students with a huge grin while she said out of the corner of her mouth, "We're in the home stretch. Only six more weeks."

"You're antsy since you'll be lying on a beach in Mexico."

"Don't forget the margarita part. That's important. Two weeks of lying on a beach doing absolutely nothing," she said with a sigh of contentment.

"Are you sure about that? You know your husband is adventure boy. How many parasailing and zip-linings has he booked?"

"We came to an agreement after Costa Rica. I get to lie on the beach, and he gets to go do all that other stuff," Alexis said with a dismissive wave of her hand. "What about you? What are your plans for the summer?"

Dylan shrugged. "Nothing specific. Hanging out, maybe take surfing lessons."

"One of Dan's buddies at the firehouse is into surfing, and he's super cute too," Alexis said, waggling her eyebrows, her dark brown eyes sparkling with mischief.

"Maybe."

Firefighter super dude? It didn't exactly sound like his type, but after an extended dry streak, he was open to the possibilities.

Alexis looked at her watch. "Ooh, gotta go. Drinks tomorrow night?" she called out over her shoulder.

"Yup, I'll be there."

Alexis might talk about lying on the beach doing nothing, but Dylan knew she was as energetic as her firefighter husband. She was a ball of energy packed into a curvy five-foot frame. They'd bonded on their first day as new teachers and as mixed kids: Dylan half Black and half White, Alexis half Mexican and half White. But unlike Dylan, Alexis came from a big family who loved unconditionally.

Dylan collected his jacket and messenger bag from his classroom. As he headed toward his car, he waved to the kids still on the playground for after-school care. He often stayed behind with them, volunteering to provide tutoring for kids who needed extra help. It was important to him to pay it forward and provide the kind of loving learning environment he'd benefited from. Dylan did his best to follow in the footsteps of the one teacher who'd changed his life, the teacher who was there for Dylan on his darkest day. Mr. Cooper had given him the support and guidance that allowed him the chance to have his own classroom.

It was Mr. Cooper who found him in the school library after the last bell the day his parents kicked him out. He'd gone to the library because he didn't know where else to go. Everything Dylan owned was in a duffel bag resting at his feet. Mr. Cooper—Kevin—and his husband, Carl, took him in, helped him become an emancipated minor, and became the parents he chose. It wasn't easy in his Kentucky hometown. Football, faith, and God were the only things that mattered. It helped that Kevin and Carl lived in the next town over, which was a little more tolerant of a gay couple. Dylan didn't go back to the school where his dad coached football and his sister was the queen bee of the cheerleading squad. Instead, he elected to finish high school online while attending community college at the same time.

Kevin and Carl didn't just take him in, they also provided a safe space where he could explore his own sexuality. Even though he hadn't been ready to tell anyone, his parents found his journal. The football coach couldn't have a gay son, and his mother wasn't willing to risk her position as head of every committee in their church. And that whole thing about twins having a special bond? Dylan would argue with any sociologist that was bullshit. He and his sister Lindsay may have been born a few minutes apart, but sharing a crib in the hospital was the only time they were ever close. When they found his journal, his parents gave him two options: conversion therapy or get out. He left.

His parents told people he ran away. Apparently that wasn't enough. Dylan's parents wanted to make sure he completely disappeared. He learned later that they'd added to the story, saying he'd died of an overdose. What was the point of disputing the lie? Kevin tried to refute it for him, but no one in their small town was going to believe Dylan's parents were anything but upstanding members of the community. The truth was in some ways it was easier for Dylan to go along with the lie and disappear. He never wanted to go back to that small town filled with people who had small minds. He might never find a place that truly felt like home, but Dylan knew that place would not be his childhood home. Dylan got to disappear, Arlene and Clay got to play the role of worried parents who tried and failed to keep their son from a life of sin to the hilt. And Lindsay became the tragic sister who lost her twin and was indulged and pampered even more as a result.

Dylan drove a few miles from his school to the Venice High School parking lot and parked. Switching his messenger bag for a small duffel bag, he headed toward the pool, flashing his membership card as he went inside. He emerged from the dressing room a few minutes later in a pair of tight, dark burgundy swim briefs. Stopping at the edge of the pool, he adjusted his goggles and swung his arms in a circle a few times before he dove in. With steady strokes, he sliced through the cool water. Most of his life with his family consisted of being criticized for his lack of athleticism. It wasn't that he didn't like sports; he didn't like the right kind, according to his father. He'd loved swimming. Carl encouraged his love of water and introduced him to kayaking. The summers he spent camping and kayaking with Kevin and Carl helped him understand there were no right or wrong activities for a man. When he moved to LA after college, one of the first things he did was seek a public pool where he could swim laps. Not only did swimming keep him in shape, but it acted as therapy for him. The steady rhythm of kicks and strokes soothed him, especially on days when he allowed himself to think about his past. Dylan wasn't the muscle-bound jock his father wanted him to be, but he'd developed a toned physique. The California sun added a golden hue to his light brown skin and a smattering of pale freckles across his nose.

When his arms turned to jelly, he hauled himself out of the pool and rested on the edge for a minute to catch his breath.

"Good form, Dylan," the lifeguard called from the tower. "You sure you don't want to join the swim team?"

Dylan peeled off his goggles and squinted up at the man with a mop of curly blond hair, sitting in the lifeguard seat. "Nah, I'm good."

As much as he loved to swim, Dylan hated competition. Another strike against him from his father's point of view.

"Any other team you'd like to join?" the lifeguard called out with a cheeky wink.

He laughed, shaking his head. The same lifeguard had been hitting on him since he joined the pool. He was cute, with dimples to go along with his charming smile and sparkly blue eyes. But two bottoms did not make a top or a lasting relationship, and Dylan wasn't interested in fooling around just for the sake of fooling around.

"No thanks," he replied in a singsong voice.

The lifeguard threw his head back with a hearty laugh.

Even though he walked to the dressing room on tired, shaky legs, Dylan felt good. The tension released, his body was loose and relaxed. He was hungry from the exercise, though, and as he jogged up the stairs to his tiny one-bedroom apartment, his stomach growled.

The apartment wasn't fancy, but it had been remodeled, and he kept it tidy, with no crosses on the walls or football trophies on the shelves.

Instead, a paddleboard stood propped against the wall next to a coatrack by the front door. Several carefully chosen pieces of vintage furniture were scattered around, and a large Persian rug in shades of cream and blue anchored the space. Leftover chicken and rice with green beans waited for him in the refrigerator. While he warmed his dinner in the microwave, he unpacked his lunch bag, rinsing out the containers to be refilled in the morning.

Instead of a dining room table, Dylan opted for a desk in the small nook of the kitchen. He didn't entertain that much, though not because he didn't have friends. Since he moved to LA, he'd gathered a small but close group of friends. He'd never been a big party guy. His club years were brief, a couple of years in college. Small dinners, movies, and game nights were more his style.

He liked his solitude. Even as a child, when his sister was out playing with the other neighborhood kids, Dylan preferred to read in the tree house his dad built in the backyard. He wondered if the tree house was still there. He didn't look for news about his parents and sister. It opened old wounds he wanted to keep closed. Dylan heard Lindsay got married right out of college, and that was about it. After his parents kicked him to the curb, no one reached out to him—no aunts, uncles, or cousins. His family would rather maintain their illusion of perfection, which looked like one of those holiday movies on a family-friendly network. His last connection to his hometown was Kevin. Kevin and Carl moved to Providence, Rhode Island, right after Dylan graduated, cutting any lingering connections.

Being rejected by his family hurt. But he was happier now. He had a good life with friends and chosen family. Accepting his parents' demands would have destroyed him. Conversion therapy would have hurt much more than losing his family did.

He ate his dinner at his desk while he reviewed his lesson plans for the rest of the year. There were less than two months left and he knew those would fly by with end of year projects and standardized tests. Dylan was already dreaming of summer hikes and camping trips.

He cozied up under the covers with his current read—a male-male romance set on Vancouver Island where a ranger rescues a lost hiker. Dylan sighed, burrowing deeper under the covers when the characters shared their first kiss. His friends teased he was a hopeless romantic, with his collection of romances that ranged from Jane Austen to Damon

Suede. They didn't understand that he clung to his favorite genre because each story was about hope and a happily ever after. Holding on to those two things helped him get to where he was now. The hope that things would get better—and they did—and the dream that he'd have his own happily-ever-after someday. That one was a little harder to believe in, so he read about fictional ever afters, the kind he wanted but secretly feared he might never have.

CHAPTER THREE

RYAN LOOKED down at his sleeping son, his bald head peeking out from under the covers. Ryan tucked the quilt around Leo and kissed his forehead before he left the room. He went down to the kitchen, where he poured himself a glass of whiskey, downed it, and refilled his glass. The amber liquid burned a trail into his belly. He set the glass on the kitchen counter and pushed it away with a heavy sigh. No amount of drinking could numb the shock of the news he'd received today.

For many months now Ryan had watched helplessly while his son underwent chemotherapy without much improvement. When Leo's medical team recommended stem cell treatment, Ryan knew his son's mixed-race heritage made finding a suitable bone marrow donor a challenge. Discovering the Be the Match registry had given him a sliver of hope, even though the chances were slim. That hope turned to shock when a match turned up immediately. Leo's doctors were thrilled but confused. Why hadn't Ryan let them know Leo had an uncle?

He hadn't told them because he didn't know. The doctors confirmed the results of the original sample Leo's uncle gave while Ryan called a private investigator.

Within an hour, he had a cursory report on Dylan McKenzie, Lindsay's twin, whom Ryan had been told died tragically from a drug overdose. Dylan was anything but the troubled child Lindsay and her parents had said he was. A second-grade teacher in Los Angeles, he wasn't a drug addict, just gay. Which, to Lindsay's parents, was worse. According to the report, Lindsay's brother had a small group of friends and lived a quiet life. Dylan became emancipated after being kicked out. He was given a full scholarship to Wesleyan University and graduated with honors, receiving bachelor's and master's degrees. What Dylan had achieved without the support of his parents was impressive as hell. And had Ryan seeing red.

With shaking fingers, he reached for his phone and called his mother-in-law.

"Was a lie more important than the life of your grandson?" he asked without a greeting when she answered.

The beat of silence on the other end of the line told Ryan everything he needed to know.

"I don't know what you're talking about," Lindsay's mother finally said, doing her best to sound innocent.

"Don't. You lied to me. Your son did not succumb to addiction. He's a schoolteacher in LA, and he's a match for bone marrow donation. A perfect match."

His mother-in-law sucked in her breath. "He can't be a donor. He's gay. He'll give him diseases far worse than the cancer. Prayer works, Ryan. You have to give it time. God will work miracles—"

"Shut up."

She tried to continue in a placating tone. "Ryan, you're upset. It's understandable. Don't forget we lost our only daughter."

"And could have killed your only grandson."

"You don't mean that."

"Yes, I do. I didn't agree with your religious beliefs when I married Lindsay. I put up with it because I wanted to respect my in-laws. But I didn't realize that you would put hate over the life you pray about in your fake church on Sunday. Let me make this clear. I will not let you kill my son with your hate."

If there was a response, he didn't hear it. Ryan disconnected and slammed the phone onto the counter. He squeezed his eyes shut, taking a deep, shuddering breath. His phone vibrated with an incoming call. Seeing Lindsay's father's name flash on the screen, he rejected the call. He may have been able to forgive the lie, but not endangering Leo's life.

He bypassed the massive living room that he never used. With its cream-on-cream-on-cream décor, it looked more like a doctor's waiting room than a home. With two exceptions, the same theme flowed throughout the house. Only his office and Leo's room showed any sign of life. When he reached his study, Ryan sat in the leather armchair by the window with a view of Lake Washington. He'd put his foot down when it came time to decorate his office. He chose a soft gray for the walls. A rug in swirling shades of gray and brown covered the wood floor. In the center of the room, his desk sat facing the window. It was a custom-made piece by a local artisan, crafted from cherry wood and meticulously sanded and polished. But it was the chair by the window where he spent most of his time in this room.

Ryan opened his laptop and read through the private investigator's report again, then clicked on the link to Dylan's Instagram account. A picture showed him sitting on a low chair, reading to a group of children all looking up at him with rapt attention. He had an animated expression, holding the picture book up so the kids could see the brightly colored illustrations. Ryan studied Dylan's face. There was no mistaking the resemblance to his wife. Dylan shared the same warm brown skin that was the legacy of their Black father, along with light hazel eyes. Only his eyes appeared kind and compassionate, where Lindsay looked at every situation with a calculated gaze, wondering how to take advantage to her benefit. Dylan wore a blue-and-green plaid button-down shirt with a pair of khakis. Ryan knew from the report that Dylan was a swimmer, and it showed in the glimpse of his toned arms where his sleeves were rolled up.

Ryan snapped his laptop closed and let his head fall back. The man who'd been rejected by his wife and in-laws was now Leo's best hope. Ryan could only hope that Dylan didn't hate them so much he'd refuse to help.

THE NEXT morning, the lake and surrounding waters of Puget Sound disappeared as his private jet ascended into the clouds. Ryan's skin itched under the starched white shirt he wore. He reached up to loosen his tie and dropped his hand, clenching his fist. He hadn't worn a suit since Lindsay's funeral. He hadn't left Leo's side since then either. This journey was important and the only reason he'd allowed himself to leave. Two and a half hours later, he touched down in Los Angeles. He checked in with Leo's nanny and nurse, Rebecca, while he waited for Dylan's school to let out for the day, watching the school children play with a pang of anguish. Would Leo ever be able to play like that again?

There was a text from his sister that he ignored. Stephanie and his parents insisted that he'd been too harsh with Leo's grandparents, and he couldn't cut them out of Leo's life. That wasn't Ryan's intention, but he was still angry. Arlene and Clay had crossed a line that would make it impossible for Ryan to ever trust them again.

Children started running out of the school with an end-of-the-day burst of energy, dragging backpacks and shouting with glee. A now familiar face appeared. He recognized his wife's twin from the pictures he'd seen, but also from the resemblance. Ryan jumped out of the back of the black SUV when he saw Dylan heading toward his car.

"Excuse me, Mr. McKenzie?"

Dylan stopped, those light hazel eyes gazing at Ryan curiously. In person, they were much more striking, almost golden in the sunlight, with flecks of dark brown and green.

"Can I speak with you for a moment?" Ryan asked.

Dylan hitched the strap of his messenger bag higher on his shoulder. "I'm sorry, are you a parent? I don't think we've met before. If you'd like to talk about your child, I'm afraid you'll have to make an appointment."

His voice had a warm quality. He spoke firmly but without a trace of frustration or disapproval for being intruded upon.

"I'm here to talk about my child, but not one of your students." He held his hand out. "I'm Ryan Blackstone, your sister's husband."

Dylan's smile faded, and his face paled. His gaze flickered between Ryan's hand and his face, clearly wary. When Dylan did take his hand, it was brief, but his grip was firm.

Dylan swallowed, his Adam's apple bobbing in the slim column of his throat. "Does my sister know you're here?"

Ryan froze. It hadn't occurred to him that Dylan wouldn't know about his sister's passing. Suddenly the conversation took on a gravity beyond his original urgent mission.

"Is there somewhere we can talk?"

"There's a coffee shop a few blocks away." Dylan shook his head when Ryan gestured to his car. "I'll meet you there. You can follow me."

Ryan kept his eyes on the red compact car ahead of them over his driver's shoulder. He'd been worried Dylan might try to escape when they'd left the school parking lot, but as he'd said, Dylan pulled up in front of a coffee shop not far from the school. Ryan jumped out and waited on the sidewalk while Dylan parked. His expression remained wary as he came toward him.

"What would you like?" Ryan asked when they went inside.

"I'll get it," Dylan replied, the warmth Ryan had heard in his voice when he introduced himself tempered to a polite coolness.

Ryan followed Dylan to a table in the corner. As soon as Dylan set his tea on the table and settled in his seat, he asked, "Why are you here, Mr. Blackstone?"

"There is no easy way to tell you this. Your sister was killed in a car accident."

Dylan gasped. He blinked rapidly, his eyes filling with tears that he did not allow to fall.

"When?" he asked in a shaky whisper.

"Almost a year ago."

Dylan dropped his chin to his chest. When he lifted his face, the pain in his expression had Ryan wanting to reach across the table and take his hands in his. "I see," he said with a tremor in his voice.

"Dylan, I'm sorry. I didn't know that you were alive. Your parents...." His jaw ticked. There was no point in doing any more harm than necessary.

"I know what my parents told people about me." He gazed out the window with a wistful expression. "It's funny. I always thought I'd know if something happened to her. Like I would feel some kind of twin bond or something. I should have known better. That bond was severed a long time ago." He looked at Ryan again. "You didn't have to come all the way here to tell me this."

"That's not why I'm here. Lindsay and I had a son, Leo. He survived the accident, but when they examined him after they found out...." He swallowed past the lump in his throat. "Leo is sick. He has leukemia."

Dylan's eyes grew wide with realization. "I'm the match." He drew in a deep breath. "I got the call a couple of weeks ago. They asked if I was willing and available to donate, but they didn't tell me anything else."

Ryan nodded. "You're the match. A perfect match. I didn't know what to think when the doctor chastised me for not letting them know Leo had an uncle who might be a candidate for a donation. I was—shock wasn't the word for it."

"Do my parents know you're here?"

"They know I've found you. They don't know I'm here."

Dylan frowned. He stared down at the cup, twisting it between his hands. "This is a lot to take in," he finally said.

"Will you do it?"

He looked at Ryan, his eyes narrowing. "Of course. This isn't about me, my sister, or my parents. I would never make a child pay for the lies they told." He cleared his throat. "I signed up for the registry, wanting to help anyone who needs a bone marrow transplant. I didn't put conditions on my donation. That's not who I am."

The steeliness in his voice couldn't hide the pain. Ryan couldn't imagine how it would feel knowing your parents would go so far to deny your existence. He was still having a hard time with the realization that Lindsay's parents' lie could have killed Leo.

Ryan exhaled. "Thank you."

"There are still tests—"

"I've made all the arrangements to have the tests expedited." He glanced at his watch. "How long will it take for you to pack?"

Dylan put his hands up. "Whoa, whoa, I'm not going anywhere with you. I can do the tests here. When it's confirmed that I'm a match, I'll come to Seattle for the transplant." He leaned forward and pushed his cup aside before clasping his hands in front of him. "I get the impression that you are used to being able to wave money around and get whatever you want, but that isn't going to work with me. You'll get my help, and my bone marrow, but you don't own me, Mr. Blackstone."

He met the anger he saw in Dylan's eyes with his own indignation. The saying "the truth hurts" came to mind. Ryan thought that was the root of the irritation he was experiencing. He'd assumed he could dictate what would happen by treating this as a situation he could manage with a big check. For the last few years he'd found he could avoid conflict and make his life easier by spending money, and with his son in jeopardy, Ryan was unwavering and unwilling to make any compromises.

Dylan's expression softened. "These last few months must have been.... I can't imagine what you've been going through. I'm sorry for your loss. I'll do everything I can to help, but that doesn't mean I'm going to drop everything and come with you to Seattle. It's not fair to my students to leave them unless I have to, and right now the next steps don't require me to be there."

"Don't you want to meet your nephew?"

Dylan looked surprised. "You—I assumed you wouldn't want me to see him."

"He's your nephew. Of course I want you to meet him."

"What did my parents say?"

"I haven't spoken to your parents since I found out about you. I've been too angry," he confessed. "It doesn't matter what they think, Dylan. I want you to have a relationship with Leo."

Dylan pressed his lips together. "I just found out my sister is dead and I have a nephew. I need some time. I'd like to meet my nephew, I would. It's just... I'd gotten used to the idea of not having any family and now...." He shook his head.

Ryan fought the urge to reach across the table and take Dylan's hand. His own family might frustrate him, but they were there for him.

"Okay," Ryan said with a resigned sigh. "Once we get the results from the next round of tests, we'll figure out the next steps."

Dylan nodded, standing up as he offered Ryan his hand. "Thank you. I'm sorry we're meeting this way."

THE DAYS that followed his meeting with Dylan seemed endless while they waited for the test results. Ryan spent most of them haunted by the pained look in Dylan's eyes and wanting to replace that hurt with something else. He'd felt off-kilter since meeting him. He hadn't been sure what to expect, but it wasn't someone who was the complete opposite of his twin. Someone whose eyes filled his dreams after Ryan returned home.

CHAPTER FOUR

"YOU'RE A MATCH."

The words hung in the air, weighted with more than the medical science. Dylan was a perfect donor candidate for his nephew. Nephew. Family. He fought back another wave of tears. He'd cry again later. Right now, he needed to pay attention to the doctor sitting across from him at the small table in the consultation room.

The simple swab on his cheek that Dylan gave for the Be the Match registry was repeated, along with more extensive blood tests. Dylan worried that his sexual orientation would disqualify him as a donor, but the doctor reassured him that gay men had been able to donate stem cells since 2015. Dylan sent a silent thank you to Mr. Cooper for insisting on educating him about safe sex practices. The first time he took Dylan to a gay men's health clinic, he'd been too embarrassed to take condoms out of the large bowl at the reception desk. Kevin gave him a stern lecture, saying there was no shame in prioritizing his and any potential partner's health. Hookups weren't really his thing, but he wasn't a monk either. He'd been tested recently and tested again as part of the matching process.

"What happens next?"

"You'll need to go to Seattle and meet with the transplant doctors. The procedure will also take place there."

"How long will it take?" Dylan calculated the time off he had. He hated the idea of leaving his kids with a long-term substitute. The school year was over in ten days. Could he wait that long? Could Leo? His nephew's health came first. If he had to leave now, he would.

"Recovery time will vary. Can be a day or up to a week. This will be a surgical procedure, and you will need time to recover. The procedure will weaken your immune system. It usually takes at least two weeks after the procedure to make a full recovery. And you'll have to be monitored for any sign of infection." The doctor referred to the tablet in his hand. "According to the oncologist's notes in Seattle, Leo will be ready in about a month."

Dylan swallowed, his already frayed nerves ticking up a notch. He nodded. "Okay."

He stopped at the reception desk when he finished with the doctor. Fishing his insurance card out of his wallet, he said, "I haven't received any billing information yet. I don't know if my insurance covers this kind of thing. Can you tell me how much I'll owe for the tests?"

The receptionist pulled up his information on her computer and smiled at him with a shake of her head. "You don't owe anything, Mr. McKenzie. Mr. Blackstone has taken care of everything."

"I see." Dylan bit the inside of his cheek. He should be thankful, but it irked him the way Leo's father kept orchestrating things without consulting him or including him in the decision-making. He didn't like feeling like a pawn.

His phone rang on his way home. Ryan Blackstone's name flashed on the screen. Based on his experience so far, he figured Ryan already knew about the latest test results. Since he'd refused to leave with Ryan that first day, the one thing Dylan agreed to do was sign a HIPAA waiver so Ryan could stay updated on the test results. It made it easier for Dylan too, wanting to keep his involvement with Ryan to a minimum.

His meeting with Ryan consumed Dylan's thoughts. Ryan Blackstone wasn't what Dylan expected. He'd always thought Lindsay would end up with some jock, not a tech guy. A tech guy with mesmerizing blue eyes and dark blond hair that enhanced his chiseled face. At first glance, Ryan seemed tall and imposing. But there was a look in Ryan's eyes that exposed a vulnerability Dylan hadn't expected. He could see the anguish and fear in their blue depths, and it made him want to know what else Ryan might be holding back.

Dylan hit the speaker button as he carefully maneuvered through LA traffic back to his apartment.

"Have you made your decision?" Ryan said in a clipped voice.

"You know what my decision is." His voice became thick with emotion. "I won't deny my nephew a chance to grow up."

There was a pause before Ryan replied. "Thank you." He cleared his throat and continued in his brusque business tone. "I have the jet on standby to bring you to Seattle. I've called your school and they'll arrange for a sub—"

"You did what?" Dylan ignored the honk from the car he cut off as he pulled over to the side of the road.

"You don't have to worry. I've made all the arrangements. A car will pick you up—"

"No. This is not how it's going to work. You don't get to take over my life so you can get what you want. I may be nothing more than a bundle of cells to you, but I am a person with a life that I have worked hard for. I won't let you control it. You don't need me in Seattle until two weeks before the donation. I'm going to finish the school year with my kids, and then I will come to Seattle."

"Dylan, I don't think you understand."

"I understand." He cut Ryan off. "Your son has leukemia, and I can make him better. You control a lot of things, but you can't control science and time. Leo needs time for his body to be ready for the procedure. When I get to Seattle won't change that." Dylan drew in a steadying breath. "I found out I have a nephew I didn't even know existed. I need to figure out where I'm going to stay while I'm in Seattle. Someone to water the plants and bring in the mail here. So you need to back off and let me figure this out."

"I'll arrange a service to take care of your apartment while you're gone, and you'll stay at my house when you're here."

Dylan clenched his jaw. Ryan had completely ignored what he said.

"I won't come until the end of the school year." They'd argue the rest later.

Following a lengthy silence, Ryan finally spoke. "Fine," he said and ended the call.

Dylan dropped his head to the steering wheel with a muttered curse. He removed the phone from its holder and dialed the contact that was always at the top of his list.

"Dylan. Carl and I were just talking about you. We were thinking about coming out to see you this summer. What do you think?"

"Hey, Dad."

"What's the matter?"

He'd called to tell Kevin what was happening, but he couldn't bring himself to burden him with the news. He'd be fine. He could do this on his own, and there was no reason to worry Kevin and Carl.

"Nothing. End of the year stress, I guess. I'd love to have you visit maybe later in the summer? I was thinking of taking a few weeks and going camping when school gets out."

"Of course. I'll send you some dates. A camping trip to decompress after a busy school year is a good idea. I remember those days well," Kevin said in a wistful voice.

"How's Pops?"

"He's good. Insisting on planting more roses even though our yard already looks like a David Austen garden display."

Dylan smiled, thinking of the little gray shingled cottage his dads moved to in Rhode Island. Carl was a landscape architect and had an obsession with roses. He'd packed the tiny yard so that it overflowed with color in the summer, often making folks stop in their tracks to take pictures.

"Well the last time you and Carl went to the nursery to buy the two roses you said he could buy he came home with six, so…."

"They had the David Austen Juliet. Do you know how hard those are to find? We had to get two of those, and then they had these double yellow shrub roses that we could put in pots by the front door."

"Okay, Dad." Dylan chuckled.

"You know I can't say no to Carl," Kevin muttered.

Kevin and Carl were Dylan's role model for what a caring, loving couple looked like. They supported each other no matter what. If Carl announced he wanted to be an astronaut tomorrow, Kevin would start researching space camps. They had the kind of relationship Dylan longed for. They gave him the first glimpse of what a family should look like.

There was never a formal adoption; they'd shared a moment during dinner when he'd flown to Providence for a visit where he'd asked if he could call Kevin Dad. Both Kevin and Carl had gotten up and came around the table, enveloping him in a hug. When they'd all dried their tears, Carl asked if he could be Pops and that was it. They were Dylan's parents, his family.

Even though Dylan hadn't told him the truth, talking to his dad when he was upset centered him, as always. Dylan hung up with Kevin and drove to his school to talk to the principal.

The principal was relieved to know he wouldn't lose a teacher this close to the end of the year. Dylan would be gone for a month, the first time he'd been anywhere other than visiting Kevin and Carl since leaving college.

Replaying the conversation he'd had with Ryan, Dylan's anger returned. The man was a jerk. If he thought he could throw money around and get Dylan to do whatever he wanted, he had another think coming.

Even though he had the love and support of Kevin and his husband, Dylan knew that the only person he could ever depend on was himself.

His independence was hard fought, and he wouldn't let Ryan come in and take over his life. He would go to Seattle and help his nephew, but he wouldn't jump when Ryan Blackstone snapped his fingers.

"EARTH TO Dylan." Alexis snapped her fingers in front of him.

Dylan looked up from the papers scattered across his desk. There weren't any shouts or laughter coming from the playground. The schoolyard was quiet; all the kids had been picked up hours ago.

Alexis perched on his desk, looking at him with a frown. "What's going on? You haven't been yourself for weeks now. I've heard rumors you're leaving."

Her statement snapped him out of his daze. "No, that's not true. I'm not leaving." He pinched the bridge of his nose and sighed. "I am leaving, but it's only for a couple of weeks."

Alexis eyed him with a worried look. "Talk to me, Dylan."

Dylan peered at his friend. He wasn't planning on saying anything. He didn't want anyone to feel like he needed help—he was fine and could handle this on his own. But Alexis was stubborn and could be like a dog with a bone when she sensed trouble.

"I have a nephew." His voice quivered. "He has leukemia, and I'm his match for a bone marrow transplant...."

Alexis got up from her perch, grabbed a spare full-sized chair from the corner, and pulled it close. She sat next to him and wrapped her arms around him. "Tell me everything," she said.

Dylan told her about the phone call notifying him he was a match, leading to Ryan's visit and the events that followed.

"Why didn't you tell me this sooner?"

"I don't know. Maybe because I'm having a hard time telling it to myself. I didn't want you to worry...." He swallowed, fighting back a wave of nervousness.

"Oh, Dylan, I wish you didn't always feel you had to handle everything on your own. Gabe and I love you, and we're here for you."

Dylan rested his head on Alexis's shoulder. Alexis and her husband, Gabe, were two of his best friends. He shouldn't feel like he was burdening them, sharing what was going on with his life. It was a defense mechanism. He knew that from therapy. He had a fear of being a burden to others, afraid of experiencing rejection again. But knowing where the fear came from didn't always mean he could keep it at bay.

He sat up, wiping his eyes. "I'm sorry."

"Noting to be sorry for. Your friends want to support you, but we can't if you don't share with us. "Now—" She stood up. "—pack up your stuff and let's go. Gabe is off tonight. You're coming over for dinner, and we'll talk about what's going to happen next."

"Thanks, Alexis."

"That's what friends are for."

DYLAN COULD have kicked himself for not telling Alexis and Gabe sooner. They gave him their unwavering support in the weeks that followed as he finished out the school year and prepared to leave for Seattle. He'd meet his nephew, make the donation, and be home in a couple of weeks. He would have the rest of the summer to find that perfect, peaceful lake to kayak across.

They threw him a goodbye dinner with their small circle of friends before he left for Seattle. Dylan boarded Ryan Blackstone's private jet the following morning. As the plane circled over Seattle before it began to dip and descend into Boeing Field International Airport, Dylan fought his rising panic. Even though his sister was gone, he was about to enter her home and the memories of her that lingered there. What made him even more nervous was facing Ryan Blackstone again.

CHAPTER FIVE

THE PLANE carrying Leo's hope for the future had landed forty-five minutes ago. Any minute now Dylan McKenzie, his brother-in-law, would arrive. When Ryan wasn't preoccupied with Leo, he would replay his meeting with Dylan in LA. He hadn't been sure what to expect, but it wasn't a soft-spoken, thoughtful man with light hazel eyes that hid nothing in their depths. They reflected hurt, disappointment, shame, and pride during their conversation. His distrust was palpable and both frustrated and angered Ryan. He prided himself on his honesty and integrity. His refusal to bend the rules often put him at odds with his board of directors, but he held firm. Others might think wealth gave them the right to access resources that weren't accessible to many. Even Ryan's parents and sister tried to argue it wasn't necessary for the company to pay their fair share of corporate taxes. It was one of the few times he used his power as the majority shareholder and put his foot down. But when Leo received his diagnosis, Ryan would pull any string and pay any amount necessary to provide his son with the best care.

Ryan glimpsed the SUV coming down the narrow driveway and stopped his pacing. Shoving his hands in his pockets, he forced himself to stand still as an unexpected wave of anticipation pooled in his gut. Dylan's face was hidden behind the dark-tinted glass. As soon as Dylan stepped out of the car, Ryan saw the flash of derision in his eyes as his gaze went to the large glass-and-iron doors of the three-story structure.

What had he expected? Dylan would be dazzled by the gross display of excess? Everyone else was. People oohed and aahed over the mansion that Lindsay made sure featured in magazines. What Dylan thought of Ryan's home didn't matter. He was here now, and Leo would get better. Knowing that didn't take away the slight sting of disappointment he felt. For some reason, Dylan's approval mattered to him.

He held his hand out as Dylan walked up the steps toward him while the driver unloaded his bags. "Thank you for coming. How was your flight?" The touch of Dylan's hand sent a shock of awareness coursing through Ryan's body, catching him off guard.

"It was fine, thank you. You didn't have to use your private plane. I would have been fine flying commercial like everyone else."

"It's the least I can do." Dylan remained silent, so Ryan continued. "Please, come in."

Dylan trailed behind him as they stepped into the grand foyer, which opened up into the living room. The wall of windows flooded the expansive two-story room with natural light and unveiled a stunning view of Lake Washington.

"Would you like something to eat or drink? I thought I would give you a tour before I took you up to the guest suite."

"Is Leo here?" Dylan asked, his voice quiet, hesitant.

"He is. He's upstairs with Mrs. Lieu, our housekeeper. Would you like to see him?"

Dylan swallowed. "I would," he said in a shaky voice. He reached into the messenger bag slung across his shoulder and pulled out a package wrapped in bright blue paper tied with green-and-white gingham ribbon. "I brought him a present. I hope that's okay."

Ryan had been unsure how to navigate this moment. His parents and sister didn't think he should share with Leo who his donor was, but that was out of the question. Dylan was Leo's uncle, he was family, and he had a right to meet his nephew.

"I'm sure Leo will love it."

He led Dylan up the sweeping staircase to the other wing of the house, where Leo's room and the guest suites were located. Ryan stopped at the small table outside of Leo's room. "You'll have to wear a mask and use hand sanitizer. With Leo's immune system so weak, we have to do everything we can to avoid infection. That's the reason I had you fly on the jet. I didn't want to risk you getting sick before the surgery."

Dylan nodded as he used the hand sanitizer and put on his mask. "I understand. I've been careful since you came to see me the first time. Is there anything else I should know? Is there anything you don't want me to say to him?"

Ryan frowned. "I don't think so. He knows you're his uncle, and he's excited to meet you."

Dylan looked surprised. "He knows about me?"

"Of course."

"Does he know I'm gay?"

Was that fear Ryan detected in Dylan's voice? A fresh wave of anger washed over him at the way his in-laws treated their son. He was angry at Lindsay too. How could she treat her twin this way? Maybe he was mad at himself as well. How could he have married someone he didn't really know at all?

"He knows he has an uncle who is a schoolteacher, who is eager to meet him, and is looking forward to being a part of his life. That's all that matters. It's up to you what you want to share with him, Dylan. I trust you."

Dylan glanced away. Even with the mask on, Ryan could see the quiver of his chin. Ryan stood by, wanting to offer comfort, feeling helpless knowing Dylan wouldn't want it from him, while Dylan regained his composure. After a minute, he took a deep breath and nodded. "Okay, I'm ready."

Ryan put on his mask and opened the door. "Hey, buddy, look who's here."

Leo looked up from the pile of Legos scattered around him. "Uncle Dylan," he exclaimed, coming toward him with his arms open.

"UNCLE DYLAN, do you like Legos?"

The little boy with his arms wrapped around Dylan's legs had already wrapped himself around his heart.

His teacher mode kicked in, and he knelt down on one knee to be eye level with his nephew, looking into the same blue eyes as his father. "I do like Legos, and I'm glad you do too. But I have one very important question for you. Captain America or Batman?"

Leo's face broke into a huge grin. "Captain America," he shouted.

Dylan clutched his heart dramatically. "What a relief," he said, handing Leo the package he'd been holding behind his back, with a grateful look at Ryan for the intel he'd provided so he could select toys and books that aligned with Leo's interests.

Leo grinned at the bright blue wrapping paper with Captain America shields scattered across the surface. He sat down and crossed his legs.

Dylan didn't miss the slight wince of discomfort on his nephew's face. He sat down next to him and held out his arms. "How about you come and sit with me, and we'll open it together?"

Leo scrambled into his lap and started tearing at the paper.

"Look, Daddy, it's Legos and books." Leo looked up at Dylan, his eyes bright despite the dark circles under them. "Will you read this one to me?" he asked, holding up a copy of *Ada Twist, Scientist*.

"Absolutely."

And just like that, as if he had known Dylan his whole life, Leo snuggled into his arms and listened to the story of a little girl and her curious questions that led to adventures learning about science, technology, engineering, and mathematics.

Ryan sat on the large window seat with pillows in bright blue, green, and red patterned fabric scattered at each end. Even though Dylan couldn't see Ryan's expression behind the mask, he could see the approval in his eyes. Ryan's phone rang, and he excused himself, leaving Dylan and Leo alone.

Little fingers reached up and gently touched his cheek. "You look like my mommy." Dylan's heart squeezed painfully tight and then shattered into a million pieces when Leo said, "Mommy made Daddy sad. Are you going to make Daddy sad?"

"No." Dylan took a breath, trying to steady his voice. "I don't want to make your daddy sad. But sometimes people hurt each other without meaning to. Your mommy never meant to leave you and your daddy so soon. Your mommy and daddy loved each other, and they both love you very much."

"Do you love me, Uncle Dylan?"

Dylan squeezed his eyes shut for a second, fighting back the wave of tears threatening to spill over. "I love you very much, Leo, and I'm so glad I'm here."

"Will you read another book to me?"

Children were chameleons, little wise people one minute, laughing and carefree the next. Leo's eyes started to droop in the middle of the second book. It was a little awkward to stand up with a sleeping child in his arms, but Dylan managed it and slipped Leo into his bed, tucking a pinwheel patchwork quilt over him.

Dylan tiptoed out of the room and found Ryan leaning against the wall, his forehead on his arm. He shuddered when Dylan put a hand on his shoulder.

"I didn't realize he knew," Ryan said in a shaky whisper.

"I'm sorry."

Ryan looked at him, his eyes red and still wet with tears. "Don't be. Thank you for what you said to him. I don't know that I would have had the right words."

An unexpected urge to take Ryan into his arms and hold him surprised Dylan. What was he thinking? This was his brother-in-law, and Ryan was straight. He had no business thinking anything.

"I've learned from my students that it's better to be honest."

Ryan nodded and took a deep breath. "I'm really glad you're here, Dylan, and not because of your bone marrow. Leo needs you in his life."

"I… I can't say I'm happy to be here. Honestly, I don't know what my feelings are right now. They're kind of all over the place."

"That's understandable." He contemplated Dylan, blue eyes searching his face with concern. "I want you to be happy here, Dylan. What can I do?"

"Can we not tiptoe around the fact that this is a little weird? You lived a life here with my sister. A life that I wasn't a part of and wouldn't have been a part of if it weren't for…." He rubbed the back of his neck. "I'm sorry. I shouldn't have." He sighed.

"It's okay." Ryan gave him a wry smile. "I think we may have reached our apology quota for today. And you're right, it does feel like Lindsay's presence is the elephant in the room."

"Is what Leo said true?" Dylan didn't want to ask, but he needed to know.

Ryan's face fell. "Yes. Lindsay and I hadn't had a genuine marriage in a long time. Lately I've been wondering if we ever had a good relationship."

They'd been standing in the hall speaking in hushed whispers since it wasn't the right place or the right time. Ryan must have had the same thought. With a glance toward Leo's room, he gestured for Dylan to follow him down the hall to the open door of a nicely appointed guest room.

"You must be hungry. I didn't mean to have you arrive and jump right into family dynamics. Why don't you take some time to unpack while I get us some lunch?"

"Thanks, that sounds good."

"I'll meet you in the kitchen when you're ready." Ryan hesitated for a moment, looking like there was something else he wanted to say before he headed down the stairs.

Dylan entered his room on shaky legs. He stared at his suitcase, which had been brought up and placed on a bench at the end of the bed. Part of him wanted to grab his luggage and go back to LA and the quiet life he'd been living. But the thought of Leo sleeping down the hall had him unpacking automatically. He'd gotten used to not having family, and within a matter of minutes, Leo had gotten under his skin. How could he not feel a connection to the little boy? He may have his father's eyes, but Dylan recognized the smile Leo shared with his twin.

There was no way he could leave now that he'd met Leo. He'd given up on the idea of having a connection with anyone in his family. It wasn't only his parents and sister who had rejected him. Even his aunts and uncles and cousins had turned their backs on him. But then Leo, with his childlike grace, welcomed him with trust and unconditional love.

And then there was Leo's father. Dylan closed his eyes and took a deep breath. He could still smell the faint sandalwood scent of Ryan's cologne. If he'd seen Ryan from across the room at a bar or club, he would have been drawn to him like a moth to the flame. The image of dancing with Ryan in a dimly lit club, his arms encircling Ryan's broad shoulders or his hands resting low on Ryan's hips as they moved in sync, intruded on Dylan's brain. Standing a few inches taller, Ryan was the perfect height for Dylan to peer into his deep blue eyes, which resembled the sparkling waters of the lake outside. With a shudder, Dylan shook himself out of his daydream. He shouldn't be having sexy thoughts about Ryan. The man was his brother-in-law and straight, absolutely off-limits.

Uncle Dylan, do you like Legos? Leo's little voice came back to him.

Dylan pressed his hand over his chest, trying to calm his pounding heartbeat. He could do this. He could spend two weeks in the house his sister had lived in with her husband and not lose his heart.

CHAPTER SIX

"SMOKING ISN'T allowed here, and it would be better if you weren't drinking around Leo."

A young woman, clearly related to Ryan and sharing the same cool blue eyes, stood in the doorway of his room. She had her arms crossed and her eyes narrowed, watching as Dylan unpacked his bag.

He put the shirt in his hand back into his suitcase and straightened, looked her in the eye.

"I don't smoke. Anything," he added with emphasis. "I'm not a big drinker, and when I do drink it's usually a glass of wine or a beer, but since I am preparing to be a donor, I've avoided both. I want to be in the best physical condition I can and provide healthy cells for my nephew."

Dylan didn't miss the slight flinch when he said "nephew."

"While you're here, I hope you'll be respectful."

"I would ask that you do the same," he replied. "I don't believe we've met." He moved toward her, holding out his hand. "I'm Dylan, by the way."

She stared at him as if he were trying to hand her a snake. "I'm Leo's aunt and Ryan's sister."

Dylan held her gaze, refusing to back down from the animosity he saw in her eyes. *They need you; you don't need them. Don't forget that*, he reminded himself.

He dropped the hand Ryan's sister refused to shake. "Since you clearly aren't here to welcome me, if you'll excuse me, I'd like to finish unpacking."

He blew out a shaky breath when she turned on her heel and walked away. Yes, they needed him, but obviously not everyone wanted him here.

He abandoned the rest of his packing and wandered around the room with its stark white décor, and a pang of longing for his apartment back in Venice washed over him. Standing at the large window overlooking the sweeping lawn that led down to the lake, he took in his surroundings. He was happy to see the azure rectangle of water below. Dylan had brought his swim trunks and goggles, thinking he'd find a public pool he could use. He probably couldn't swim for a week or two after the surgery, but he could enjoy the pool now, and it would keep him away from the soulless mansion. He replayed his encounter with Ryan's sister. Her comments about drinking and smoking implied she'd heard the lies his parents had told about him and, even worse, believed them. The heaviness in his chest he grew up with returned, reassuring if depressing. He knew this feeling well—and how to survive with it. It might not make sense, but it felt familiar in an unfamiliar place.

A knock on the door pulled him from his musings.

"Do you have everything you need?" Ryan asked, looking at his half-unpacked suitcase with a frown.

"I appreciate your offer to stay here, but I'm not sure if this is a good idea." The words tumbled out of his mouth before he'd had time to formulate a plan.

"Why? You can see I have plenty of room," he said, sweeping his hand over the bedroom, which was twice the size of Dylan's apartment.

Dylan wrapped his arm around his middle. "I think it would be better if I stayed in a hotel. I don't expect you to pay," he said in a rush, throwing things back into his suitcase....

He needed to get away before the rising panic he felt overwhelmed him. Why did he think he could come here and act like this was all normal? Ryan's sister wouldn't be the only one who believed his parents' lies about him. Who else would pass judgment, disapproving of his existence?

"Dylan, wait." Ryan moved to his side and gently wrapped his hand around his wrist to stop him. "What's going on?"

"It doesn't matter. You don't have to worry. I won't abandon Leo, but I can't stay here."

Ryan let go of his wrist but didn't move away from him. "It does matter. You matter, Dylan. Talk to me."

Dylan bunched up the shirt in his hand and threw it down into his open suitcase before turning to face Ryan. "Can you honestly tell me that a small part of you doesn't wonder if the story my parents made up is true?" He held out his arm. "Do you want to check for tracks? You've seen my medical tests. You know I don't drink or smoke, but do you really believe that?"

"Whoa." Ryan wrinkled his brow. "Where is this coming from?"

"Your sister's welcome was less than friendly. It's hard enough to be here with reminders of my sister. Knowing your family believes the lie my parents told, I... this is too hard."

Ryan sighed. "My sister lost her best friend when Lindsay died. She's struggling."

"And that makes it okay for her to warn me against doing drugs around her nephew?"

Ryan looked taken aback. "No, of course not. She wasn't trying to offend you. She's very protective."

The situation was impossible. Why would he think Ryan would defend him from his sister? She was his family; he was nothing more than a donor, no matter what Ryan said.

"Give us a chance, Dylan. You can't stay by yourself after the surgery. You'll need help."

His jaw ticked. "I've been on my own for a long time. You don't know what I can and can't do."

"You're right. You can take care of yourself, but you don't have to, not this time. And I'd like to have the chance to get to know you if you'd let me."

How could anyone look at the sincerity in Ryan's blue eyes and not have their resolve falter?

"If you won't stay for me, will you please stay for Leo? I want him to get to know his uncle," Ryan continued.

"Now you're not playing fair."

Ryan's lip tipped up in a half smile. "Is it working?"

"Yeah, it is. I'll stay, but I'd appreciate it if you would make it clear to your sister that I'm not the drug-addicted junkie my parents want to pretend I am."

"I'll talk to Stephanie."

Dylan nodded, but it was an empty gesture. Everyone else believed his parents' lies without question. Would anything Ryan said to his sister really make a difference?

"You must be hungry," Ryan offered. "Come with me and I'll introduce you to Mrs. Lieu."

Dylan followed Ryan through a grand dining room, a spacious family room, and into a massive kitchen. This room, unlike the rest of the house, had warmth despite the white cabinets and gleaming white marble countertops. Dylan recognized that the warmth in the room originated from the diminutive woman with sparkling brown eyes and short salt-and-pepper hair framing her light tan face. Wiping her hands on a colorful floral apron, she came toward him with a warm, friendly expression on her face.

"I was about to come and find you to introduce myself to you if you didn't show up soon," she said.

"Dylan, this is my housekeeper, Mrs. Lieu," Ryan said, putting his arm around her shoulder, looking as proud as if he were introducing Dylan to his mother.

He held out his hand and was swept into a hug instead. Mrs. Lieu couldn't have been more than five feet tall, but that compact frame was all muscle as she practically squeezed the life out of him.

"It's nice to meet you." He chuckled, returning the hug a little more gently.

When she let go, she put her hands on his cheeks and said, "Beautiful boy. Don't you worry, I'll take good care of you. I have a nice lunch ready for you." She ushered him toward the kitchen table that sat in front of a floor-to-ceiling window with a view of the lake.

"I hope you like banh mi," she said, going to the counter, returning with two plates, and setting them in front of Dylan and Ryan.

The smell of the Vietnamese sandwiches she placed before them—crusty bread rolls spread with pesto, mayo, Asian ham, pickled vegetables, green onion, and coriander—made his stomach rumble.

"I love banh mi. Thank you," Dylan said.

"Mrs. Lieu makes the best banh mi in Seattle."

Mrs. Lieu laughed. "Seattle has a lot of wonderful Vietnamese cuisine. Ryan doesn't know what he's talking about since he'll only eat my cooking."

"But that's because yours is the best."

Mrs. Lieu rolled her eyes and went back to bustling around the kitchen.

Ryan turned to Dylan with a smile. "I don't know what I would do without Mrs. Lieu. She keeps me fed and the house running."

"How long has she worked for you?"

"More than ten years now. I hired her when I started my company. If I hadn't, I wouldn't have ever had clean laundry, and I would have starved to death."

"Ugh." Mrs. Lieu pinched her nose. "That boy would have been willing to live in a pigsty, he gets so caught up in his work."

"It wasn't that bad," Ryan said with a pout.

"Remember the time you pulled out a smoothie I made for you from the freezer and then forgot about it?"

"You're never going to let me forget that, are you?"

Mrs. Lieu laughed. "He put it in the kitchen sink and then forgot about it for two days. The smoothie fermented and then—" She clapped her hands together and made a rocket motion. "—boom, it exploded. And when the lid flew off, it left a dent in the ceiling."

"How was I to know a smoothie could become a guided missile?"

Dylan enjoyed watching the banter between the two of them. It was clear they cared for each other. This was a side of Ryan he'd never seen before. He was—Dylan searched for the right word—lighter, around Mrs. Lieu. Dylan felt like he was seeing the real Ryan for the first time. A movement outside caught his eye.

"Whoa, was that...?" The large object passed again, swooping low across the water. "Wow, a bald eagle."

Ryan chuckled. "I forget most people don't see bald eagles on a regular basis."

"Definitely not," Dylan said, watching the enormous raptor dive and swoop, hunting for its lunch. "You must love living on the water with these views."

Ryan's gaze followed Dylan's out of the window. "Honestly, I don't enjoy it as much as I wanted when we bought this house."

"Ryan spends too much time working and not enough enjoying what he's worked so hard for," Mrs. Lieu said, coming back to the table with a plate of cookies.

Dylan eyed the dock at the edge of the property. "Do you have a boat?"

"No." Ryan shook his head.

"I'd get a kayak and be out on the water every day," Dylan said wistfully.

"Would you like a tour of the grounds?"

"Sure."

With a parting wave to Mrs. Lieu, Dylan followed Ryan through a set of french doors out to the upper flagstone patio that ran the length of the house. The pool Dylan had seen from his bedroom window was on the next level, followed by a third tier that led to a massive lawn going down to the water.

"This is incredible." Dylan stood at the end of the dock, craning his neck to look up and down the lake. "I can't even see where it ends."

"It's almost twenty-two miles long."

"It's probably too cold to swim in," Dylan murmured to himself.

"It's colder than it looks, even in the summer. You can swim in it, but you should be careful. Maybe it would be better if you didn't."

"Don't worry, I won't do anything to jeopardize my health before the surgery."

"That's not what I meant. I just… I don't know, people drown out there," Ryan said, flinging his arm toward the water.

He'd lost his wife in an accident, so Dylan realized where Ryan's caution was coming from and rolled his shoulders, forcing himself to relax.

"I'm more of a pool swimmer anyway. I'd rather kayak when I'm on a lake."

"You're a water person, aren't you?"

Dylan looked out at the glimmering dark teal water. "I am. Yet another thing that disappointed my parents. Instead of a football player, they got a swimmer."

"Can I ask what happened?"

"Will knowing change anything, make any difference?"

"I'm not trying to pry. I'm still wrapping my brain around the fact that your parents would lie and keep you a secret when they knew you were out there and you could help Leo."

"Prejudice isn't rational. People can justify anything if they want to."

"How did they find out you were gay?"

"My mother found my diary. Pretty classic story for a lot of gay kids." Dylan sat down on the edge of the dock and clasped his hands in his lap. "My parents were waiting for me when I got home from school. They gave me two choices: conversion therapy or get out. I knew what conversion therapy could do, and I knew—" His voice broke and he took a breath. "—I couldn't do it."

Ryan moved to sit next to him. "You did the right thing."

"I've never had any regrets. That decision cost me, but it saved my life."

"You must have been terrified."

"I didn't know what I was going to do. I walked out of my house with a backpack and a duffel bag. I didn't know where to go, so I went to school. I always hung out in the library. It was my safe space. One of my teachers, Mr. Cooper, saw me. He took one look at the bag at my feet and he understood what happened. He brought me home, and he and his husband, Carl, took me in. I couldn't go back to school. It was too hard to walk down the halls and see my sister walk past me as if I didn't even exist. Plus my dad was the coach. A football coach in a small southern town has more power than God. They didn't waste any time spreading rumors about me being a troubled child. Everyone knew it wasn't true, but no one was going to call Coach McKenzie a liar. I switched to an online high school and finished my junior and senior year."

"How old were you?"

"I was fifteen when my parents kicked me out."

Dylan watched Ryan process the information, his expression morphing from disgust to anger and then sorrow.

"I-I don't know what to say," he said, his voice gruff.

"There's nothing to say. You didn't know. How would you?"

Ryan grabbed his arm, sending a jolt of awareness where his hand touched Dylan's skin. "That doesn't mean I don't care that what happened to you was wrong. If I'd have known, I don't think…." He let go and turned away.

Dylan's breath hitched. Was Ryan going to say he wouldn't have married Lindsay if he'd known?

Ryan got up, dusting his hands on his jeans. "I'm going to check on Leo. Make yourself at home."

He was halfway across the lawn, walking with long strides, his hands fisted at his sides, before Dylan stood up. Dylan watched him retreat into the mansion, the water and trees reflected in the wall of windows. Money could buy a lot of things, including grand houses, but it couldn't fill a house with love.

CHAPTER SEVEN

WITH EACH measured, even stroke, Dylan sliced through the water, leaving behind only faint ripples on the surface. From his office window, Ryan watched the play of muscles on Dylan's back as his lean legs and arms propelled him through the water. It occurred to him that no one had ever used the pool for actual exercise before. Lindsay didn't use it at all except to lounge around it with her friends. The pool was another excuse for a fashion show more than something fun. How many times had he invited her to join them when he played with Leo in the pool? A picture of the three of them splashing and laughing in the water together formed in his mind. In his vision, Leo was healthy, but it wasn't Lindsay he was laughing with. It was Dylan.

He exhaled, leaning his arm against the glass. The first few days after Dylan arrived had been awkward. It was Leo who brought them together and helped them find balance. Dylan was wonderful with him. Even playing with Legos, Dylan skillfully integrated science, math, history, and reading into the activity. There was more laughter in the house than before, making it feel more like the home Ryan always wanted. Dylan's presence also reinforced how dysfunctional his marriage to Lindsay had been. Stephanie and his parents reassured Ryan that he'd made the right choice marrying Lindsay, and he'd be happy when he settled into married life. Ryan thought he wanted a wife and children. The children part, yes, but he wanted more than a wife. He wanted a partner, someone he could talk to at the end of a long day. A relationship where they would inspire each other to be the best versions of themselves. But instead of growing together, he and Lindsay grew apart. Lindsay was available to talk, but their conversations were limited to Lindsay sharing gossip Ryan didn't care about or where they should go on their next vacation. Ryan hoped Leo's birth would bring them closer, but Lindsay viewed Leo as more of a burden than their child.

The knowledge shattered him, leaving him alone in accepting the hard reality that his marriage was over while everyone else turned a blind eye.

Now that he'd met Dylan, Ryan was even more disgusted with himself for the choice he'd made. Marrying Lindsay, or anyone who could be so hateful and callous, would be out of the question for him. He felt a deep sense of regret for believing the lies that Lindsay and her family had told about Dylan. From the moment they'd met, Ryan knew that there wasn't a shred of truth to what he'd been told about Dylan.

Dylan pulled himself out of the pool, water sliding off his body, leaving tiny droplets that glistened in the sun against his tan skin. No, Dylan's actions reflected his caring and compassionate nature. He was so sweet with Leo, the two of them instantly bonding. The reality was Dylan had all the qualities Ryan'd hoped to find in his twin.

Ryan turned away and let out a deep, shuddering breath, feeling the familiar tug in his gut that he had thought successfully banished.

"Ryan, are you okay?"

His sister walked into his office with a worried look. She came toward him, looking over his shoulder with a frown.

"I see he's already making himself at home."

"He's a guest, Steph. He can use the pool."

She turned to him with an apologetic look. "Sorry, I didn't mean to sound like I didn't approve. I'm anxious about, well… everything."

Ryan put his arm around her shoulder. "I know. This is…." He shook his head with a sigh. "I still can't believe it—the last year feels like it's been a dream, or a nightmare."

"Once we get through the transplant, things will get better."

"I hope so. There's still a chance it won't work."

"It will. It has too."

She spoke with the confidence Ryan wanted to have. Over the last year, his understanding of hope had changed drastically. How many times had he said something as thoughtless as "I hope it doesn't rain today?" Now he spent his time hoping his son didn't die. Hope was a funny thing, a tiny spark that could ignite or extinguish in a heartbeat. Hope could bring so much joy, but it could also break your heart. Especially when the thing you wanted, hoped for, wasn't what you needed when you finally got it.

He nodded and looked back down at Dylan, who was drying himself off.

"Are you sure you don't want me to move in? I can help keep you keep an eye on him while he's recuperating." Stephanie asked with a slight sharpness to her voice.

There was something in his sister's tone that set his teeth on edge.

"I don't need a babysitter," he snapped.

Stephanie frowned. "Of course not. It's not you I'm worried about." She nodded toward Dylan.

"Why would you be worried about Dylan?"

"What do we really know about him? Lindsay's parents told me—"

Ryan cut her off. "When did you talk to Lindsay's parents?"

"Just because you're angry with them doesn't mean I am. They're Leo's grandparents, and they have a right to know what's going on with their grandson."

"The grandson they almost killed with their secret."

"They're grieving, and they weren't thinking straight. They understand how important this is now, and they're so sorry. You know how much they love Leo, Ryan. You need to give them a break."

"I can't stop you from talking to them, and I won't keep Leo from his grandparents, but I have nothing to say to them. At least not right now. As for Dylan, there were no red flags in the private investigator's report."

He bit the inside of his cheek. He didn't agree with what Stephanie was saying, but Leo was Lindsay's parents' grandson. Their only grandson.

Stephanie patted his shoulder. "You'll see. Once we get through this procedure, things will get back to normal."

What was that supposed to look like? What was normal, and was that what he wanted? Ryan didn't want to go back to living a life where he was passing time waiting for... something. There was a hole in his life that he didn't know how to fill because he couldn't define what was missing. He'd had occasional moments in the past when he believed he knew what he was missing, but he didn't have the will or desire to go against his family's beliefs.

Thankfully, Stephanie changed the subject. "I had a nice visit with Rebecca. I told you she would be a great fit."

"Thanks for taking the time to vet all the candidates. Finding a nanny with a nursing degree was a good idea."

His sister gave him that look that always twisted his stomach in nervous knots. "She's pretty, too, don't you think?"

Ryan clenched his teeth. "Don't start, Steph."

"Leo needs a mother and you need a wife. It's not too soon to start thinking about it. It's important you have the right woman at your side."

Ryan noted his sister didn't say anything about love. What mattered to her was who would look good in pictures.

"And I'm not interested in dating anyone."

"All I'm saying is Rebecca has the right qualities you need."

Coldness swept over him. It was the same argument his sister had used to convince him Lindsay was the woman for him. It had worked then, and he'd made a mistake. He thought about how his life would have been if Lindsay survived the accident, and how these months with Leo fighting for his life would have gone. Neither of their families believed in divorce. He would have lived a ghostlike life. Looking down, he saw Dylan sitting on the edge of the dock, watching the boaters on the lake. He wasn't going to repeat the same mistakes he'd made before. He wouldn't get pushed into a relationship his heart wasn't into.

He moved away from his sister. "I'm not having this conversation. Drop it."

Stephanie frowned. His sister didn't take well to being told what to do. He watched her, calculating how hard she could push.

A second later, her frown morphed into a soothing smile. "Of course. Once Leo gets his transplant, things will change."

"Is there anything else, Steph? I have a lot of work to catch up on. I expect I'll be at the hospital most of the day for Dylan's procedure tomorrow."

His sister's frown returned. "Why are you going to the hospital?"

"Because that man"—he pointed toward the window—"is doing something that will save my son's life, and the right thing to do is to be there when it happens." When his sister opened her mouth in what he knew was going to be an argument about why he didn't need to go, he cut her off. "This is not open for negotiation, Steph."

He pictured teenaged Dylan, alone and scared, sitting in the school library, and shuddered. Dylan wouldn't be alone at the hospital tomorrow. He'd make sure of it.

He studied his sister. There it was, that calculating look again. Had she always looked at him the same way she looked at a client, trying to figure out how much she could gain from them?

Her face brightened, but her eyes were still cold. "Of course, you're right."

She was placating him. What was that saying how once you see something you can't unsee it? History was trying to repeat itself. His sister had pushed him into a relationship with Lindsay, and now she was trying it again with Rebecca, the nanny she'd carefully selected for him. He'd gone along with her choice. Rebecca was the right candidate. He would have hired her himself, but it was also easier to give in to his sister than argue with her.

A knock on the doorframe interrupted their standoff.

"Excuse me." Dylan hovered in the doorway. "Mrs. Lieu asked what I'd like for dinner, and I wanted to make sure you wouldn't mind if we had salmon? Is that something Leo would like?"

"Sure, that would be fine. Mrs. Lieu makes salmon nuggets for Leo. He'll love them."

"Okay, thanks."

As soon as Dylan was out of sight, Stephanie scowled. "I hope he's not going to walk around like that in front of Leo."

"He's wearing a bathing suit."

Stephanie scoffed and rolled her eyes. "What is it with those types always strutting around?"

Anger surged through Ryan. "Stop it." His sister's eyes widened at the sharpness in his tone. "Stop trying to find fault with Dylan. He's not doing anything wrong, and he's doing something wonderful for Leo. Dylan's going in for surgery to donate his bone marrow tomorrow. Or did you forget that?"

Color flushed his sister's cheeks, and she looked away, her mouth turned down. Ryan wasn't surprised she refused to answer. Even when they were kids playing board games, Stephanie would walk off in a huff rather than acknowledge defeat. He gestured to the three monitors on his desk filled with numbers. "I have work to do. You'll have the new algorithm for the Commerce Bank later tonight. I also sent the list of my recommendations to fill the vacant board position. That should be everything you need before I'm officially on PTO for Dylan's donation and Leo's transplant." With a stern look, he said. "Dylan will only be here for a couple more weeks, and I think the least we can do is to treat him like the guest he is."

Stephanie lifted her chin, and her eyes locked with his with a challenging glint. Ryan forced himself to hold her gaze. Usually he'd give in when they disagreed. It was easier than arguing. His parents would side with his sister; they always did. Everyone knew what was best but Ryan. Dylan was the only other person he'd ever refused to compromise on, apart from Leo and Mrs. Lieu.

"He won't be here much longer. I doubt our paths will cross that often," Stephanie finally said.

"When you do, you'll be polite."

"Of course," she said with a brittle smile.

RYAN WAS relieved when his sister declined to stay for dinner. He didn't want to make Dylan uncomfortable. Tonight would be the last night they would be together until after Leo received Dylan's donation. The next few weeks would be filled with hospitals and anxious waiting. Their family dinner included Mrs. Lieu, Rebecca, Leo, Dylan, and Ryan.

"I've got one," Dylan said, his eyes lit up with laughter and the sugar rush from Mrs. Lieu's decadent chocolate cake. "Why is Spiderman good at playing baseball?"

Leo shook his head, bits of chocolate clinging to the corners of his mouth.

"He knows how to catch flies," Dylan said.

Dylan's joke got belly laughs from Leo and a groan from the rest of the table. Dylan and Leo had been exchanging bad superhero jokes through dinner. Watching the two of them, some of Ryan's worry eased. For the first time in months, Ryan felt a sense of calm. The weeks ahead would be difficult, but everything would be okay.

CHAPTER EIGHT

A DEEP VOICE called out gently, "Dylan, can you wake up for us?"

Gradually, he emerged from the haze of anesthesia and opened his eyes. A face pinched with worry replaced the voice.

"What are you doing here?" he croaked.

Ryan gently placed a straw at his lips, trying to keep Dylan still by placing a comforting hand on his shoulder. "Drink some water and stay still."

He drank, looking up at Ryan's face, which was clouded with concern.

"How do you feel? Are you in pain? Do you need the nurse?" Ryan's words tumbled over themselves as he waved for someone out of Dylan's vision. A nurse appeared at his side. "Are you sure he's not in any pain?" Ryan asked.

Dylan lifted his hand, which still felt like it was filled with sand, and pushed the cup away from his lips. "I'm fine. I just need a minute. The anesthesia...."

"He's okay, Mr. Blackstone. This is normal after surgery." The nurse peered down at Dylan with a friendly smile. "You did great, Dylan. You'll be able to go home in a few hours, okay? If you start to feel any pain or discomfort, you let us know." She pointed to the call button on the side of the bed and left.

As soon as they were alone, Ryan pulled a chair up to the side of the bed and clasped Dylan's hand in his. "Thank you," he said in a gruff voice. He shook his head, his eyes shining with unshed tears. "Thank you so much."

His hands were warm and soft, and Dylan was too weak to pull out of his grasp, nor did he want to. Ryan's heightened emotions were too much. Suddenly, Dylan felt overwhelmed by his own. He closed his eyes, swallowing, trying to get a grasp on his feelings.

"I need to call Kevin and Carl and let them know you're awake," Ryan said.

"You told them?" Dylan gasped.

"Yes, of course." Ryan frowned at him. "They were understandably upset you didn't say anything to them."

"I didn't want them to worry," Dylan mumbled. The anesthesia was doing its best to pull him back to sleep again.

"Here." Ryan held the phone for him. If his mind wasn't so fuzzy, Dylan would have questioned why Ryan had their number in his phone.

Kevin answered on the first ring. "Ryan, how's he doing?"

"Dylan's awake now. I'm putting him on speaker."

"Hi, sweetheart. Carl's here too. How are you doing, kiddo?"

"I'm okay. A little fuzzy trying to wake up. They said everything went well."

"Honey, I'm so proud of you," Carl said in a teary voice. "But honey, why didn't you tell us?"

"Didn't want to burden you…." Dylan's voice drifted off.

"It's okay. Rest and we'll check on you later, okay?" Kevin said.

Dylan nodded, his eyelids growing heavy. He felt the phone slip out of his hand as his eyes closed. He heard Ryan quietly reassuring his dads he was okay.

"Dylan," a voice called out. He opened his eyes, and there was Ryan again. He wrinkled his forehead. Hadn't he been talking to Kevin and Carl? Dylan struggled to sit up, wincing at the ache in his back as he tried to look around and get his bearings.

Ryan was at his side in a flash, his arm around his shoulders to support him. "Hey, take it easy. You're okay. We're still at the hospital. You fell asleep again." Ryan gave him another sip of water and adjusted the bed so he could sit up. "How is your pain level?"

Dylan took a breath and assessed how he was feeling. "I'm sore, that's all. It's not too bad."

"The doctor said that was to be expected, but I don't want you in any pain. If you need more medication, let me know. I have your prescriptions ready, but if you need something before we leave the hospital, I can—"

"Ryan, it's fine," he exhaled.

A different nurse came in, bustling around his bed, taking the pulse oximeter off his hand. He stared down at the small bandage where his IV had been. She turned to Ryan. "If you'll give us a minute, I'll finish getting Mr. McKenzie ready to go home."

Ryan hesitated, looking at Dylan with a worried expression before stepping into the hallway.

"He hasn't left your side since you came out of surgery. He insisted on holding your hand as we wheeled you down the hall to your room," she said as she went about removing the catheter and helping Dylan sit up. "He certainly is devoted to you. It always warms my heart when I see someone so in love with their partner."

"He's not my partner."

"Well, however you want to define your relationship, I hope I can find someone someday who looks at me the way he looks at you."

With the nurse's help, he put on the sweats he had brought to wear after the surgery. The moment she called out that Dylan was ready, Ryan was by his side, wrapping his arm around his waist to support him as he stood up.

An attendant came in with a wheelchair, and Ryan gently lowered him into it and then dropped to his knee to arrange his feet on the footrests. Ryan stayed glued to his side, giving him anxious looks as the attendant wheeled him out. He kept a firm grip on Dylan's hand as he helped him into the car and leaned across him to buckle him in. He paused as he pulled back and they were face-to-face, their lips a hair's breadth apart.

Ryan's breath hitched, and his eyes darkened. "Let's get you home," he murmured.

Dylan swallowed and closed his eyes, nodding.

Ryan asked a hundred times between the hospital and home if he was okay. He cursed at every bump on the road that might cause discomfort to Dylan. He meant well, but the attentiveness was too much. Dylan wasn't used to this kind of devotion. Ryan put care and concern in every touch and glance. It created emotions in Dylan that spread over him like the lapping waves of the lake and threatened to pull him under.

When they arrived at the house, Dylan didn't even have time to reach for his door before Ryan was at his side.

"I got it," he growled when Ryan reached for the seat belt again.

The ache in his back had intensified during the journey home, and all he wanted now was to crawl into bed.

Ryan gently steered him inside, up the stairs, and to his room. Dylan stopped short in the doorway and looked at him in surprise.

"I thought this would be more comfortable for you," he said as he gestured to the new adjustable bed.

Dylan could only nod. He shuffled to the bed, wincing as he got under the covers. Again, Ryan was right there, hovering at his side. He handed Dylan the remote control for the bed. "I'll give you a minute to get comfortable."

Dylan nodded again. It was too much. He didn't want someone taking care of him. Ryan hesitated for a moment, reaching out as he gently brushed his hand across the furrows on Dylan's forehead. "I'll check in on you in a little while."

"Okay," Dylan said, swallowing back tears.

When Ryan left, Dylan leaned back with a sigh. Ryan should be at the hospital with Leo, not here with him. He was the donor, nothing else. Leo was what mattered.

Ryan returned with a tray. The smell of chicken soup wafted toward him, and his favorite tea, Earl Grey, with sugar and milk. Ryan set the tray on the nightstand and perched on the side of the bed. "You're in pain, but I need to get some food in you first so the meds don't upset your stomach." He held out the tea. "Let me know if there's enough sugar."

Dylan took a tentative sip. "It's perfect, thank you. You don't have to stay. I can take care of myself. You should be with Leo."

"My sister is with him. I'll be at the hospital tomorrow, but today I'm going to take care of you."

Dylan bit down on his lip and turned his head away, struggling to take a breath. His stomach twisted.

"What's wrong?" Ryan pried the cup Dylan had been clutching out of his hand. Setting it aside, he took Dylan's hand in his.

"Nothing, I'm… it's the anesthesia wearing off."

"You must be starving." Ryan reached for the bowl of soup and handed it to him.

Dylan's hand trembled as he lifted the spoon to his mouth and let the warm broth slip between his lips. Suddenly he dropped the spoon into the bowl and set it aside.

Ryan cupped his cheek, brushing the wetness away from his eyes. "Dylan, what's going on? Are you in pain?"

"Why are you doing this?" he sniffed.

"Doing what?" The gentleness in Ryan's voice broke Dylan apart even more.

"Taking care of me. You don't have to do this. I can take care of myself. I've done what you needed me to do. You don't have to feel guilty or anything for leaving me alone now."

Ryan leaned forward and pressed a kiss to his forehead. "You're more than a donor to me." He sighed. "You had a significant medical procedure, your body is weak, and you're hungry and tired. Let me take care of you." Ryan picked up the soup and held a spoonful to Dylan's lips.

"I can feed myself."

"Maybe, but I'm going to help you anyway."

Dylan didn't have the mental or physical strength to argue. He opened his mouth and let Ryan feed him. By the time he finished and made his way to the bathroom, sleep was trying to claim him again. The covers were tucked in around him. Dylan wasn't sure if the soft caress over his forehead and the murmured words were part of a dream or not.

The sky was dusky blue when he opened his eyes. Ryan stirred in the chair next to the window.

Ryan came over and sat on the edge of the bed. "What do you need?"

"I'm—I'm not sure." He stretched gingerly, testing his limbs. "I feel… heavy. Like I'm made of sand."

Ryan nodded. "You're going to be weak while your body rebuilds the marrow that was taken. You don't have to do anything but rest for now."

"I'm not sure I know how to do that."

Resting was for people who didn't worry about being left alone without any support. Even when he took the time to relax with a book, there was always a part of him that felt guilty. He should have been taking on another tutoring client, or maybe even get a second job to keep his modest bank account healthy. Working himself to the point of exhaustion in college and when he'd first moved to LA, he'd learned to force himself to take breaks, but it was always a battle between what his body and spirit needed and his fears.

"Are you hungry?" Ryan checked his watch. "You should have some food in your stomach." At the mention of food, Dylan's stomach grumbled. "I guess that answers that question," Ryan said with a smile. "Mrs. Lieu has been cooking all day. We've got chicken potpie, the vegetable potstickers you like, and pho. If there's something else you want, let me know."

"Pho sounds good, and maybe a couple of egg rolls?"

Ryan jumped up. "Got it."

Mrs. Lieu came in fifteen minutes later with a tray filled with food. She set the tray down and fussed over Dylan, adding pillows and blankets to the bed until he was almost buried under layers of down before she kissed his forehead. "Beautiful boy, you'll get better now. Mr. Blackstone is too selfish with you. I'm making him take a shower and eat. It's my turn to look after you."

"Ryan hasn't eaten?"

She shook her head, *tsk*ing while she put the tray in his lap. "I told him he doesn't do you any good if he gets sick too. He can't spend all his time watching you."

Mrs. Lieu tucked a napkin into the neck of his shirt and lifted the lid off the pot of pho and egg rolls. She poured a cup of fragrant jasmine tea. "I put beef in the pho. You need protein to get your strength back."

"Thank you, Mrs. Lieu, this looks wonderful." He realized how late in the day it was and looked at his nightstand. "Do you know where my phone is? I should check in with my folks."

She smiled and opened the drawer of the nightstand to retrieve his phone. "You don't have to worry. Mr. Blackstone had been talking to your Kevin and Carl. He calls every hour to tell them you're okay."

The room blurred with a fresh sheen of tears. "It's too much," he murmured, shaking his head.

"No," Mrs. Lieu said emphatically. "It's just right. You need to learn how to accept kindness from people. You have us now: Ryan, Leo, and me. We will be your family."

He held his hand out. "Thank you, Mrs. Lieu."

She put her hand in his with a squeeze, gave his cheek a peck, and patted his shoulder. "My beautiful boy," she said before leaving.

Ryan hadn't left his side.

His hands shook as he dialed his dad's number. Kevin answered on the first ring, and Dylan spent the next few minutes reassuring his fathers that he was okay. Ryan had made a good impression, and they couldn't stop talking about how kind he'd been with his updates.

"It's reassuring to know you're in good hands," Carl said.

"Yeah, I—it's kind of hard," Dylan admitted.

"What do you mean, son?"

"They're all being so nice to me, wanting to take care of me."

"Ah, I see. I know you've heard Carl and I say this before, and we're going to keep telling you this. Maybe someday you'll believe it. You're worth being loved, Dylan. It's okay to let people take care of you."

Dylan tried to blink back tears, but they escaped anyway. "Love you, Dad," he said in a shaky whisper.

"We love you too," Kevin said. "You're tired and weak. Get some rest and we'll check in with you later."

"Let us know if there's anything you need," Carl added.

"Okay."

Dylan sniffed. He hung up and let the phone fall from his hand onto the mattress, his gaze going to the pink sky outside his window that cast a purple glow on the lake. He looked away from the setting sun to the doorway, wishing Ryan would come back. Dylan was sure he was with Leo, where he was supposed to be, but when Ryan held his hand, Dylan felt safe and cared for.

Dylan's eyes drifted closed again, and he dreamed of waking up with Ryan holding his hand, their fingers intertwined.

CHAPTER NINE

RYAN STOOD under the hot spray, letting the water sluice over his body. With a shudder, he finally let go. Tears mingled with the water swirling down the drain. Relief mingled with hope, but he wouldn't be able to really breathe until Leo's procedure was done.

When he felt a little more centered, he shut off the water and stepped out of the shower. Wrapping a towel around his waist, he leaned against the bathroom counter, staring at his reflection in the mirror. The dark circles under his eyes matched Dylan's. Only his came from worry and not from sacrifice. The haunted look Ryan saw in Dylan's eyes every time someone showed him compassion made Ryan want to do more. As he watched Dylan sleep, Ryan wrestled with the growing need for more. He couldn't stop himself from reaching for Dylan's hand. All he could allow himself was to hold him. Taking care of Dylan was a small gesture, and it wasn't enough to express his deeper feelings. He wanted Dylan. He wanted to make up for all the times Dylan wasn't loved the way he should have been. The attraction that pulled at him—mind, body, and soul—had been building since their first meeting. Ryan couldn't stop it, and this time he didn't want to.

Ryan panicked when Dylan talked about going home. He wasn't ready for him to leave; he didn't want him to leave.

His phone flashed with an incoming call from his sister.

"Is Leo okay?" he answered.

"He's fine. Three bedtime stories and he's fast asleep."

Ryan exhaled. "Good. That's good."

"I reached out to Lisa. The jet is on standby to take Dylan back to LA on Thursday, and his follow-up appointments have been scheduled with his doctor."

"You did what? I didn't tell you to do that."

"No, you didn't, but you have enough on your plate, so I thought I'd go ahead and take care of it for you."

"Thursday is the day after tomorrow. It can take a week to ten days to recover from surgery."

"We can hire a private nurse to travel with him."

Stephanie's dismissive attitude set his teeth on edge. "Call my assistant back and cancel everything. Dylan is staying here until he recovers. Actually, Dylan is staying for the summer. He'll be tutoring Leo to help him keep up with school." The plan took shape as he spoke. It was reckless and selfish, and he didn't care. Ryan only hoped he could convince Dylan to go along with it.

He ignored his sister's exasperated huff. "We can hire—"

"No, we can't," he cut her off. "He's Leo's uncle, and he should get to spend time with him."

"I don't think it's right for him to worm his way into the family. Leo shouldn't get too attached. It's not like he'll be seeing him on a regular basis after this."

"That's not what he's doing, Steph." He softened his tone. "Look, I know Lindsay was your best friend, and it's been hard for you. You need to take the time to get to know Dylan."

"He's not like Lindsay at all." The words came out sounding like an accusation.

"No, he's not. And that's not a bad thing."

"I'll try," she finally said.

"Thanks, Steph, that's all I ask."

He hung up with his sister and went back to the guest room. He carefully perched on the edge of the bed, looking down at Dylan's sleeping form. Without the registry, the odds were Leo wouldn't have survived, and without the registry, Dylan never would have come into their lives. The thought of never meeting this kind, caring man made him shudder. How was it possible for anyone to believe the lies Dylan's parents told about him after meeting and getting to know him?

His sister's actions caught him off guard. Yes, she'd been overly protective of Ryan, but she'd also always been his closest confidant and advisor. His parents weren't the kind who were super engaged in their children's lives. They were raised with a series of nannies who, although kind, couldn't make up for their parents' absence at school events or missed birthdays. Maybe that's why he and Stephanie shared a bond that was closer than most.

Dylan stirred and rolled to his side with a slight wince. Ryan checked his watch. It was too soon for him to take any more pain medication.

That had been another point of worry. Dylan refused to take anything more than an over-the-counter painkiller, rejecting any kind of narcotic. Ryan suspected the root cause was the lies Dylan's parents spread about him. Were they aware of the profound and enduring effect their cruelty had on their son? Of course not. They'd made it clear they didn't care.

"*Con*," Mrs. Lieu whispered from the doorway. "Leave him be." She motioned for him to join her. "There's nothing you can do but let him sleep," she said when he met her in the hallway.

"He'll need more pain medication in—" He checked his watch. "—an hour and a half."

"I know. I'm keeping track."

Ryan ran his hands through his hair. "But he's hurting now."

Mrs. Lieu gave him a sympathetic look. "And so are you. You always want to take on everyone else's pain."

"I'm fine."

"No, you're not," she said with a stern shake of her head. "Come down to the kitchen. I made fettuccine." She gave him a gentle push toward the stairs and followed him down to the kitchen.

The pasta was rich and creamy, with the perfect balance of garlic and parmesan, and was exactly what he needed.

"You're falling asleep at the table." Mrs. Lieu rested her chin on her palm, smiling at him.

His protest came to a halt when a yawn interrupted him.

"Go to bed. I'll make sure Dylan gets his medicine."

"Thanks," he said around another yawn.

On his way to his room, he poked his head in Dylan's room for one last check and found him struggling to sit up in bed.

"Whoa, whoa, what are you doing?' Ryan rushed over and gently pushed him back down.

"It's fine. I needed to use the bathroom," he said in a sleepy mumble.

"I'll help you."

Ryan put his arm around Dylan's waist and helped him slowly stand. Dylan winced, letting out a slow hiss.

"They should have kept you in the hospital," Ryan said as they carefully made their way toward the bathroom.

"Ryan, it's fine. The doctor said soreness was normal."

Ryan shook his head with an exasperated sigh and grabbed Dylan's hand while he kept his arm around his waist with the other. "Take it easy."

This close he could feel the firm muscles in Dylan's back that he'd only seen from his office window while he watched him swim. The soft curls on top of Dylan's head tickled his chin. Ryan breathed in the rosemary-and-mint scent of Dylan's shampoo. He almost tripped himself at the jolt of awareness that had his cock straining against his zipper.

"Ryan?" Dylan looked up at him with concern.

He didn't realize he'd come to a stop midway between the bed and the bathroom.

"Sorry," he said in a hoarse voice. "I wanted to make sure you were okay."

The way Dylan looked up at him, Ryan was close enough to see the flecks of green and black in the soft brown depths of his eyes. He only had to drop his chin and Dylan's lips would be a breath away.

He jerked back, making Dylan wince. "Sorry." He got Dylan to the bathroom and left him at the door. "I'll let you…." He backed away.

Ryan turned and fled. In the hall, he pressed himself against the wall, breathing heavily, trying to get his body back under control. What the hell was happening to him? He didn't lose control. He couldn't lose control.

He squeezed his eyes shut. "Don't do this," he said in an anguished whisper.

"Ryan," Dylan called out from the bedroom.

He drew in a deep breath and walked back in. "I'm here."

Dylan had returned to bed on his own, his face pinched with pain. "Could I have some ibuprofen or aspirin, please?"

He felt like an ass hearing the strain in Dylan's voice. "I'll get you something."

He rushed back downstairs, filled a pitcher with fresh water, and grabbed the bottle of painkillers Mrs. Lieu had left on the counter, waving her off when she came into the kitchen offering to help.

Dylan was sitting up against the pillows with his eyes squeezed shut, beads of sweat on his forehead, when Ryan returned. He poured a glass of water and shook out a couple of pills for Dylan.

"Thanks." Dylan took the glass from him with a shaky hand. He swallowed the pills and sat back with a sigh.

Ryan noted how pale he looked. "Is there anything else I can get you?"

"Maybe more of Mrs. Lieu's pho if there's any left."

Ryan chuckled. "Are you kidding? She's made enough to feed the entire UW football team. I'll get you some."

Ryan was relieved to see the pain on Dylan's face had eased when he returned with a bowl of broth.

But his hand was still shaking and the bowl almost tipped into his lap when Dylan tried to take a sip from the spoon.

"Here." Ryan took the bowl out of his hands and dipped the spoon in the broth, holding it to Dylan's lips.

"I can—"

"Nope," Ryan said with a wry smile, tipping the spoon into Dylan's mouth before he could finish his protest. "I'm a dad. I've got experience dealing with a stubborn, sick kid. Don't argue with me."

Dylan's lips twitched, and he opened his mouth in response.

"You're a really good dad, Ryan," he said after another sip.

"Thanks." He cleared his throat, surprised at the emotions Dylan's compliment brought up. Besides Mrs. Lieu, no one else had ever told him that before.

He put the spoon to Dylan's lips again.

"Was my sister a good mom?" he asked quietly.

Ryan put the spoonful of broth back in the bowl. "I—" Why didn't yes come instantly? "Lindsay loved Leo, but… being a mother. It's a challenging job for everyone. Your sister did the best she could."

Dylan nodded with a grim expression that let Ryan know he didn't have to say anything more.

He fed Dylan another couple of spoonsful.

"I should have brought a napkin," he said, wiping a drop from Dylan's chin with his thumb.

Dylan licked his lips. "I think I'm done now," he said with a slight quiver in his voice.

Ryan looked down at the empty bowl. "Yeah, okay." He got up and hesitated. "Do you need anything else?"

"No, I think I'll read for a little while," Dylan said, reaching for his e-reader on the bedside table.

"What do you like to read?"

Dylan's face flushed. "You'll think it's dumb."

"No judgment, I promise."

"I like to read gay romance."

Ryan's eyebrows shot up.

"Remember, you said no judgment," Dylan said.

"What? Who's your favorite author?"

"I have a couple: Damon Suede and Lily Morton."

"If I was going to read one, what book would you recommend?"

Now it was Dylan's turn to look surprised. "Oh, I… why?"

"I haven't read anything new in a while. Maybe I'll try one."

"Well, Damon Suede writes pretty sexy stuff, and Lily Morton writes fun snarky dialogue. I guess it depends on what you're into." Dylan's face flushed. "I didn't mean that the way it sounded."

Ryan looked Dylan in the eye. "I don't mind."

Dylan clamped his mouth shut and looked away.

The man was sick, and Ryan was flirting with him. Kicking himself, he took another step toward the door. "I'll let you get some rest. If you need anything, promise you'll text me or Mrs. Lieu."

Dylan nodded but kept his gaze focused on the twinkle of lights from the houses on the other side of the lake outside his window.

What had gotten into him, flirting with Dylan? It was so natural. He'd wanted to keep going to see the flush of color spread over his cheeks and the slight dimple that appeared on one cheek when Dylan smiled. He struggled when he'd first started dating, always feeling awkward and unsure of what to say. But he didn't feel that way around Dylan.

The sky started to tinge pale pink as Ryan finished reading his first gay romance. He'd chosen a Lily Morton book to start with. By the time he finished, he headed straight for the shower to jerk off.

The story of a single-dad actor and a male model had him laughing and, at times, wiping away tears. And the sex scenes had him replacing the fictional characters with a vision of himself exploring Dylan's body.

He'd never given in to his fantasies like this before. A part of him felt like he should feel guilty, but he didn't. His thoughts and feelings were a jumble, but one thing was clear. He was attracted to Dylan, and he wanted to explore the feelings Dylan had awakened in him. He felt like he'd been sleepwalking through life and had just woken up ready to face a new day.

CHAPTER TEN

"HOW ARE you feeling, son?"

"I'm good, a little tired, but that's to be expected." Dylan squinted at the boats on the water from his lounge chair by the pool. He needed a few more days to recover before swimming again, but he preferred sitting outside in the Seattle summer sun rather than being indoors. For all its opulence, he hated Ryan's house with its stark white oversized rooms that held no warmth except Leo and Ryan. They brought color and life to the house. A day after his surgery and he was already feeling cooped up.

"Carl and I are so proud of you," Kevin said. "You've done an amazing, selfless thing."

"I wish I felt that way. I feel guilty. Everyone is being so nice, trying to take care of me."

"That's hard for you, isn't it?"

"I don't want to inconvenience anyone."

"Dylan, you're not an inconvenience. Carl and I have watched you grow into the kind and caring man you are today. I hope someday you'll realize you're never an inconvenience to people who love you. Caring for someone is an act of friendship and love."

Dylan caught a movement out of the corner of his eye and looked up to see Ryan standing on the balcony off his office. He mouthed "You okay?" and gave him a thumbs-up with a little smile.

Is that what Ryan wanted from him—friendship? Is that why he was being so nice to him? Guilt had Dylan's stomach in nervous knots for the thoughts he'd had of Ryan as more than a friend.

Dylan flashed his own thumbs-up with a nod. "I promise I'll try to do better letting people take care of me."

"How are you getting along with Ryan?"

Dylan's gaze went to the empty balcony where Ryan had been standing a few moments before. "Fine. It's… strange."

"How so?"

"It's hard to explain. He was married to my sister. Everything I believed he was or how I thought he would be isn't how Ryan is at all. He's always trying to make sure I'm happy. He's so caring. It's hard to picture someone like him with Lindsay. They don't match at all."

"I see," Kevin said, softly.

"There's no sign of Lindsay here other than a photo in Leo's room. It's like looking at the pieces of a broken mirror. There are just fragments, and you can't put the pieces together to make a complete picture."

"Have you heard anything about your parents?"

"No. I know they call to check in with Leo. Ryan hasn't mentioned anything about them to me. I think he doesn't want to make me uncomfortable, or any more uncomfortable than I already am."

"You'll be home soon, and you'll have the rest of the summer to process this experience."

Dylan sighed. "I'm going to miss Leo. He's a great kid. Ryan keeps telling me he wants me to be in Leo's life, but I'm not sure what that looks like. What happens when my parents know I'm spending time with Leo?" He could hear Kevin suck in his breath. "It won't be good," he finished with a slight tremor in his voice.

"If Ryan is the person you say he is, he won't let Arlene and Clay come between you and Leo."

"I don't want to cause any trouble."

"You wouldn't be." Ryan's deep voice interrupted the conversation. Dylan jerked his head up to see Ryan standing next to him.

He shoved his hands in his jean pockets and gave him a sheepish look. "I wasn't eavesdropping, I promise." He gestured to the phone. "If that's your dads, please tell them I said hi. I'll just…." he gestured toward the dock as he started in that direction.

"I guess you heard that," Dylan said, watching Ryan walk away.

Kevin chuckled. "I did. Tell Ryan we said hello."

"I should go. I need to talk to Ryan about what he heard me say."

"All right, son. You're still healing, so take it easy, okay?"

"I will. Love you, Dad."

"Love you too."

Dylan hung up and looked toward the dock. Things were already so awkward with Ryan, and now he was going to have to talk to him about his concerns with his parents. They were valid concerns. His parents weren't going to be okay with their gay son spending time with their only grandchild. They would blame Dylan's influence if Leo didn't grow up to be a straight-and-narrow jock. But what if that wasn't what Leo wanted to be? Dylan clutched his chest, fighting to catch his breath. The thought of Leo being cast out the way he was chilled him to his bones. Of all the reasons he needed to be in Leo's life, he needed his nephew to know that he always had someone he could call for any reason, any time, no questions asked.

His panic had him almost running toward Ryan on the dock.

"What's wrong?" Ryan asked when Dylan stopped in front of him, trying to catch his breath.

"I want to talk about my parents and Leo. Promise me you won't let them force Leo to be someone he isn't. Don't let them convince you Leo should go to a conversion camp or therapy—" His voice broke. He knew he was rambling, but he couldn't stop. "If anything happens, you have to let me know. It doesn't matter when. I'll come." He grabbed Ryan's arm. "Promise me."

"Dylan, breathe." Ryan put his hands on his shoulders, but Dylan couldn't catch his breath. "Dylan, you're having a panic attack." Ryan gently grasped his chin. "Look at me."

He tried to focus on Ryan's face, but it took all of his energy to get enough air into his lungs.

"Dylan, name five things you can see," Ryan said, brushing his thumb along his jawline.

Dylan's gaze darted around wildly. "Lake, trees—" He took a breath. "—boat, mountain"—his gaze finally landed on Ryan's face—"eyes."

"Good. Now name three things you can hear."

"Airplane, water… your voice."

"Almost there. Tell me two things you can feel."

"Sun, your fingers."

"Can you take a deep breath for me?"

Dylan nodded. He took three more breaths before Ryan let go and stepped back with a slight smile.

"I think you're okay now."

"I haven't had a panic attack in…. It's been a long time."

Ryan put his hand on Dylan's back, guiding him back to the chairs by the pool. "Here," he said, pointing to a nearby lounger and urging him to sit down. Ryan grabbed a blanket from the back of another chair and dropped it around Dylan's shoulders.

"How did you become an expert in panic attacks?"

Ryan sat down on the side of the lounger next to him. "One of my roommates in college."

"Thank you."

"Do you want to talk about it?" Ryan asked.

"No." Dylan looked down at Ryan's arms, admiring the way the sun made the hair on his arms look like golden floss in the summer sun. He wrapped his arms around his knees to keep himself from reaching out and brushing his fingers against Ryan's warm, sun-kissed skin. "Maybe." He sighed. "I was telling Kevin about how you want me to stay in Leo's life, and then I thought about what my parents are going to say when they find out. And then I-I guess I had a flashback to how I was raised and my dad's idea of what it meant to be a man." He shuddered. "The idea of Leo being put through that kind of torture, I just...."

"Dylan, I promise you, I won't let that happen."

The sincerity in Ryan's voice wrapped around him like the blanket over his shoulders. "I know that, I do. I don't know why I panicked."

"Because what your parents and Lindsay did was terrible, and it's understandable that you have some trauma. Add that you donated bone marrow and your immune system is rebuilding. You get to have as many emotions as you want."

Dylan nodded, blinking back tears. "I probably overdid it this morning. I think I'll go back to bed for a while."

"Do you need help?"

"No, I'm okay." He shook his head even though he wanted to say yes. Maybe he wasn't thinking straight from being overly tired, but his first thought was how nice it would have been to have Ryan tuck him in. He got up and paused. "Thank you for helping me when I lost it."

"I'm glad I was here."

"I… I should go," he said, even though he was reluctant to leave.

"Would you like to have dinner with me tonight?" Ryan asked.

A chance to spend more time with Ryan? Butterflies fluttered in his stomach at the idea. And then disappeared when Ryan continued, "I wanted to talk about your going back home."

"Oh. You don't have to have dinner with me. We can just talk about it."

Ryan took a step closer. "What if I want to have dinner with you anyway?"

Why was Ryan looking at him like that? What game was he playing?

Ryan reached out, his fingers gently brushing against his. "Have dinner with me, Dylan."

"I-I'm not feeling well. I don't think that would be a good idea."

Ryan's face fell. "Of course, I wasn't thinking. Do you think you'll be okay to be with Leo on Zero Day? He asked for you to be there."

Ryan's request took him by surprise. He hadn't expected to be included on the day Leo received his bone marrow. The offer touched him and left him feeling even more confused.

He nodded. "Tell Leo I'll be there."

No matter how he felt, Dylan wouldn't let his nephew down.

"Thank you. It means a lot to Leo and to me."

Dylan wasn't lying. A dull headache had been building, making the sun too bright and the air too hot.

"I really need to lie down," he mumbled.

He stumbled, jerking back when Ryan reached for him. "Don't, I'm fine, I don't want you."

Dylan didn't realize he'd said want instead of need until he made it to his room. With a groan, he climbed into bed, too tired to care. It didn't matter what he wanted anyway, he'd put away wants with the rest of his childhood the day he was kicked out. Trading wants for needs. Food, shelter, education. Dylan knew how lucky he'd been that Kevin found him in the library that afternoon. He knew how many kids weren't as lucky, and even now with a job, an apartment, and a little money in the bank, he still worried about something happening that would leave him alone and without a safety net. Being away from home and his friends, he felt even more vulnerable.

And then there was the way Ryan kept trying to take care of him. That wasn't so bad, but the way he kept looking at him as if…. "He's not thinking of you like that," he whispered to himself.

But what if he was? a small voice in his heart whispered. Suppose he had made a mistake about Ryan? Was it possible he was bi? Dylan rolled over with a grunt of discomfort mixed with frustration. He had to stop wishful thinking.

CHAPTER ELEVEN

RYAN HOVERED outside of the guest suite. Dylan looked pale as he slept. Worry gnawed at Ryan's gut. He'd been sleeping a lot since they came home from the hospital. The doctor reassured him that was normal, but it was unsettling, too, how weak Dylan was. He was about to go in when a tug on his arm kept him in place.

"Let him sleep." Mrs. Lieu gently pulled him away. "He's fine. Rest and more of my soup is what he needs now."

"You're right." He sighed. "I… he's saving Leo's life, and I feel responsible."

"I know"—she patted his arm—"and Dylan knows it too. He doesn't expect you to watch over him."

"But I want to. I know I need to be with Leo, and I'll go to the hospital soon, but I want to make sure Dylan is okay too."

They were making their way downstairs. Mrs. Lieu paused at his declaration. She studied him for a moment before she continued to guide him down to the kitchen. As he settled at the kitchen island, the aroma of freshly brewed tea filled the air, and she turned to face him with a sympathetic gaze.

"You like this man, don't you?"

"Dylan has been very gracious. I—"

"No." She reached across the island and grasped his hand. "That's not what I mean. You're attracted to him."

Ryan clenched his jaw and looked away.

"My *con*, I can see it in your eyes. This is a look I've never seen before. I've wondered if I would ever see it. It's okay to let yourself care for Dylan. You are always wanting to please everyone else. It's time for you to be happy. I think Dylan could be someone who makes you happy."

"I've only known him for a few weeks."

"Our hearts don't know weeks, days, hours, or minutes."

Ryan blinked back tears. "You don't seem to be surprised that I'm attracted to another man."

"I've always known that you have a big heart that is capable of caring for the right person. The sex of the person doesn't matter. How they love is what counts."

She turned around and went to the stove, leaving Ryan to contemplate what she'd said. He'd read articles on demisexuality. Was that what Mrs. Lieu was talking about? Was that why he never felt the sexual attraction he was supposed to feel with Lindsay? The soothing chamomile and lemongrass fragrance drifted toward him. He gratefully accepted the cup she pushed toward him. Whenever he was stressed, Mrs. Lieu would always make lemongrass and chamomile for him. Typically, it would be accompanied by a serious lecture about working late. This time it was served with a gentle nod, filled with love and understanding.

"I have a lot to think about."

"Don't try to carry everything on your shoulders alone. I'm here if you need me, and when you're ready, I think you should talk to Dylan." She checked her watch. "Go to the hospital and be with Leo. I'll let you know when Dylan wakes up again and how he's feeling."

"Thank you." He got up and came around the island to give Mrs. Lieu a hug.

"My boys." She patted him on the back. "You will all grow healthy and strong again."

Ryan kept turning his conversation with Mrs. Lieu over and over in his mind as he drove across the bridge toward the hospital. How much of himself had he given up to make others happy? He'd never wanted to start Blackstone Financial, but he knew it would make his parents happy. He tried to think about what his parents had done to make *him* happy and came up empty. The road and the trees became hazy by the time Ryan took the exit off the bridge. He gripped the steering wheel tightly, following the road blindly as his chest grew tighter and tighter. Before he could make it to the hospital, it became too much and he pulled over onto a side street. A sob tore through him, and then another. He hadn't mourned for his wife like this; now he grieved for… everything.

When he could catch his breath again, he finished his drive to the hospital.

"Daddy, your eyes are all puffy," Leo observed when Ryan walked into his room.

"I got something in them."

He hoped the lame excuse would be enough.

"Is uncle Dylan back from the hospital?"

"He is." Ryan perched on the edge of Leo's bed. "He did great, and now he's home resting."

Leo nodded, his large eyes holding a hint of worry. "Aunt Stephanie says he will go home now, but I don't want him to."

"No, sweetheart, Dylan isn't going home for a while. He needs to recover, and he should be here for your transplant, don't you think?"

"Grandpa McKenzie said he did the only thing he's good for. I don't know what that means."

Ryan inhaled a sharp breath, fighting not to show Leo his anger toward Dylan's father. "Your grandpa McKenzie is wrong. Your uncle Dylan is a great uncle, and we are so lucky we found him."

"Will he read to me some more?"

"Absolutely. As soon as you're both feeling up to it. In the meantime do you think I can be his substitute?"

Leo nodded and reached under the covers to pull out an issue of *Captain Underpants*. Ryan spent the rest of the afternoon reading stories, playing games, and watching movies to keep his son entertained. The day after tomorrow would be Zero Day, transplant day. Then the process of engraftment would begin. If it was successful, over the next month Dylan's donated cells would begin to grow and produce new blood cells.

Before they finished the book Leo started to slow blink, his head falling against Ryan's chest. Mrs. Lieu sent a text letting him know Dylan was awake, had eaten, and was insisting Ryan stay at the hospital with Leo.

Ryan carefully tucked Leo under the covers, making sure not to jostle the port on Leo's arm that would connect to the IV that would feed Dylan's healthy cells into his body. Once he had Leo settled, Ryan stepped into the hall and called Dylan.

"How are you feeling?" he asked when Dylan answered.

"I'm fine. Mrs. Lieu's pho can make anyone feel better. How's Leo?"

"He's okay. He's been asking for you. Apparently, you're a better story-time reader than I am."

Dylan laughed softly. "I can't wait to see him again. It's funny how you can know someone for such a short amount of time and feel such a strong connection."

"I know."

Dylan had been in his home for a short time, and Ryan was having a hard time imagining what life would be like when he left.

"I should go and let you rest."

"I'm not tired," Dylan said around a yawn.

"That's not what it sounds like to me. I'll check on you in the morning."

Ryan hung up and stared at his phone with a frown. He hadn't heard from his parents in the last couple of days.

"Ryan, is something the matter?" his mother answered.

"I was going to ask the same thing. Why haven't you called to check in?"

"Check in on what?"

"How Dylan's donation went."

"I assumed if there was a problem, you'd let us know."

"And I assumed you'd have the decency to care about Leo's donor," he said with his jaw clenched.

"He's a donor, a stranger, and we don't know if it will work or not yet."

"He's more than a donor, and Dylan is not a stranger. He's Leo's uncle, and he's saving your grandson's life."

"You don't know if it will work."

"It's going to work."

"How do you know?"

"Because unlike you, I have faith."

He hung up before he said anything he would regret. Ryan had never challenged his mother's callousness before. He'd always accepted her coolness rather than make waves with the family and ask for more. This time her lack of empathy had him seething with anger.

"Ryan, is everything okay?" Joy Anderson, Leo's patient-care coordinator and, along with her husband, a personal friend, came toward him with a worried frown.

Ryan glanced at his watch. "You're working late tonight."

"I'm just finishing up. How's Leo? I checked in with his doctor, and everything was on track for the transplant."

"Leo's good. I'm tired, anxious, worried, all the things, I guess."

"Of course you are. It's important to remember this isn't a sprint, and you need to give yourself time to rest."

"Thanks," he sighed. "You're right. It's hard knowing you don't have any control of the process—you feel helpless waiting for time and the science to do their work."

"You've got my number. I'm here whenever you need me."

"Thanks, Joy, I really appreciate that. You've gone above and beyond."

Joy gave him a gentle pat on the shoulder. "You're more than a client. You know that. Jason and I are here for you whenever you need us."

"Thank you, I appreciate that. And tell Jason I said thank you, too."

Joy gave him a quick hug and headed down the hallway toward the exit, leaving Ryan thinking about the status of his friendships... or the lack of them. Friends had been another point of conflict with Lindsay. He didn't want to hang out with people who only wanted to talk about their wealth or who wanted to pester him with questions about how to make even more money. The few friends he had weren't glamorous enough for Lindsay. Her only interest in his friendship with Joy and her husband, music star Jason Anderson, was to ask for VIP tickets to one of his shows.

Any hope Lindsay would bond with his friends was dashed quickly. She constantly bothered Jason for celebrity gossip and completely ignored Joy. Eventually Ryan stopped including Lindsay and interacted with them on his own. It wasn't very often, despite Jason and Joy's reassurances that he was welcome to hang out any time. Ryan avoided interacting with them partly from embarrassment about Lindsay's behavior, and because it was easier than arguing with his wife about who he chose to be friends with.

One of the oncology nurses came down the hall toward him. "Hey, Mr. Blackstone, were you planning on staying the night with Leo? I can grab an extra blanket for you if you need it."

"Thanks, Thanh, and please call me Ryan. I was trying to decide. Leo's donor is staying at my house, and I'm feeling torn, needing to be in two places at once if I'm being honest."

Thanh gave him a sympathetic smile. "I'm on duty tonight, and Leo's favorite nurse, Noelle, will be here in the morning. Why don't you go home where you can check on your guest and sleep in your own bed. We're almost to Zero Day, and we still have a long way to go. You need your rest as much as Leo does."

"Thank you, Thanh. You're right." He liked the nurse, who always had a glint of laughter in his brown eyes.

"Can you tell my husband that? I've been trying to convince him I'm always right for a while now."

A handsome man with creamy brown skin and a cap of short curly hair, wearing a white coat, came up and put his hand on Thanh's shoulder, dropping a kiss on his cheek.

"Do we need to talk about that time you thought you should be a blond again?" he said.

"One time. You're never going to let me live that down," Thanh muttered.

The man chuckled and held his hand out to Ryan. "I'm Milo, Thanh's husband."

"Hi. Ryan." Ryan shook his hand.

"Ryan is Leo's dad," Thanh explained. "Milo is an ER doc," he said, looked at his husband with pride.

"Leo's a great kid. Thanh introduced me to him. Congratulations on finding a donor. It can be really difficult with a biracial child. Thank goodness for the Be the Match registry."

"Thanks, I still can't believe it. Without Be the Match, we wouldn't have had this opportunity. I'm incredibly grateful."

Thanh sniffed. "Is that Santorini's lasagna I smell?"

"Yup," Milo said, holding up a lunch bag.

"Let me finish and I'll join you." Thanh gave Milo another kiss on the cheek. "Go home, Ryan. Get some sleep and I'll see you tomorrow." Thanh waved goodbye before heading into one of the patient rooms.

Ryan watched Milo's gaze following Thanh. The love between them was palpable.

"Can I ask, how long have you been married?"

"Almost five years now." Milo glanced around. "We met right here. I knew the minute I laid eyes on him Thanh was special." Milo shook his head. "My friends and family were all surprised. He wasn't my usual type. But after our first date, I knew he was my person."

Ryan listened, an invisible band tightening around his chest. Milo was describing the feeling Ryan had always hoped to have.

When he got home, he crept into Dylan's room and hovered over his sleeping form, watching his chest rise and fall. He reached out and brushed his fingers over Dylan's slightly damp curls. He frowned and put the back of his hand on Dylan's forehead. Was he warm? He'd been told that a slight fever was normal while his body rebuilt blood cells, but knowing that didn't ease Ryan's worry.

He never thought he'd have that moment when he looked at someone and knew that person was special. Until he met Dylan. The moment he saw him in the parking lot at Dylan's school, he felt a pull that he couldn't explain. At first he thought it was because of the connection to Lindsay. But he knew deep down it was something more.

CHAPTER TWELVE

"YOU'RE NOT eating enough." Mrs. Lieu frowned at him.

Dylan forced himself to lift a forkful of the fluffy omelet stuffed with spinach, mushrooms, and feta. It had been three days since they'd extracted his bone marrow, and he felt fine, just tired.

Mrs. Lieu placed a slice of homemade bread slathered with butter and honey in front of him. "It's a big day today. Your body needs fuel."

Thanks to Mrs. Lieu, he'd been on a steady diet of iron-rich foods since his surgery. He'd hoped to be back in the pool by now. He missed the feeling of the water on his skin, but he didn't have the energy yet. As much as he appreciated all the care and concern, he was feeling a bit stifled. It didn't help that he'd been avoiding Ryan since their conversation the other day. He felt like a coward. Avoiding Ryan wasn't going to delay his return home. There was no reason to stay. His feelings were still all over the map. Ryan always made the time to seek him out, usually finding him curled up under a cozy blanket in a chair by the window in his room, where the soft sunlight filtered through the window and he could watch the boaters on the lake. The other rooms were too big and stark to feel comfortable in. Often Ryan would ask him about the book he was reading and if he needed anything, always looking at him with concern and wanting to know how he felt.

It was the caring look in his eyes that made Dylan's heart beat faster. He knew it was wrong, and there was no way he'd ever... do what, try to kiss him? That's what had colored his dreams the last few nights.

"Dylan, are you sure you're okay with doing this?"

He jerked his head up, realizing he'd been on the verge of slipping back into that dream state sitting at the kitchen island.

He shoved one more large bite of omelet into his mouth, followed by a chunk of toast, chased it with a gulp of tea, and jumped up from his seat. "Ryan will be here soon. I should grab my things." Dylan came around the island and dropped a kiss on the crease along Mrs. Lieu's brow. "Thank you for breakfast and for taking care of me. Don't worry about me. I'll be fine."

She shooed him away with an affectionate pat on the arm and a frown that showed she didn't agree. Thank goodness she didn't catch him having to stop midway up the stairs to blink away the black spots that suddenly danced across his vision. He'd already packed a few books for Leo and a change of clothes for himself when he got up that morning. He grabbed his backpack. Ryan was waiting for him when he appeared at the top of the stairs, looking up at him with a wide smile and excitement in his eyes.

"Are you ready?" he asked as Dylan came down the stairs.

Before he could answer, the room tilted, and he pitched forward, missing the last step. Ryan's arms wrapped around him, saving him from falling to the floor.

"Are you okay?" His warm breath tickled Dylan's ear.

Dylan looked into Ryan's blue eyes, searching his face. "I'm fine," he said, straightening up, but Ryan kept his grip on him. One of Ryan's hands moved from his shoulder to Dylan's waist, creating a sudden surge of awareness in him.

He turned away before Ryan could see anything that would have him sending Dylan on the first flight back to LA, thinking he was trying to hit on him.

"We should get going," Dylan mumbled, pushing past him.

"Dylan, wait." Ryan chased after him.

"I'm fine. Don't worry about me. I wasn't paying attention to what I was doing."

Dylan kept moving. He had to get some distance and his body under control. It must be because he was still recovering. That was it. All his defenses were down. His body's response wasn't because he was attracted to Ryan; his body was out of sync right now. A few more days of healing and he'd be fine. It didn't matter; he would be back in LA in less than a week.

AFTER SO many weeks of tests, doctor's appointments, and then his procedure, Zero Day was finally here. After all the preparation and worry, it came down to watching Dylan's bone marrow flow from an IV bag down through a tube into the small port in Leo's hand.

It was silly to think there would be some magical transformation, like the fairy godmother waving her wand in *Cinderella*. And yet he and Ryan hovered over Leo, watching the slow drip from the IV bag.

Please let it work. He couldn't face what would happen if he lost the only family member who loved him.

They'd been taking turns reading the books Dylan brought to Leo. Now Ryan was stretched out on the bed, propped up against the elevated back with his arm around Leo, who slept tucked up against his side. Dylan got up from where he'd been sitting next to the bed and gently tucked a blanket around Leo's shoulders.

"Thank you," Ryan whispered, looking up at him. The look of gratitude in his eyes seemed to be for more than just making sure Leo was warm.

Dylan hovered over them. Ryan's upturned face tempted Dylan to reach out and touch Ryan's lips with his fingers... and with his mouth. He slowly straightened. "Can I get you anything else?" Dylan asked.

"Yes. You can take a rest." Ryan tipped his head to the window seat with a pillow and blanket folded at one end, wide enough for someone to sleep on.

Dylan nodded and picked up his tablet before taking a seat on the bench and pulling the blanket over his lap. He tried to focus on the words in his book, but they soon blurred and his eyes closed.

This time it was Ryan tucking a blanket over his shoulders. Dylan yawned and sat up.

"Sorry, I was trying not to wake you."

"That's okay." Dylan glanced over at the bed where Leo was curled up, still sleeping soundly. "How's he doing?"

"Leo's fine. Why don't you and I get some dinner? Leo's favorite nurse is here. He's in good hands."

Dylan stood up and swayed. "Still sleepy," he mumbled when Ryan grabbed his elbow. "I'm okay."

Dylan moved away from the lure of letting Ryan's firm hands keep him from falling.

"Why don't you want to let people take care of you?" Ryan asked softly.

"I could ask you the same question."

The corner of Ryan's mouth tipped up. "Who could have guessed we'd have so much in common?"

"There are a lot of things about you I didn't expect."

"Tell me about them over dinner," Ryan said.

Dylan swallowed, trying to quell the butterflies in his stomach. This needed to stop happening. The worst thing that could happen would be to catch feelings for his sister's husband. He had a hard time picturing Ryan and his sister together. They didn't seem like they had anything in common, but then again, he hadn't seen his sister for a long time.

"Sorry I can't take you somewhere with a little more ambiance," Ryan said, entering one of the smaller hospital cafés. "I promise I'll make it up to you and take you somewhere nice next time."

Next time. That wasn't going to happen, but Dylan couldn't help the image that formed in his mind of sitting across from Ryan at a candlelit table. Dylan stifled a groan. What was wrong with him? Why couldn't he stop thinking about Ryan as someone he wanted to wake up naked in bed with? There were too many reasons he shouldn't, but they weren't enough to keep him from saying, "That would be nice."

They ordered a couple of sandwiches and found a small table in the corner.

"So what are the other things you didn't expect about me?" Ryan asked.

"Honestly. I thought you'd be more of a snob. You're…." He paused, trying to find the right words to explain the disconnect. "You know the expression don't judge a book by its cover?" Ryan nodded. "You don't match your surroundings."

Ryan wrinkled his forehead. "I'm going to need you to elaborate."

"You live in this enormous fancy house. But you're not fancy. You're a millionaire, but you don't act like one. You married my sister, but you don't seem religious or conservative. I can't figure you out."

Ryan laughed with a snort. "Neither can I."

"What does that mean?"

"I've been thinking a lot about what you said lately. I don't feel like I fit in my own life. I've never really felt comfortable in my skin."

"I know what that feels like."

Ryan nodded.

"Have you ever thought about moving?"

"I have. Stephanie and my parents think it's too soon after Lindsay's passing to move Leo. It's the only home he's ever had."

"You're close to your sister and your parents, aren't you?"

Ryan shrugged. "Yes and no. We were really close as kids, but I don't have much in common with the rest of my family. I'm more of an introvert. That's why it works well to let Stephanie work face-to-face with Blackstone clients. When she suggested taking over sales and communications, I was happy to focus on the tech, which is what I really love to do anyway."

Dylan chewed a bite of his sandwich, listening thoughtfully. Why wasn't he surprised it was Ryan's sister's idea and that he went along with it?

They finished their sandwiches and started back toward Leo's room.

"But would you if you wanted to?" Dylan asked.

"Would I what?"

"Live in a different place."

Ryan's face twisted. "In a heartbeat. I hate that house."

"Then why did you buy it?"

"It's what Lindsay wanted." Ryan shrugged. "She and Stephanie and my parents all thought we should have a place where we could entertain clients."

"So it didn't matter what you wanted?"

"It was easier to make everyone else happy."

Dylan shook his head. "I'm glad that worked for you. I couldn't go along with what would have made everyone else happy."

Ryan scowled. "That was a line no one should be asked to cross."

"No, but it happens. And you can't say what you'd be willing to do in order to hold on to the only life you've ever known." Dylan hesitated for a second before reaching out and squeezing Ryan's hand. "I hope you get to live in a place that you love someday."

When Ryan looked down at their joined hands, Dylan pulled out of his grasp, shoving his hands in his pockets. A nurse coming out of Leo's room ended their conversation.

"He just woke up," she said.

"Noelle, this is Leo's uncle, Dylan McKenzie. Dylan, this is Noelle Wright."

"It's so nice to finally meet you. Leo's a big fan of his uncle Dylan," she said, shaking his hand.

"I'm guessing you're the nurse Leo's been telling me about."

"The one and only." She chuckled. "I'm going to order him some dinner, and I'll check back in a while."

"Thanks, Noelle." Ryan gave her a warm smile. "The staff here is wonderful," he said to Dylan as she walked away, "but Noelle charmed Leo from the first day. She told me it's a mixed thing."

Dylan nodded. "It's a funny phenomenon, but people who are mixed race—we recognize a kindred spirit or something. One time I was sitting at the airport waiting for a flight, and this little boy came over and climbed into my lap. He couldn't have been more than three. His mom was White and his dad Black. They chased after him, apologizing and embarrassed. Their little boy looked up at me and put his hand on my cheek, and we smiled at each other while I explained kids like us recognize each other."

"That's really sweet. But I think that little boy recognized a kind soul when he saw one."

Dylan felt his face heat from Ryan's compliment. "Anyway my point is, I bet if you asked, Noelle would tell you the same thing."

"That she recognized a kind soul when she met you?" Ryan said with a hint of amusement in his voice.

Was Ryan flirting with him? No, that was wishful thinking, and he had no business making wishes that weren't going to come true.

"Come on, let's see if Leo wants to watch a movie." Dylan turned his back on Ryan's enticing smile and opened the door to Leo's room.

CHAPTER THIRTEEN

RYAN COULDN'T resist the temptation to make Dylan blush. He'd never considered himself a flirt, but there was something about Dylan that made him want to be the one who made him smile and laugh. He'd become addicted to it. Small moments like the one in the hospital hallway outside Leo's room became something he craved.

They'd brought Leo home two days ago and fell into a routine. Dylan spent the mornings with Rebecca and Leo, working with him on small academic tasks that would keep him caught up when it was time to go back to school. Dylan made lesson plans with Rebecca for Leo for when Dylan returned to LA. Ryan worked in his home office in the morning, and they all had lunch together. Then they spent the afternoon keeping Leo entertained as they waited for his body to accept the new cells from Dylan's bone marrow.

It felt like everyone was collectively holding their breath, waiting.

The house was quiet now. Leo was asleep. Mrs. Lieu was out for her monthly book club meeting. Rebecca was in her room watching a movie, leaving Ryan to seek Dylan.

He found him on the patio, sitting by the fire pit with a blanket wrapped around his shoulders. Even in the moonlight, Ryan could still see the faint shadows under his eyes.

"Hey. Do you mind if I join you?"

"I hope it's okay that I turned it on," Dylan said, pointing to the flames.

"Dylan, you don't have to ask. Of course it's okay." Ryan sat down on the long outdoor sofa next to him. "Are you okay?" he asked, noticing Dylan's gloomy expression.

"I'm going to miss him," Dylan said with a slight quiver in his voice. "I didn't think it would be so hard to leave."

"Then don't." Dylan turned to him with wide eyes. "Stay for the rest of the summer. You've been wonderful tutoring Leo. If you stay, you'll be able to help him so that he won't be behind when school starts.

He doesn't want you to go and—" He swallowed. "—I don't want you to go either. I… it's been nice having you here. To feel like a family again."

"I-I'm not sure, Ryan." Dylan looked at him, his expression clouded with uncertainty. "I can't replace her, you know that, right? I know we're twins, but I'm not—" He pressed his mouth closed, blinking rapidly.

Ryan grabbed his arm. "I know that, and I don't want you to be. That's why I want you to stay, because you're different from Lindsay and her parents. I want Leo to know that he has family, an uncle who is loving and accepting."

"I need time to think about it. The time I've had with Leo means a lot to me. But staying in this house filled with memories of my sister, I don't feel any connection to her. It's strange because she was my twin, but I don't feel any sadness or loss. What kind of person does that make me?"

"I wonder what kind of person I am for feeling the same way. Lindsay was my wife, the mother of my child, and while there's a hole in my heart, it's a void that doesn't come from missing her. Since the accident I've been on a roller coaster. Some days I'm angry, some I'm sad, others relieved, but I haven't missed her. What does that say about me?"

"I'm sorry," Dylan whispered.

Ryan couldn't stop himself from reaching for Dylan's hand. He needed contact. Every time he touched Dylan, he felt grounded. Without thinking, he moved closer and wrapped his arm around Dylan's shoulder. Side by side, they stared into the flames, the heat from their bodies mingling with the heat from the flames. Dylan shuddered and dropped his chin to his chest.

"I'll stay," he said in a small voice.

Ryan fought the urge to wrap both his arms around him. He wanted to hold Dylan closer, haul him into his lap and…. he was hard as a rock. It hit him so fast he grunted.

"Are you okay?"

No, he wasn't okay. Feelings both physical and emotional engulfed him, threatening to drown him. For the first time, he couldn't put his feelings aside. They were too close to the surface to push down anymore and too big to ignore. He shifted, angling his body away, but he couldn't bring himself to let Dylan go.

"Thank you." He'd been saying those words to Dylan a lot. Only "thank you" didn't express his emotions. How did you express gratitude to someone who gave so much, some of it without even knowing? How do you thank someone who brought you to life when you didn't know you were dead? "It means a lot to Leo and to me to have you here. We... care about you. You're important to us."

To me.

Dylan stifled a yawn. "Sorry, I'm still tired more than I usually am."

"I've been worried about you."

"You don't have to worry about me. The doctor said I might feel like this for a while. It's totally fine."

Dylan got up, and Ryan stood also. "I'm going to bed."

Ryan wanted to follow him, climb into bed, and hold Dylan while he slept.

"I'm going to stay out here a little longer. These summer nights go by quickly."

Dylan looked up at the sky. "I bet away from the city light, the stars are even more amazing."

"I'll take you somewhere you can see them before the summer's over."

Was it the emotion in his voice that made Dylan's breath catch? Ryan's eyes locked with Dylan's, silently begging for understanding, unsure of how to take the first step and fearing what would follow.

"I should go," Dylan murmured.

Ryan could only nod and watch Dylan walk back into the house. As soon as he was out of sight, Ryan sat down and dropped his head in his hands. What was he doing? Did he really want a physical relationship with a man? Without hesitation he knew the answer was yes. He'd been questioning his feelings, his needs and desires, since he met Dylan. For a long time, he'd wondered if he was asexual. Except he'd been attracted to people before. His first crush, a boy in the second grade. Another boy in junior high. When his sister teased him about how he was always talking about his friend Sam, he saw the sharp look in his father's eyes and knew what he felt was wrong. By the time he began questioning those beliefs, he was married with a child. Demisexual would have fit, except his attraction to Dylan was immediate and so strong it took his breath away.

He lifted his head and clasped his hands tightly in his lap, staring into the flames. "I think I'm gay," he whispered.

He held his breath for a few moments and then exhaled. Saying it out loud wasn't as scary as he thought it would be. Whispering it to himself alone in the dark wasn't the same thing as telling your friends and family. Or Dylan.

He looked across the lake. It wasn't too late. Jumping up, he went into the house, grabbed his car keys, and drove across the bridge.

"Ryan, what are you doing here? Is everything okay?" Joy Anderson asked, opening the door wide to usher him into the house.

"Sorry to barge in on you like this. I-I wanted to talk to someone, and you and Jason, well, you're the only friends I have." He shook his head. "God, that sounds pathetic, doesn't it?"

Joy gave him a sympathetic smile. "I'm glad you came. Jason's in the living room. Come on in. I'll get you something to drink, and then we can sit and talk."

Ryan didn't sit. Instead he almost wore a hole in the carpet while he paced and spilled out everything he'd been thinking and feeling. Eventually he dropped into a chair facing Jason and Joy, who'd been sitting on the couch listening without comment.

"I'm sorry. That was a mess."

Jason got up, walked over, and grabbed his hand, pulling Ryan up into a bear hug. "Thanks for trusting us. I'm so fucking proud of you, man."

When he pulled away, it surprised Ryan to see tears in Jason's eyes. "Since I've known you, it's always seemed like you"—Jason put his hand over Ryan's heart—"had this void."

Ryan blinked back tears and nodded. "Me too."

Joy came over and Ryan found himself sandwiched in a group hug. "We love you and hope you know you can always count on us to listen and support you."

"Thank you," he said with a teary laugh, wiping his eyes. "You're the first people I've told. I don't know if or when I'm going to tell anyone else."

"But you're going to tell Dylan, right?" Joy said.

"I don't know what to say. What happens if… what if I'm wrong and when we're together, it… doesn't work?"

Jason looked at him skeptically. "Do you really think that will happen?"

In his heart, he knew that being with Dylan, being able to touch him and kiss him, would be nothing less than wonderful.

He sighed. "I don't think so. No, I know what I feel is right."

"Do you think Dylan is attracted to you?" Joy asked.

He thought about the look in Dylan's eyes when he left him by the fire. The small moments that had passed between them since Dylan arrived. There was nothing he could define other than a feeling in his gut. The attraction he felt was mutual.

"I think so. I hope so."

"Why don't you bring Dylan over for dinner sometime? We'd like to get to know him. Anyone who can make you smile the way you do when you talk about him is someone we'd like to be friends with," Joy said.

"I appreciate you guys. I know I haven't been a very good friend—"

Jason shook his head. "Stop it. Friends don't keep a scorecard. Joy and I know you've been dealing with a lot. I've been hoping you'd reach out, but I didn't want to add to your stress. You were already spreading yourself so thin, trying to make everyone else around you happy."

"Do me a favor—next time add to my stress. I've realized I need friends in my life. I know your schedule is crazy with touring, but if you're up for it, I'd like it if we could grab a drink sometime."

Jason smiled. "Anytime."

Jason and Joy made him stay for a late-night snack. It was nice to relax and catch up with them. Joy talked about what it was like growing up with two dads and offered a welcome perspective on her experience. Jason shared that he'd cut back on his touring so he'd have more time to mentor up-and-coming artists. Before he left, Jason gave Ryan a tour of his remodeled studio space.

"This is really amazing," Ryan said, looking at the scattered rugs and high-end microphones in the recording room, separated from a massive soundboard on the other side of a glass partition.

"I'm offering mentorships to emerging country artists who come from historically excluded communities. They'll be able to live in the apartment above the garage while I work with them in the studio for a month."

"Exactly what does 'historically excluded' communities mean?" Ryan asked.

"Dating Joy was an eye-opener. It was pretty depressing to learn how many people still associate country music, even the lifestyle, with whiteness." He scowled. "The hate people directed toward Joy for being a Black woman dating a country musician turned my stomach. There was a young person I had spotted busking in Nashville. No one would give them a break because they were nonbinary. They're really talented and deserve a chance, so I decided to do something about it. Same goes for Black artists. Black, Asian, Hispanic, and people across the LGBTQ spectrum don't get the same access that I got, and I want to support them."

"It never occurred to me that was a problem."

Jason raised an eyebrow. "It happens in every industry, including yours."

Ryan pinched the bridge of his nose. "I've been hiding from reality for a long time. And not only my sexuality, but a lot of things. I have a lot to learn."

"Joy will tell you it's an ongoing process. I used to be arrogant enough to think I'd just get it one day and wouldn't make any more wrong assumptions. Boy, was I wrong. Joy is the one who taught me no matter who you are, people who want to hate will find a reason to dislike you. You have to love more and keep loving no matter what."

"You married a smart woman."

Jason grinned. "Trust me, I'm grateful every day. I'm so damn lucky, and I hope you'll have a chance to be happy someday." His face fell. "I'm sorry that Lindsay died, but you weren't happy, Ryan. If Lindsay hadn't died, it was only a matter of time before your marriage did."

"I don't know. I would have stayed out of obligation or guilt."

"But that doesn't mean Lindsay would have stayed," Jason said in a grave voice.

Ryan's gut tightened. He couldn't unsee the hint of guilt in Jason's eyes. "Is there something I should know?"

"She's gone. Would knowing make it any better? It was only a rumor, Ryan."

His jaw ticked. "But you think it's true, don't you?"

Jason dipped his head. "You weren't happy, but it was pretty clear the few times we hung out together that Lindsay wasn't happy either."

Jason was right, and Ryan knew it.

"I'm sorry, Ryan. I didn't want to hurt you."

"I know that, and the truth is, deep down I knew. I just wanted to pretend it wasn't true. It feels like the ripple effect from Lindsay's accident keeps going. It's like a whirlpool trying to suck me down, and I'm terrified."

"And now you have feelings for her twin brother." Jason shot him an anxious look. "When the news comes out, it won't sit well with some people. Are you prepared for that?"

"About as prepared as I am to out myself. So no, not at all."

"Whatever you need, you know Joy and I are here for you."

Driving back across the bridge toward home, Ryan wrestled with his fears and concerns. He'd already come too far to go back, and he didn't want to. He couldn't live the life he'd led before. Was there any way he could move forward and not cause any more pain? Would he be able to convince his family that he would still be the same loving son, only now he wasn't as willing to put his own needs aside? The one thing Ryan was sure of when he crossed the bridge was that he'd wake up tomorrow ready to start a new chapter of his life.

CHAPTER FOURTEEN

"HE'S BEEN tired today," Dylan whispered to Rebecca.

"That's to be expected," she said with an understanding nod.

"He fell asleep halfway through our lessons."

"Not to worry. I'm here, so you go ahead and take a break." She eyed him with a frown. "You have circles under your eyes. Are you feeling okay?"

Dylan ran his hand through his hair. "I didn't sleep well last night."

He'd lain awake after sitting with Ryan next to the fire and agreeing to stay for the summer. He couldn't bring himself to say no. Not when Ryan had his arm around him, smelling like sandalwood and the summer evening air. There was a moment between them when he thought Ryan might kiss him. His heart started hammering again as he replayed it in his mind.

"When is your next doctor's appointment?" Rebecca asked, looking at him with a critical eye.

"I don't have anything scheduled. They told me I don't have to come back unless I'm having any problems."

She frowned. "You're still at risk for infection, Dylan. You need to take care of yourself. Get some rest, okay?"

"Yeah, I will."

Rebecca patted his arm. "I'm serious, Dylan. Take care of yourself. I was happy to hear from Ryan that you'll be staying for the summer. Leo loves having you here, and I know Ryan feels the same way."

"I will."

He appreciated Rebecca's concern, even if it wasn't necessary. He liked Leo's nanny. Dylan thought of her as a friend almost as soon as they met. Rebecca was a few years older and had been working as a traveling nurse until this job came up. Apparently, Ryan's sister offered her a ridiculous amount of money to work for Ryan. Rebecca also suspected that Stephanie had selected her as the new Mrs. Blackstone. Since Rebecca wasn't remotely attracted to Ryan and had been seeing someone since she came to Seattle, she found it all completely ridiculous.

Dylan said goodbye and headed downstairs, hoping a bowl of Mrs. Lieu's pho would alleviate the dull headache that he'd been fighting the last couple of days.

He asked me to stay.

Until that moment, Dylan hadn't realized just how much he didn't want to leave. Leo wasn't the only one he was reluctant to leave behind. Over the last couple of weeks since he arrived, he'd realized his first impression of Ryan was completely wrong. The idea of having more time to spend with him sent a nervous shiver through Dylan and made him anxious to seek Ryan out to see those deep blue eyes and his smile.

Dylan stopped outside the kitchen, hearing Ryan's voice filled with frustration and an undercurrent of anger. His breath hitched at the disdain in Ryan's sister's voice. It wasn't his intention to eavesdrop as he stood frozen, listening to the two of them argue.

"All I'm saying is you should be careful, and I think you could find someone better to tutor Leo."

"Who would be better than his uncle, who also happens to be a teacher?" Ryan said.

"Lindsay's parents said he was a difficult child who—"

Ryan cut her off. "How many times do I have to tell you they lied?"

Dylan took minor consolation from the anger in Ryan's voice. But his anger didn't lessen the sting of Dylan's parents' lies about him.

"Even if what the McKenzies said isn't true, what about his lifestyle? Do you really think having a man like that around Leo is a good idea?"

"What are you talking about? He's a schoolteacher who lives in LA. What about his lifestyle would be inappropriate?"

"He's a gay man living in LA, Ryan," Stephanie said as if she were explaining the obvious to a child. "Do you really want a person like that to have an influence on your child?"

Her insinuation made Dylan physically ill. He clutched his stomach, blinking back a wave of tears.

Ryan's voice trailed off as Dylan was abruptly pulled away by a small hand gripping his elbow.

He looked down as Mrs. Lieu pressed a finger to her lips and pushed him toward a long hallway leading to another wing of the house. As they walked, Mrs. Lieu's hand moved from his elbow to his hand, giving it a reassuring squeeze as she said in a hushed voice, "Not to worry. I'll make tea."

"Tea and sympathy," Dylan said under his breath.

"I've always loved Deborah Kerr."

They'd reached a doorway at the end of the hall. Mrs. Lieu opened the door and pulled him into an open-floor-plan kitchen and living room with a large window looking out on the lake. Instead of the stark white of the rest of the house, the walls were painted a soft light tan. Fuchsia-and-marigold-yellow pillows adorned a chocolate-brown velvet sofa, matching the colors of an overstuffed floral chair. Warm-toned wood cabinets and stone countertops with veins of gold and brown anchored the kitchen and added to the cozy feel of the space.

Mrs. Lieu pushed him down onto one of the leather stools at the kitchen island and put the kettle on.

"I have some lovely green tea with blackberry. Doesn't that sound nice?"

Dylan nodded. "Thank you, but you don't have to do this."

She paused, her dark brown eyes studying him for a moment. "But I think I do."

Dylan rested his chin on the palm of his hand and watched Mrs. Lieu bustle about putting sugar cookies on a small plate.

"I love old movies, don't you? They don't make them like that anymore. What's your favorite?" she asked, sliding the plate in front of him.

Dylan took a cookie and bit into the flaky, buttery dough with a hint of lemon, thinking as he chewed.

"Now, Voyager."

"Ah, that's a good one. It seems like people either love or hate Bette Davis. Personally, I love her. Why do you like *Now, Voyager*?"

She set a cup of tea next to the plate of cookies. Green notes mixed with blackberry wafted toward him, smelling like summer in a cup.

"I like how her character learns to stand on her own and be her own person. There's this line her character says. I used to repeat it to myself when I'd get overwhelmed or discouraged when I first left home. 'It's not difficult, it's just in the doing.'"

Mrs. Lieu sat next to him, watching him over the rim of her cup as she took a sip. She swallowed and looked at him thoughtfully. "You had to deal with a lot at a young age." She sighed. "The Blackstones are… hard people. Like Charlotte Vale in the movie, you didn't fit in with your family, and Ryan doesn't fit in with his."

"I would never hurt Leo."

"Oh, sweetheart." Mrs. Lieu put her hand over his. "I know that, and so does Ryan."

"But his sister and his parents believe the lie my parents told."

"Maybe they're searching for any excuse not to face their own deficiencies."

"So they get to destroy my reputation to save their own?"

Mrs. Lieu shook her head and took another sip of her tea. "Desperate people will do desperate things to keep a lie alive."

There was a knock on the door, and Ryan poked his head in. "Mrs. Lieu, I was looking for—oh, there you are."

Dylan stood up and wrapped his arm around his middle, trying to quell the nervousness that suddenly swept over him. Had Stephanie convinced her brother and Ryan was here to tell him to leave?

"It turns out our Dylan and I share a love of old movies. We've been talking about Bette Davis," Mrs. Lieu offered.

"What did you need?" Dylan asked.

"Oh, I, uh… I just wanted to know where you were."

Ryan hovered in the doorway, looking unsure of what he wanted to do.

"I should go. Thank you for the tea and sympathy," Dylan said, giving Mrs. Lieu a quick kiss on the cheek before making his way toward the door. He brushed past Ryan, mumbling, "Excuse me."

Ryan fell in step beside him. "Are you feeling okay?"

"I'm fine," he said.

"Did I say or do something? You seem upset."

Dylan stopped when he reached the end of the hall, glancing toward the kitchen. "Is your sister still here?"

Ryan's face fell. "You heard, didn't you?"

"I wasn't—I didn't mean to eavesdrop. Look, if you think I would ever hurt Leo or do anything inappropriate around him…."

Ryan reached for his arm. "I know you would never do anything to hurt Leo. The things Stephanie said were… misguided."

"They were lies. Nobody wants me here, Ryan. I'm only good for my cells, and you've got those, and now I'm nothing again." He shook his head with a sardonic laugh. "I'm the Henrietta Lacks of the Blackstone family."

Dylan jerked back when Ryan reached for his hand. "Your cells aren't the only reason I want you here. You're more than that to me and to Leo. You should know that by now. I—"

"Don't." Dylan put his hand up. "Don't make excuses. Your family doesn't like me, and I doubt they ever will. And—" He winced at the way his voice broke. "—over time they'll wear you down and convince you too."

"No, that's not true."

Dylan eyed him skeptically. He'd already seen Ryan give in rather than argue his point. Now he stood in front of him, gazing at Dylan as if he really cared. It was too much. He needed to get away from this empty house full of broken people and this man who stirred feelings in him. Feelings that he shouldn't have for his brother-in-law.

"I need to go."

Ryan grabbed his wrist. "Don't go. Don't leave us."

"I'm not leaving. I need a break, that's all."

Instead of letting go, Ryan's grip tightened as he moved closer. "Dylan, I need—we need you."

"Ryan." The name came out as a whisper.

"Dylan." Ryan moved his hand to hold his. "Stay with us."

Three words and his heart tumbled.

Dylan looked down at where their hands were joined. "What are you doing?"

Ryan's gaze followed. "I don't know."

Dylan shivered and closed his eyes, trying to calm his racing heart.

"Dylan, Dylan, are you okay?"

Ryan's voice echoed from far away as suddenly Dylan felt like he'd been plunged into a warm pool of blackness.

It was a perfect sunny day on a clear blue lake. Peering over the side of the kayak, he saw water that was fathomless, growing darker and darker without end.

"If we begin, we'll keep going down, never ending." Ryan's voice echoed through the water. "But we'll be together." His voice drifted further away. Ryan's face appeared beneath the surface of the water, and his hands stretched out for Dylan, but he kept drifting deeper into the dark. Dylan pushed himself over the side of the boat, sinking into the depths, reaching for Ryan's hands. When he caught him, Ryan smiled and pulled them farther down, but as they sank into the depths, Ryan's expression became blank. When the blue morphed into an inky black, Ryan let go. Dylan strained, reaching for him, but he started floating upward, shaking his head sadly.

"Dylan. Don't cry, I'm here." Ryan's voice echoed from a distance.

A hand reached down, pulled him out of the midnight blue depths and into Ryan's arms.

CHAPTER FIFTEEN

"DYLAN. DYLAN, wake up."

Ryan's voice grew louder and sounded like he was nearby instead of so far away. Dylan opened his eyes and gazed around at an unfamiliar room.

"What?" he croaked and tried to swallow. Greedily, he drank cool water through a straw pressed against his lips. "What happened?" he asked as the room came into focus. Why was he in a hospital room?

Ryan grasped the hand that didn't have an IV sticking out of it, looking at Dylan with worry. "You have an infection. But you're going to be fine, thank God. I should have paid more attention."

Dylan was trying to process what Ryan was telling him when the doctor came in. "Mr. McKenzie, you're looking a little better, I see."

"I… I'm…. I don't understand."

The doctor gave him a reassuring smile. "You've been fighting a high fever for the last twenty-four hours and unconscious for most of that time. It's understandable that you're feeling a little confused."

As the doctor's words sank in, Dylan struggled to sit up and gasped. "I had a fever? Leo. Is he okay? I didn't make him sick, did I?"

Ryan jumped up and gently pushed him back down against the pillows. "Leo's fine."

"You had an infection. It's always a risk after bone marrow donation. Your body is vulnerable while it rebuilds the blood cells that were lost. You had a fever, but you weren't contagious," the doctor said as he checked Dylan's pulse and took his temperature.

Dylan looked from Ryan to the doctor and back again. He felt so heavy, as if he'd stayed in the pool for too long and his body was waterlogged.

He closed his eyes and took a deep shuddering breath.

"We want to monitor you overnight and let the antibiotics do their job before we release you," the doctor continued. "You'll need to take it easy for the next week or so and let your body recover. Mr. Blackstone has assured me he has a private nurse on hand who can keep an eye on you."

"I'll take care of him," Ryan said to the doctor, continuing to hold Dylan's hand.

The doctor said some other things that Dylan didn't hear as he drifted back to sleep. When he woke up again, the night sky outside his window had an eerie bluish glow from the city lights.

There was a movement by the bed, and Ryan's face hovered near his.

"Hey," Ryan said with a smile as he adjusted the bed and gently helped Dylan sit up against the pillows. "Do you want some water?"

"Yes, please."

Ryan held the cup to his lips again, and Dylan drank, the cool liquid sliding down his throat and quenching his thirst.

"Well, that's a good sign," Ryan said when Dylan's stomach let out a loud rumble.

"How long have I been asleep?"

"Most of the afternoon." Ryan reached into a bag at his feet and pulled out a thermos. He opened the lid and the fragrant aroma of lemongrass and beef broth wafted toward him.

Ryan poured the broth into a bowl that was sitting on a side table. "Mrs. Lieu insisted you would not eat hospital food when you woke up."

Ryan held the bowl and dipped a spoon in, held it to Dylan's lips.

"I can feed myself."

Ryan shook his head. "Maybe later, but for right now, I'm going to feed you."

Reluctantly, Dylan opened his mouth. He sighed when the rich liquid settled in his stomach.

"Good?" Ryan asked, giving him another spoonful.

Dylan nodded. Ryan fed him the broth until the bowl was empty and Dylan was feeling more human.

"Have you been here the whole time?"

Ryan grasped his hand. "Yes."

HAD HE been there the whole time? His heart had stopped when Dylan slumped in his arms. Ryan demanded to ride in the ambulance with him and hadn't left the hospital or his side since then. He'd spent the hours watching Dylan sleep, cursing himself for not seeing how worn down Dylan had been.

Ryan would make up for it now.

Dylan frowned. "You should be with Leo."

"Leo's fine. Mrs. Lieu and Rebecca are with him, and I'm sure my sister has stopped by."

"But you—"

"Dylan, don't argue with me. I'll leave the hospital when I bring you home."

"I didn't mean to cause trouble."

Ryan reached for Dylan's hand, which he'd been holding almost nonstop. He couldn't help himself. He needed the reassurance the contact gave him that Dylan would be okay.

"You didn't cause trouble, but you did scare the shit out of me. How long were you not feeling well?"

"I… I'm not sure. I guess I thought I was just tired from being stressed."

"That's my fault."

"No." Dylan squeezed his hand.

Ryan swallowed, blinking back a sudden rush of tears. He'd told Dylan he'd take care of him, and he'd failed.

"You didn't say anything to Kevin and Carl, did you?"

"Of course I did."

Dylan let his head fall back against the pillows with a groan. "I wish you wouldn't have. I don't want them to worry about me."

Ryan brushed his thumb over Dylan's knuckles. "Did your parents break you so much that you don't think you deserve to have anyone care about you?"

Dylan's eyes grew wide before he pulled his hand out of Ryan's grasp and wrapped it around his waist.

"I'm sorry, I shouldn't have said that."

Dylan turned his head away. "You can go now."

Ryan got up slowly. "I'll go, but I'm not leaving. I'll be in the waiting room."

Dylan didn't respond. Ryan stopped at the nurses' station to let them know Dylan was awake and then slumped into a chair in the small waiting area by the elevators.

"Fuck," he muttered, dropping his head in his hands.

"Mr. Blackstone?" He looked up to see a nurse hovering in front of him, looking at him with concern. "Can I get you anything?"

"No, thank you."

"Mr. Blackstone, why don't you go home and get some rest? Shower and change."

"I can't leave."

The nurse knelt down in front of him. "We'll take care of Mr. McKenzie. I don't want to offend, but you need a shower. You can bring back some clothes for your friend so he'll have something fresh to wear home."

Ryan nodded. He hadn't thought of that.

"Yeah, okay." He pulled himself up from his seat and headed for the elevator. Outside, he took a minute to get his bearings. He'd forgotten that he didn't have his car. While he waited for an Uber, he made a list of what he'd need to bring back for Dylan.

It was late when he stumbled in. Mrs. Lieu came out of her room wrapped in her robe as soon as he got back.

"How is he?"

"Good, better. The antibiotics are working, and he'll be released day after tomorrow. How's Leo?"

Mrs. Lieu gave him a reassuring smile. "Our little lion is fine."

"Good, that's good." Ryan's voice broke, and he found himself embraced by Mrs. Lieu's comforting arms.

"Oh, my sweet boy. It's all right. Dylan is going to be okay. You'll bring him home, and we'll take good care of him."

"But I didn't before."

Mrs. Lieu pushed him toward the stairs. "You need a hot shower. I'll make you something to eat, and then we'll talk."

He nodded numbly and pulled himself up to his room, stopping to peek in on his son sleeping soundly. The adjoining room was slightly ajar and the light on. He went next door and knocked.

"Everything okay?" he asked when Rebecca answered.

"We had a great day. I used one of Dylan's lesson plans, and we had a scavenger hunt. He had more energy today. How's Dylan?"

"Better. He'll be able to come home tomorrow. I know it's not part of your job, but I'm hoping you can help monitor him. I'll pay you, of course."

Rebecca waved her hand. "Don't worry about that. It's the least I can do." Her expression sobered. "I should have caught the signs. I feel terrible."

"We all do. I'm going to make sure I pay more attention."

After saying goodbye to Rebecca, he stumbled into his room and swiftly shed his clothes. Unfazed by the icy water, he stepped into the shower and let the water warm until steam enveloped him, turning hotter within a minute. It was then that he let go.

When he'd gotten the news about Lindsay, he'd been shocked. But he never felt fear the way he felt when he held Dylan unconscious in his arms. He wasn't afraid of losing a woman he'd known for years, shared a life with, had a child with. But that ambulance ride with Dylan and the thought of not seeing his smile or touching him…. Ryan shuddered and pressed his hand against his heart. The thought hurt more than Lindsay's death ever had, and that knowledge terrified him. When his fingertips were pruned, he finally shut off the water.

Despite feeling bone-tired after his shower, he felt better after changing into clean sweatpants and a long-sleeved T-shirt. Ryan made his way back downstairs, where Mrs. Lieu was waiting with a plate of chicken and rice.

"Feel better?"

"I do," he said around a mouthful of chicken.

"Do you want to talk about it?"

Ryan sighed and set his fork down. "I feel guilty."

"It's not your fault. We all missed the signs."

"That's not what I feel guilty about."

"Oh, I see."

It wasn't what she said, but the look in her eye when she said it that made him feel exposed.

There was a moment of silence before he asked, "Do you? Do you see?"

"I see that you have feelings, deep feelings, and that they scare you. But Ryan—" She grasped his hands, looking him in the eye. "—don't run away from what you feel. Dylan has brought a light to your eyes that I've never seen. I've been worried that I might never see it. Don't ignore that."

"I'm scared," he confessed.

"What frightens you more—continuing to live this life where you try to make everyone else happy but yourself, or finally having a chance to love and be loved?"

Ryan pressed his hand against his mouth, trying to stifle another sob. Mrs. Lieu was right, but that didn't lessen the fear he felt. Mainly that when he told Dylan how he felt, Dylan would reject him.

"My *con*, don't be so afraid of what you might lose that you give up what you really want."

"I don't know." He shook his head.

"I think you know. You're just not ready to say it yet." She tilted her head, staring at him with a critical eye. "Or is it you're worried about what other people will think?"

He dropped his chin, unable to look Mrs. Lieu in the eye.

"*Con*." Ryan flinched at the sharpness in her voice. She came over and grasped his shoulder, giving him a little shake. "How long are you going to let people dictate to you rather than saying what you really want?"

Ryan's heart hammered in his chest. "I don't know," he said in a gruff voice.

"Well, you'd better figure it out before you lose him." She pulled him into a tight hug. "I love you, and I want you to be happy."

Mrs. Lieu let go and walked out of the kitchen, but not before Ryan saw her wipe away the wetness from her eyes.

As he walked back through the house and climbed the stairs to his room, exhaustion washed over him, both physically and emotionally. He lay down and covered his eyes with his arm. Even though he was exhausted, his mind raced, grappling with a flood of overpowering emotions he couldn't control.

CHAPTER SIXTEEN

DYLAN LOST track of the days, sleeping through most of them. Three days in the hospital and he could finally go back home. Every time he woke up in the hospital, Ryan was by his side, holding his hand.

For the first time in a very long time, Dylan wanted to be taken care of.

"Whoa, where do you think you're going?" Rebecca said with a scowl, catching him making his way down the hallway.

"I wanted to say hi to Leo. It's been almost a week since I've seen him."

"That's fine, but you can't overdo it. You had a serious infection, Dylan, and your immune system is still weak."

"I'm not overdoing it. I'm feeling a bit cooped up, that's all. I promise I'll be good."

"Make sure you do." Rebecca's lips quirked. "I don't think Mrs. Lieu and I can handle Ryan like that again." She sobered. "You gave us all quite a scare. Ryan was...." She sighed. "He was frantic."

"Ryan was that upset?"

"He was appropriately upset when someone he cares about was lying unconscious in his arms."

"Oh."

The knowing glint in her eyes had the heat rising in his cheeks and his pulse quickening.

Rebecca offered him her arm. "Come on. I'll give you and Leo an hour, but then you both need a nap."

Dylan chuckled. "Thanks, Mom."

Rebecca opened the door to Leo's room and gave him a playful slap on the back. "Don't be cheeky."

He turned and gave her a kiss on the cheek. "Thanks. I really mean it. Thank you."

It was nice to spend the next hour with Leo. They started out playing Legos but ended curled up together, reading and eventually falling asleep.

RYAN LOOKED down at Leo, sleeping in Dylan's arms. The shadows under both of their eyes were less pronounced than they had been in the last week. The bone marrow donation was working. Of course he'd have to wait for the doctor to confirm it, but Ryan *knew* it was working.

He crouched down and gently reached out to caress Dylan's cheek. He was still too pale and had lost weight with the infection.

Dylan's eyes fluttered open, and he smiled. "Hi." He glanced down at Leo curled up next to him. "How long have we been asleep?"

"Not long enough. I didn't mean to wake you up. I wanted to check on you."

Ryan stood as Dylan carefully untangled himself from Leo, tucking him under the blankets before getting up.

Ryan reached for Dylan's arm. Dylan didn't need the support, but Ryan needed the contact.

"Are you hungry? Mrs. Lieu has enough food made to feed almost all of Seattle."

"Not really." Dylan gave him a wry smile. "But I know you won't take no for an answer, so I'll have something." He cocked his head. "You know I never would have taken you for the stern nurse type."

Ryan raised his eyebrows. "Sometimes you have a difficult patient who needs a firm hand."

Dylan dropped his head, his cheeks turning bright pink against his tawny-brown skin.

"It's a nice day. Do you want to eat out on the dock?" Ryan offered.

"I'd love that. I could use some fresh air. Let me grab some things from my room."

When Dylan was ready, Ryan guided him down the stairs, ignoring his grumblings about not needing him to hover. The last few days had been harrowing, and he was going to indulge in his worries and keep a close eye on Dylan no matter how much he complained. Or anyone else for that matter. Stephanie and his parents had done nothing to lessen the stress of the last few days. Their constant digs at Dylan and criticism of the time Ryan was spending with him only made things worse.

It didn't matter now. Dylan was okay and back home.

Mrs. Lieu insisted on overpacking a basket with fried chicken, potato salad, green salad, peaches, and brownies. It was so heavy Ryan let out a grunt when he lifted it.

He pulled two Adirondack chairs from the lawn to the dock and set the basket between them.

"Are you warm enough? Do you want your sunglasses? You should wear sunscreen."

"Ryan, stop." Dylan wrapped his hand around Ryan's wrist. "I'm fine. I put on sunscreen, I've got my sunglasses in my pocket, and you brought three extra blankets."

He looked down at Dylan's hand, resisting the urge to weave their fingers together, and nodded. "You really scared me, Dylan. I want, I need, to make sure you're okay." Ryan shifted his chair, angling it toward Dylan. "Will you tell me your side of the story?"

"My story? What do you mean?"

"I'd like to hear from you what happened with your family."

Dylan eyed Ryan. "You know what happened from the private investigator you hired."

"I do, but I'd like to hear it from you. I want to know what really happened."

"Will hearing the story from me make any difference?"

"Maybe if I hear your side of the story, I'll understand why you are the way you are. Why you are always saying you're fine even when you're not."

Dylan sat forward, resting his forearms on his thighs, clasping his hands in front of him. He took a few deep breaths and began.

"I think I always knew I was… different. I tried to play sports, to be the version of a son my father wanted so badly. The harder I tried, the more I disappointed him. I had a journal—I needed someone to talk to, and it was all I had." He looked at Ryan. "You've been to my hometown. It's a small place with small minds. Family, faith, and football." He smirked. "If you didn't fit in to those three neat little boxes, well… you just didn't fit. My mom is in leadership at their church, my dad is the football coach, and my sister a cheerleader." He winced. "Was a cheerleader. I kept them from being the perfect family. And then they found my diary."

"You don't have to say any more. I shouldn't have asked."

"But you did. I didn't have the luxury of making the conversation stop when it got uncomfortable. You asked me for my side of the story, not for the parts that don't make you uneasy."

Dylan was right. When Ryan tried to speak, he held his hand up. "Don't you dare try to tell me you didn't want me to feel uncomfortable. Nothing about this entire situation is comfortable." He poked himself. "I'm not uncomfortable with who I am."

Ryan grabbed his hand, gently pulling it away from his chest. He held it between his. "You're right, and I'm sorry. I'm ready to listen to anything you want to share."

Leaving his hand between Ryan's, Dylan took a deep breath and nodded. "I woke up late that morning. I was rushing to get to school, and I forgot to hide it. When I came home, my parents were sitting at the kitchen table with the diary in the middle of the table. I was completely numb with panic. They gave me two choices. Go to a special camp or leave. I knew they were talking about conversion therapy before they showed me the brochure for the camp." Dylan hated the tremor in his voice. "I tried to be strong enough to agree, but I… I couldn't do it. They gave me twenty minutes to pack my stuff and get out. I didn't know where to go, so I went back to school. The school library was always my refuge, the place where I felt safe, and that's where Kevin—Mr. Cooper—found me."

"What about Lindsay?"

Dylan smirked and pulled out of Ryan's grasp. "Yeah, that whole thing about twins being bonded?" He shook his head. "Maybe for some kids, but not us. Lindsay came home from cheerleading practice as I was leaving. She let me know in no uncertain terms that I was an embarrassment and it would be a relief to have me out of her life. My parents and Lindsay didn't waste any time telling people the story I'm sure you heard."

"That you had a drug problem, ran away, and died of an overdose?"

"So much better than having a gay son, right?"

"Dylan, I—"

"Whatever you're going to say, don't. I don't blame you. Why would you question your wife? You were in love, and I hope you were happy."

Ryan dropped his head. "We weren't happy."

Dylan opened his mouth and closed it again. "I thought…."

"Everyone did. We put on a convincing performance as a happily married couple. But that wasn't the reality. Lindsay and I had different goals and values. I thought with time we would grow into our marriage, but we grew further apart instead of closer together." He drew in a shaky breath. "It wasn't easy before Lindsay died, and now it's even a bigger mess. You said the more you tried to be the perfect son, the more you failed. I know what that feels like. The more I tried to be the perfect husband, the more I felt like I failed."

"It was the same for me and my dad, it's a two-way street, Ryan. Both people have to be open to wanting a relationship. Being different isn't a flaw if two people will accept each other for who they are with love and respect." He sighed, rubbing the back of his neck. "I don't know what I'm trying to say. I guess I'm saying if you love someone unconditionally, you shouldn't have to feel like you have to be perfect for the other person. Lindsay should have accepted you as you are."

"She should have done the same thing for you."

Understanding filled the silence that surrounded them.

"You must be starving by now," Ryan said.

"Not really, but I'll eat something for you."

The way Dylan said "for you" had Ryan's gaze focusing on his lips.

"I, uh…." He cleared his throat and started digging through the basket of food. He needed to do anything to stop thinking about Dylan's lips and what it would feel like kissing them.

"You said you weren't hungry, but you devoured that plate fast," Ryan observed, a smug smile on his lips as he glanced at Dylan's empty dish.

"I guess I was hungrier than I thought," Dylan admitted.

"Can I get you anything else?" Ryan asked, taking their plates and packing everything back in the basket.

"Could we walk down there?" Dylan pointed to the small stretch of beach next to the dock. "I wouldn't mind stretching my legs a bit."

They made their way down to the beach. Ryan picked up a smooth, flat rock and skipped it over the water.

Dylan slipped off his shoes and dug his toes into the rocky sand. "I miss sandy beaches, but the view?" He shaded his eyes, scanning the shoreline. "It's magical here."

"I love these long summer days," Ryan said, looking at a picture-perfect view of Mount Rainier in the distance. "But don't get lured in.

People come up here and fall in love during the summers, and they decide to move here. Then winter hits, and it's so dark and gray you don't see that"—he pointed toward the mountain—"for weeks on end."

"But think of all those dark and cozy winter nights."

The late afternoon sun created a golden halo around Dylan. A good meal and time outside made his lips pink and brought some of the color back to his face.

Ryan groaned, "Dylan," and reached for him, grasping his waist as he pulled him closer.

Dylan gasped, his eyes growing wide. "Wh-what are you doing?"

"Something I haven't been able to stop thinking about for a while now," Ryan whispered.

"But you can't. You're not gay. You can't like me," Dylan sputtered.

Ryan cupped his cheek. "You're wrong. I do like you and—" He drew in a breath. "—I've been hiding who I am from everyone, including myself, for a long time." Dylan closed his eyes and shuddered when Ryan brushed his thumb over his lips. "When the sun shines so bright, you can't hide anymore. Your light blinded me when we met," he whispered, inhaling the sunshine and citrus on Dylan's lips from the lemonade they had at lunch. A low hum rumbled in his chest when his lips finally met Dylan's.

So this is what a kiss was supposed to feel like. Soft and firm. The slight abrasion of Dylan's stubble on his skin. Dylan's lips parted. Even though they'd just eaten, Ryan was hungry all over again. Ryan delved into Dylan's mouth with his tongue. He cupped the back of Dylan's neck in his hand, pulling him closer, but it still wasn't enough. When he finally released Dylan's mouth, Dylan dropped his head to Ryan's chest, his breath coming out in soft pants. Ryan shifted, pressing his hard cock against Dylan's, and almost exploded right then.

"I knew it," he whispered, cradling Dylan's face when they broke apart. "I knew you would taste sweet and so good. I want more. I want all of you. I've been wanting to kiss you for so long."

Dylan regarded him, his eyes searching Ryan's face. "I didn't want to be attracted to you, but—" He licked his lips. "—I wondered what it would feel like to be like this with you, and it's so much more than what I imagined."

"I may not know what I'm doing, but I know what I want, and I want you, Dylan." He smiled and caressed Dylan's cheek again. "So I need you to get better so we can do more than kiss. I need you in my bed, where I can explore and taste every inch of you."

Dylan's face fell, and he pulled out of Ryan's hold. "I can't do that."
Ryan's stomach dropped. "I thought you wanted…."

"I do, but I can't—" Dylan shook his head. "Not in the same bed you shared with my sister." His lips trembled. "What are we thinking? We can't do this. I-I'm confused," he finished weakly. When he looked up at Ryan, Dylan's eyes filled with anguish. "I remind you of Lindsay. You're confused. You aren't gay."

"Stop." Ryan grasped his shoulders and kissed Dylan's forehead. "Don't compare this to what your sister and I had, because this between us is completely different. I never felt like this with Lindsay or anyone before. This isn't a random impulse, Dylan. I've had feelings before, but I was scared, and I never acted on them. I thought I could ignore them and they'd go away. You're not Lindsay, and that's why I'm attracted to you. I desire you because you're a man. A man I want to make love to."

Dylan's eyes were shiny with unshed tears as they searched Ryan's face. "I want to believe you," he said in a shaky whisper.

"I'm telling you the truth. I shouldn't have ambushed you like that. It's… I couldn't hold it in anymore. When you collapsed, I realized I didn't want to continue on pretending to be someone I'm not." Ryan reached out and brushed his hand against Dylan's. "When you relapsed, I was scared of losing you, but now I'm even more frightened by the possibility of never knowing the feeling of holding you in my arms."

CHAPTER SEVENTEEN

RYAN COULDN'T stop thinking about kissing Dylan. One kiss wasn't enough, and he craved more.

He couldn't ignore the attraction that had been building since he first met Dylan. He had kept the knowledge to himself for weeks, but seeing him in the hospital made him realize he couldn't hide his feelings any longer. Watching over Dylan, wanting to kiss him, to feel his body pressed against his in bed, was driving him to distraction. Now that he'd acted on his impulse, it was even worse. He'd put off work projects and returning to his office, letting deadlines fall by the wayside.

He pressed the heels of his palms against his eyes. There'd been that boy in high school and others over the years who'd given him butterflies and an awareness that he didn't feel with a woman. Including the person he'd vowed to spend his life with. Instead, he put that part of himself away, never acting on those feelings. His parents made it clear when they talked about their friends who had children come out what a disappointment it was. Maybe that's why Stephanie was constantly encouraging him to date her friends. Did she know? It didn't matter now. This time something was different. Maybe he was different, older, and after sacrificing so much of himself over the years, he'd hit a wall. But it was also Dylan, and the way he looked at him with those large brown eyes, and the way his hair curled at the nape of his neck when he got out of the pool. Ryan finally had to admit he wanted Dylan. He understood Dylan's misgivings, but his comment that Ryan only thought of him as a replacement for his twin hurt. His feelings for Dylan were so different from any he ever held for Lindsay.

Ryan had been a bit surprised when Stephanie brought Lindsay home for the weekend and made not-so-subtle suggestions that he should ask her out. Half-Black girls were okay; dating a guy, absolutely not. It was a harsh realization. Family was everything to him. Maybe it was the fear of never having his own family and losing his parents' love that made him pursue a relationship with Lindsay that wasn't really in his heart. He'd always been a pleaser. He'd been the kid who was happier going along with the crowd than being the leader. Ryan never liked confrontation and found it easier to conform to what others wanted than to argue.

Now here he was, thirty-four and never having lived the life he wanted.

"I can't do it anymore." He sighed.

A soft tap on the door brought him out of his reverie.

"Ryan, are you okay?" Dylan hovered in his doorway doing that thing he did, looking at him as if he really saw him, really cared.

"I—" He closed his mouth and shook his head. No, he wasn't okay, and he didn't know how to explain.

Dylan came toward him. He still looked too pale but much better. He'd been lying on one of the deck chairs, sleeping in the sun. Ryan had been trying to get caught up on work, but he kept wandering over to his office window to check on him.

Ryan's libido. Lust pooled in his belly when he caught the scent of warm sunshine on Dylan's skin. "Don't," he said in a shaky whisper.

Dylan stopped, wrapping his arms around his middle. "I thought this might happen. It's okay if…. What happened last night was a mistake. You got caught up in a moment. It's fine. It happens."

"Dylan, stop." Ryan's voice was gruff. "If you come any closer, I'm going to want to kiss you again."

"Oh." A blush colored Dylan's cheeks. "Would that be a bad thing?"

Dylan's response brought a smile to his lips. "Yes and no. Kissing you again definitely wouldn't be a bad thing, but I'm not sure if I can stop with a kiss. That kiss unlocked a part of me. It set me free, and now—" Ryan frowned, shaking his head. "—I can't go back to being numb, and I don't want to anymore."

"What do we do now?"

Ryan got up and stood in front of Dylan. "I know what I need. What's more important is what do you want?"

"I want…." Dylan paused, his tongue darting out to lick his lips. "I'd like to kiss you again, and I think I want more, but I'm… I don't know, scared, worried, and… a lot of things."

"I wish I could let you." Dylan wrinkled his forehead, looking at him with confusion. "Never mind. Was there something you needed?"

"Leo and I have been reading books about camping," Dylan said. "Well, not really camping, but about national parks, and I wondered if I could take Leo camping."

"What?"

Dylan shook his head with a small smile. "I didn't mean camping for real." He glanced out the window. "I thought if it was okay with you, I'd get a tent and we could camp in the backyard. Unless you have one and it would be okay with you if I borrowed it."

"No, I don't have a tent."

"That's okay, I can get one. I think Leo's feeling better. He's got a lot more energy these days. So what do you think?"

Dylan looked at him with a hopeful expression that made Ryan's heart do a little flip-flop. And then he smiled. Ryan was willing to do anything to be the reason behind Dylan's smiles.

"I think that's a great idea. We could go to REI this afternoon."

"I'd like that. I have a membership, and I was hoping to see the flagship store while I was here," Dylan said.

Ryan glanced at his watch. "Can you give me an hour to finish up?"

"Yeah, sure, that would be fine. You don't have to take me. I can get a rideshare and go myself."

Ryan groaned. "I forgot." He went to his desk drawer and pulled out a set of keys. "I meant to give you these when you arrived. It was so busy, and then you were sick." He held a car key out to Dylan.

Dylan stared down at the key in his hand, rubbing his thumb over the Mercedes logo on the key fob. "I can't take your car."

"It's to the SUV. I don't think Lindsay used it more than a dozen times since she bought it. It's the latest model."

Dylan's expression clouded. "I can't," he said, holding the key back out to Ryan. "I don't think I would feel comfortable using Lindsay's car."

Ryan's stomach sank. "I didn't think. Of course you'd feel uncomfortable. That was thoughtless of me."

"I don't want to be an inconvenience."

Ryan had reached his limit. He reached out to Dylan and pulled him closer, gripping his shoulders. "You're not an inconvenience," he said, giving him a little shake. "You have every right to feel the way you do."

Dylan sighed, his body relaxing into Ryan's. He splayed his hands on Dylan's back. Eventually, Dylan tensed and stepped out of his arms.

"I shouldn't have done that. I'm sorry."

"Don't be sorry. I want to be here for you. You've been through a lot, Dylan. You deserve it."

"You need to stop doing that."

"Doing what?"

"Wanting to take care of me."

Ryan gently caressed Dylan's cheek. "I like taking care of you. I like you, Dylan. Taking care of you makes me happy."

He didn't want to scare Dylan away, so he stepped back and held out his hand. "Give me back the key." Dylan passed it to him, and Ryan continued, "I'll get you something else you can drive while you're here." When Dylan protested, Ryan put his finger to his lips. "Don't you dare say anything about inconveniencing me. Let me take care of it and don't worry. And we'll go to REI together."

Dylan clamped his mouth shut and nodded.

"I'll meet you downstairs in an hour, okay?"

Dylan nodded again and backed out of the room.

Ryan wasted no time after Dylan's departure calling his assistant to organize the pickup and trade-in of Lindsay's SUV for a new compact SUV to be delivered the next day. He didn't want Dylan to feel like a prisoner while he was here.

"RYAN, YOU'RE being ridiculous. We don't need all this for camping in the backyard," Dylan said.

They'd been making their way through the flagship REI store for the last hour. As soon as they walked in, Ryan wasted no time in adding items to their cart while Dylan remained fascinated by the towering climbing structure near the entrance.

Ryan tried to look innocent as he held a top-of-the-line camp stove hovering above the cart. "Maybe we don't need it for camping in the backyard, but if Leo likes it, I'd like to take him camping for real."

"I'm not going to be able to reason with you, am I?"

"Nope," Ryan said, adding the stove to the cart. "Let's go look at tents."

Ten minutes later, Dylan put his foot down. "Absolutely not. You do not need a ten-person tent."

Ryan tapped his lips, walking around the enormous tent on display one more time before looking at Dylan. "Okay, what do you suggest?"

Dylan grabbed Ryan's arm and led him over to a display of tents with a guide that listed all the different tents with a chart comparing the various features. He eyed Ryan, who was staring at the guide with a furrowed brow.

"Have you ever been camping before?"

Ryan gave him a sheepish smile. "No."

The random assortment of items in the cart made sense now. Dylan's frustration melted into compassion that had him reaching for Ryan's hand and giving it a reassuring squeeze. "That's okay. This will be good practice when you and Leo are ready to venture into the wilderness."

Dylan tapped a picture on the guide. "I think this is a reasonable option. There's plenty of room for you and Leo."

"But what about you?"

"Well, I thought I'd—"

"Nope." Ryan shook his head. "Don't do that thing you do where you don't include yourself. This could be the beginning of a tradition. We can take Leo camping every summer."

Dylan looked down and realized he was still holding Ryan's hand. He let go, unsure Ryan was ready to show affection in public. Ryan didn't loosen his grasp right away. Dylan's heart fluttered in his chest. He found it difficult to accept that Ryan was attracted to him. This smart, kind, deadly sexy man wanted him. It was intoxicating.

"What about this one, the next size up? Would that be big enough for the three of us?"

Dylan studied the model Ryan was pointing at. "That would be perfect."

Next they added three sleeping bags to the cart, along with camp chairs and a portable campfire, which Ryan insisted they needed in addition to the propane camp stove.

"This is the one thing you can't argue with me about," Ryan said, holding up three stainless-steel roasting sticks. "We can't go camping without making s'mores."

"Of course not." Dylan grinned.

While they waited in line with their cart overflowing, Dylan looked around the two-story timber framed structure. "Someday I'd like to have this."

Ryan wrinkled his forehead. "A store?"

"No," he chuckled. "I'd like to have a little cabin in the woods. By a lake where I could go snowshoeing in the winter and kayaking in the summer."

"That sounds perfect. My family has been trying to get me to buy a vacation house, but they want me to buy in a resort with perfect sandy white beaches."

"What do you want?"

"Something simple where I can unplug and relax. A place that isn't designed to impress anyone or entertain clients. Your cabin in the woods sounds like a perfect place where I could just… be."

"I'd love to have you and Leo come visit if I can ever make my dream come true."

"I'd love it if Leo and I could be a part of your dream," Ryan said softly, with a look that made Dylan catch his breath again.

Ryan's sister was waiting for them when they returned, with a dismissive glance at Dylan and some urgent business with Ryan.

It seemed like everything was urgent with whatever Stephanie needed her brother to do. As his sister led Ryan away, Dylan imagined a scenario where he and Ryan would stay in a secluded cabin, watching the snowfall from their shared bed.

Dylan organized the camping gear on the patio and went to tell Leo about this plan.

"Yay!" Leo threw his little arms around Dylan's legs, gazing up at him with an enormous smile. "Are we gonna roast marshmallows, Uncle Dylan?"

"Of course. It wouldn't be a camping trip without making s'mores."

"You can't take him camping." Acid dripped from Stephanie, who was glaring at him from the doorway.

"Don't worry, we're camping in the backyard."

"Don't tell me what to do," Stephanie snapped. She crouched down next to Leo with a fake smile. "Leo, can you ask Rebecca to take you to the kitchen and have Mrs. Lieu give you a treat?"

Leo hesitated, his eyes flickering with uncertainty, looking to Dylan for reassurance.

"It's okay, Leo. We can read another camping story later, and we can plan our camping trip."

"Okay, Uncle Dylan." Leo ran out of the room calling for Rebecca.

"Never correct me in front of my nephew ever again," Stephanie seethed at him.

"He's my nephew too, and I only have his best interests at heart. The camping trip is a learning experience. Leo's feeling better. He has more energy, and this is a safe way for him to have an adventure."

"This isn't about Leo. It's about you thinking you have any place in this family or any right to influence my brother."

Dylan looked Stephanie in the eye. "Believe me, I know my place. I learned it the day my parents kicked me out. You won't intimidate me, Stephanie. I haven't done anything wrong. I came here to save Leo. There's no other agenda. At the end of the summer, I'll be going back to LA. But I will be a part of Leo's life. That's all I want." He took a deep breath. "Actually, that's not true. There's one other thing I want."

Stephanie smirked. "I knew it."

Dylan shook his head, looking at her with pity. "I want Ryan to stop living his life making everyone but himself happy. But I can't change that. It's up to him."

"Stay away from my brother," she warned, her voice filled with a mix of anger and protectiveness. "You don't know what he wants or what he needs."

"And you do?"

She folded her arms. Anger radiated from her in waves. "I'm Ryan's sister. It's my job to take care of him. It's always been my job. I've kept him from straying down the wrong path my entire life, and I'm not going to let you ruin it."

Her words sent a chill through Dylan. What did she mean by keeping Ryan from straying down the wrong path?

"You don't have to worry about me."

"But I do," she said before turning on her heel and walking away.

Dylan wrapped his arms around his middle. Despite what he'd said, Stephanie's words worried him. She was going to look for any excuse to find fault with him. Did she think he'd try to seduce Ryan? Is that what she meant about keeping him from going down the wrong path? At first he scoffed at the idea and then thought about the mixed signals he'd been getting from Ryan. The hand holding and heated looks weren't something a straight man would do. Was it possible Ryan was bi?

No, it couldn't be. Ryan was reaching out to Dylan because he reminded him of Lindsay. Despite Ryan's denial, it couldn't be anything more, even if there was a small part of Dylan that wished it could be.

CHAPTER EIGHTEEN

"WHERE ARE you taking me?" Dylan followed Ryan through the house, trying not to think about how hot Ryan's ass looked in the gray sweatpants he was wearing.

Not to think about how amazing Ryan's lips felt against his had been Dylan's main focus since the day before last when they'd kissed on the beach. His emotions were all over the map since then. He was definitely on board for more kissing. Kissing Ryan felt like coming home, or coming home to the home he'd always wished for as an adult. Warm and cozy, a safe place where he felt... loved.

That was the scary part. Was this nothing more than a phase for Ryan? Was he merely curious? Did he have some kind of weird twin fetish? The thought made Dylan shudder, and he immediately rejected it. Ryan wasn't the type for something like that. But he still wondered if he reminded Ryan of Lindsay and that was the reason for the attraction, even though Ryan denied it.

"Movie night." Ryan smiled at him over his shoulder.

The way Ryan smiled—his eyes filled with excitement and a slight dimple in his chin—tempted Dylan to overcome his fears and go wherever Ryan led him. He hadn't seen Ryan much since they'd returned from shopping for camping gear. Stephanie had been there with some kind of work emergency that had kept Ryan locked away in his office for the day, leaving any time together limited to secret smiles and brief touches. The time apart only intensified Dylan's longing. Sparks of anticipation tingled under his skin when Ryan took his hand.

Dylan glanced at his cotton pajama bottoms and T-shirt. "I'm not dressed to go out to a movie."

Ryan inspected him up and down with a glint in his eye that turned those sparks into a flame. "You're dressed perfectly for where we're going."

"Where are we going?" Dylan asked as they went to another wing of the house he'd never explored.

Ryan opened a door with a flourish. "Welcome to Cinema Blackstone."

"The rich are different from you and me." Dylan murmured the quote attributed to F. Scott Fitzgerald under his breath. He took in the middle of a home-theater room that was much nicer than any movie theater he'd ever been in.

The windowless room had three rows of four plush black leather reclining seats arranged on a tiered floor, ensuring every occupant a view of the massive screen on the opposite wall. The walls and ceiling were painted a dark charcoal color, as were the built-in speakers, so that they were barely noticeable. Gray-and-black speckled carpet covered the floor and added to the soundproofing. The room was designed to create the ultimate movie experience, from the low lighting to the theater-style popcorn machine and candy counter, to the glass-fronted beverage cooler stocked with soda, beer, and wine.

"Well?" Ryan looked at him anxiously. "What do you think?"

It was cute how much Ryan wanted him to like it. Dylan closed the door behind them, walked over to Ryan, and wrapped his arms around his neck. "It's wonderful," he whispered against his lips.

Their lips clashed like two starving men devouring each other. All of the promises he'd made to himself to hold back and not lead with his heart evaporated under Ryan's onslaught. This wasn't a mistake; this was fate, an unexpected match that made Dylan whole.

"I haven't been able to think of anything but this. I've wanted to kiss you so bad," Ryan mumbled against his mouth. His warm lips captured Dylan's again in another kiss that left him breathless and wanting more.

Ryan backed him toward a chair and twisted his body as they fell into it so that Dylan was in his lap. He shifted, straddled Ryan's thighs, and held his face in his hands, looking into his lake-blue eyes and finding want and need in their depths. Ryan opened his lips when Dylan ran his tongue across them before opening his mouth with a groan. He grabbed Dylan's ass, pressing him into his groin. Dylan let go of Ryan's face and pressed his hands against Ryan's chest, releasing his mouth with a soft pop. With their gazes fixed, Dylan delved into the waistband of Ryan's sweatpants. He grinned, realizing it was the sole layer of fabric covering Ryan's long shaft. Ryan gasped when Dylan wrapped his hand around his length. His head fell back, and his eyes closed.

"Don't," he hissed. But when Dylan let go, Ryan covered Dylan's hand with his, holding it against his erection. Dylan's eyes popped open. "I'll come," Ryan said in an anguished whisper.

"I can help with that. Do you trust me?"

He answered with a jerky nod. Dylan slid off his lap, kneeling between Ryan's legs. Nuzzling them apart, he pulled Ryan's sweatpants down far enough to free him. Ryan's cock was long and thick, cut, nestled in a thatch of trimmed dark blond hair.

Dylan looked from the drop of precum at the tip to Ryan's face. "How long has it been?"

"A year? I don't know. I can't remember," he answered in choppy, strained bursts.

Dylan nuzzled the hair at the base of Ryan's cock, breathing in his musky scent. "This first time may not last long, but don't worry, we have time," he said. Before Ryan could answer, Dylan took him in his mouth, exploring his veined length with his tongue.

Ryan made a sound like a wounded animal, his back arching off the chair. Dylan stretched his hands under Ryan's shirt, spreading his palms against his firm chest, pushing him back in the chair. It only took seconds before he could feel Ryan's cock pulse.

Ryan threw his arm over his face. "Oh God, Dylan, I'm—" He didn't finish. Ryan's release filled Dylan's mouth.

At first Dylan thought the wetness on Ryan's face was from sweat, and then he realized Ryan was crying.

He clambered into his lap and held Ryan's face, looking at him anxiously. "I'm so sorry. I don't know what I was thinking. I shouldn't have—"

Ryan grabbed Dylan's wrists. Leaning forward, he stopped Dylan's babbling with a kiss, plunging his tongue into his mouth. When he released him, Ryan pressed his forehead against Dylan's. "Never apologize for what happened between us again. I'm not crying because there's anything wrong. I'm crying because for the first time in my life everything is right."

Dylan wrapped his arms around him, nuzzling his neck with a nod. Now it was Dylan's turn to fight back tears. He understood what Ryan was saying. He'd never felt so powerful. Even though he was the one giving Ryan a blow job, the way Ryan called out his name and reached for him when he climaxed made Dylan feel like he was the one who was cherished and cared for. It was new, thrilling, frightening, and filled him with hope.

After a few minutes, Ryan gently grasped Dylan's chin, tilting his face so he could look into Dylan's eyes. "I didn't bring you here to.... I didn't think this was going to happen, you know that, right?"

Dylan caressed his cheek. "I know, but I'm happy it did." He wrinkled his forehead. "Why *did* you decide to bring me here?"

"Mrs. Lieu said you liked old movies."

"What movie are we going to watch?"

"*Desk Set*. Mrs. Lieu said I'd like it."

Dylan laughed and kissed him. "It's perfect."

"What's so great about *Desk Set*?"

"It's about a guy, Spencer Tracy, who loves computers more than anything until he meets Katharine Hepburn."

Ryan raised his eyebrows. "So you're telling me I'll like it because it's about a computer geek?"

Dylan laughed and squirmed out of Ryan's arms when he tickled his ribs. Ryan stood up and hauled him back into his arms, his hands skimming down Dylan's sides before wrapping around his waist. "It doesn't matter what the movie is about. I'll like it because I'm watching it with you."

Amid their kisses and caresses, Dylan wondered how they were able to get the movie playing. They started in separate seats, but as the opening credits ended, he found himself sitting on Ryan's lap with Ryan's arms around him, watching the movie.

EVEN AFTER watching the movie, Ryan still couldn't tell you what *Desk Set* was about. But he could describe in detail what it felt like holding Dylan in his arms, the softness of the skin, of his cock, the slickness of his release on his hand, the musky smell and the sweet, salty tang when he smeared it on Dylan's lips and kissed him.

Despite Dylan's insistence, Ryan didn't need to worry about his own release. Ryan had other ideas. Driven by the need to see Dylan's face when he came, Ryan couldn't keep his hands off him. He wouldn't allow Dylan to refuse him the satisfaction of taking care of him in a different way. And now he knew what it was like to feel free, alive, and scared for what happens next. He couldn't let Dylan go. He knew that now. The question was, how did he make a life where he could love him the way he deserved to be loved?

The movie credits had faded from the screen, and Dylan was relaxed, asleep in his arms. He'd never felt so emotionally and physically connected with anyone like this before, and he wanted more. He wanted to claim Dylan in every way.

Dylan stirred in his arms. "I'm sorry," he said with a sleepy smile.

He kissed the top of Dylan's head. "It's okay, you're still recovering."

"Oh, I think I'm fully recovered now," he said with a mischievous glint in his eye.

Ryan could feel his face heat and his body beginning to respond. He shifted in his seat and Dylan bit his lip, looking at the bulge in his pants.

"Does this mean you don't have any regrets?" Dylan brushed his hand over Ryan's cock.

He pulled Dylan up so that he straddled his lap, grabbed his face, and kissed him. "No regrets," he said in a low, husky voice when he finally tore his mouth away.

Now it was Dylan's turn to blush. "I'm glad."

Ryan glanced at the closed door and sighed. "I wish we could stay in here."

"But we can't. Hiding from the world won't make what we have to face next disappear, Ryan."

He blew out a shaky breath and nodded. Dylan was right. They couldn't hide, but he wasn't ready to come out yet. He didn't want to face the battle that he knew was coming. A small part of him wanted to think his parents and his sister would be okay with his choice, but a bigger part of his heart knew that wasn't true. For a person who spent most of his life avoiding conflict, what was coming terrified him. But not as much as thinking about what his life would look like when Dylan went back to LA.

"One more kiss before we go back to the real world?"

Dylan nodded and lifted his face. One kiss turned into two that turned into both of them coming when Dylan held their cocks together and jerked them off.

"That wasn't supposed to happen," Dylan panted, looking down at the come splattered across both their pants.

Ryan gave him a kiss on the forehead. "Hold on a minute."

He went to the small doorway at the back of the room and returned with two towels.

"The way the door is built into the wall, I didn't even notice there was a bathroom there," Dylan said, wiping at his pants.

"See, we could live here if we wanted to. We have everything we need," Ryan answered with a cocky grin.

"We can't live on popcorn, Milk Duds, and soda. Plus we're missing one important element."

"Leo," they said in unison.

"What would he think about... us?" Dylan asked.

"I don't know. I have a lot to think about and some big decisions to make. This is all new, thrilling, and overwhelming. Can you... will you be patient with me while I figure it out?"

Dylan nodded, giving him a tender kiss that brought Ryan to tears again. Ryan kept his hand on Dylan's back as they walked out of the room. He stopped at Dylan's door. "I have to say good night or I'm going to want to follow you inside," he whispered.

CHAPTER NINETEEN

RYAN THREW his head back and laughed. Leo giggled, with more chocolate on his face than on his graham cracker, while in the other hand he held a roasting stick over the campfire as a marshmallow engulfed in flames slid off into the fire.

"I need another one, Daddy," Leo said.

"I think you've had more than enough, buddy." Dylan took the skewer from Leo's sticky fingers. "Let's get you cleaned up and into your jammies."

"And then we get ghost stories?"

"Yup, I've got three for us to read," Dylan said, leading Leo toward the outdoor kitchen on the patio to wash up.

Ryan was finally having the family experience he'd always wanted. It was all because of Dylan. He'd organized the day to make it a learning adventure for Leo. Leo's backpack was filled with all the essentials for a camping trip, including a compass and a custom-drawn backyard map. They embarked on a "hike" through the dense "woods," identifying different plants in the backyard and discovering the little plastic forest animals Dylan hid in the surrounding bushes. Dylan taught Leo how to use the compass to mark the location of each animal on his map. Even putting up the tent became a math lesson, using the tent poles to learn about measurements. Leo took a nap in the tent after eating the roast turkey sandwiches made by Mrs. Lieu. Dylan scattered wood pieces around the yard for Leo to collect for the campfire.

"You're an amazing teacher." Ryan kissed Dylan's cheek as he used stencils and water-soluble spray-paint to create animal tracks around the yard. "Where did you get all this stuff?"

"I ordered it and had it delivered overnight."

"Let me reimburse you."

"It's fine, Ryan. It didn't cost too much, and I'm happy to do it." Dylan rested his hands on his hips, eyeing his handiwork. "I think I'll do something like this for my kids next year."

Ryan's heart fell. It was selfish, but he wanted Dylan to stay beyond the summer. But what could he offer him? He couldn't ask Dylan to stay and keep their relationship a secret. That wasn't fair to either of them.

He reached for Dylan's hand. "I never could have come up with anything like this. Thank you."

Dylan smiled. "Consider it training for when you can take Leo on a real camping trip."

"You'll be there to keep me from straying off the trail and getting us lost in the woods."

Dylan's smile faded, replaced with a worried look.

"What's wrong?"

"Nothing. It's—I hope you know I would never. I didn't mean to… lead you astray," Dylan said with a slight wince.

"Whoa, where is this coming from?"

"I… your sister is worried I'll influence you, and I don't want you to think I'm…." He shoved his hands in his pockets and shrugged. "I would never make you do something you didn't want to do."

Ryan's jaw ticked. "Exactly what did my sister say?"

"She was worried about Leo camping, that's all."

"That's not all."

"She's your sister. I'm not going to get in the middle of your relationship. Let it go, Ryan. It's fine. I'm a big boy, and I know how to take care of myself."

But he couldn't let it go. He put it aside while he spent the rest of the afternoon collecting firewood with Leo and doing the other activities Dylan planned. After roasting hot dogs for dinner and making s'mores for dessert, Leo sat in Dylan's lap reading silly camping ghost stories with a flashlight while Ryan thought about his earlier conversation with Dylan. He'd told Stephanie to back down, and she didn't listen. He was mad as hell. She'd crossed a line. She might interfere with other aspects of his life, but Dylan was off-limits.

"Ryan," Dylan called out softly.

His head jerked up from the hypnotic dance of the flames to see Leo curled in Dylan's arms, fast asleep.

He got up and went over to gently extract his son from Dylan's arms. Dylan entered the tent, adjusted the lantern, and prepared Leo's sleeping bag to make it easier for Ryan to tuck Leo in.

Ryan glanced at Dylan kneeling by his side. It felt so right. This was the family he'd hoped for, the family he wanted. He tipped his head toward the front of the tent and motioned for Dylan to follow him outside.

As soon as they stepped out of the tent into the warm summer night, Ryan reached for Dylan, pulled him close, and kissed him. Dylan melted into him, parting his lips, welcoming Ryan in. Ryan devoured the perfect wet heat of Dylan's mouth, mapping every inch with his tongue. When he broke the kiss, Dylan looked up at him, his lips wet and pupils dilated with lust.

Ryan's fingers caressed the smooth column of skin at Dylan's throat.

"I've been waiting all day to kiss you by firelight," Ryan murmured, his heart pounding in his ears. Dylan's fingers tangled in the hair at the nape of Ryan's neck. He leaned in and kissed the spot between Ryan's neck and the curve of his shoulder.

"I've been thinking about you all day."

Ryan sighed, pressing his forehead to Dylan's. "I've been reading some of those authors you told me about. I've read about it, watched people in movies talk about it, but I've never known what kissing was really supposed to feel like until I kissed you."

He began walking Dylan backward until they reached a chair by the fire. Ryan turned Dylan around, sat, and pulled him into his lap, as he had that memorable time in the movie room. Dylan straddled his thighs and took Ryan's face in his hands, his eyes searching Ryan's for a moment before he captured his mouth in another bone-melting kiss. Ryan's body responded, becoming almost painfully hard.

He tore his mouth away. "Dylan, stop," he panted. "I need more. I need to touch you."

Dylan leaned back and ripped his shirt off. Ryan leaned forward and pressed a kiss over Dylan's heart, breathing in the fine smell of chlorine, rosemary, and mint that was uniquely his. He let his hands trail down Dylan's abs, tight and toned from his time in the pool. Dylan reached down and palmed Ryan's cock. As their mouths clashed, Ryan started thrusting his hips, seeking release.

"More," he said between clenched teeth.

Dylan leaned in and nuzzled his neck. "Hold on, sweetheart. I'll take care of you," he whispered in Ryan's ear before dropping to his knees and unzipping Ryan's shorts.

Ryan pressed the back of his hand against his mouth, stifling a shout when Dylan's lips wrapped around the head of his cock. The feeling of being enveloped in the warmth of Dylan's mouth had him instantly on the edge.

"I'm going to come if you don't stop," he managed to get out.

Instead of stopping, Dylan took him deeper, increasing the pressure, leaving Ryan in a mindless haze of lust. He grabbed Dylan's silky curls as his release hit him, leaving him light-headed, with spots dancing before his eyes.

Dylan looked up at him with a shy smile. "Are you okay?"

Ryan hauled him back up and kissed him, tasting himself on Dylan's lips. He grabbed Dylan's ass, fusing their bodies together.

"Now it's my turn," he growled in Dylan's ear.

Ryan reached into the waistband of Dylan's shorts. Dylan threw his head back with a low moan when Ryan grasped his cock.

They exchanged sloppy kisses while Ryan slowly jerked Dylan off, his release spilling into Ryan's hand. Dylan sighed, dropping his head to Ryan's shoulder. This time when they kissed, it was slow and tender.

"Next time we're doing that in a bed," Ryan said, his voice gruff.

Dylan wrapped his arms around Ryan's neck. He would have been happy to stay like that all night except for the mess they'd made. They used the bathroom by the pool to clean up. Exchanging soft smiles and shy glances, they walked back to the fire arm in arm. Ryan added more wood to the fire and pulled Dylan back into his lap. Staring into the blaze, his thumb brushing back and forth along the back of Dylan's neck, he watched the flames twist and flicker the same way his heart was.

"Daddy," Leo called out.

Dylan gave him a quick peck on the lips and stood up. Ryan snagged his hand and pulled him toward the tent with him.

"We're here," he said as he poked his head through the flap.

"I have to go potty," Leo said with a sleepy yawn.

"Okay, buddy."

Leo was already half asleep again in Ryan's arms when he carried him back from the bathroom. Dylan had put the fire out and had Leo's sleeping bag ready for Ryan to tuck him into, with a sleeping bag for each of them unrolled on either side of Leo's.

They took turns getting ready for bed, and once they'd turned out the light and were in their sleeping bags, Ryan whispered in the dark, "Thank you. For today. For giving Leo this experience. He'll never forget it."

"I'm going to miss this, miss you when summer's over," Dylan said with a slight quiver in his voice.

"Leo and I could come to California for winter and spring break, or you could come back here."

"It would be fun to take Leo to Disneyland."

"I bet you look pretty cute in mouse ears," Ryan said.

Dylan chuckled, and then Ryan heard him sigh softly. "We can't pretend like this is going to be easy."

Ryan lay back on his sleeping bag, staring at the ceiling of the tent. "I know, but can we pretend for a little while longer that it's just us, and nobody else matters?"

Dylan didn't answer for a long time. "We can pretend, but other people won't. What happens then?"

"I don't know."

Eventually he heard Dylan's soft, even breathing in sync with Leo's, but Ryan couldn't sleep. His heart felt heavy and light at the same time. Dylan's concerns were valid. Ryan would have to face his family at some point. Dylan's parents weren't going to accept their relationship either. Ryan brushed his fingers over his lips, remembering the warmth and firmness of Dylan's lips and wanting more. Every intimate touch he shared with Dylan confirmed Ryan's sexuality. A door had been unlocked, and now that he'd walked through it, there was no going back. But Ryan's feelings for Dylan weren't solely based on Dylan being a man. He challenged Ryan. Dylan was creative and smart, compassionate and thoughtful. Those qualities made him as attractive as his looks. Ryan loved the way Dylan's eyes lit up when he laughed, and the little dimple that formed on his cheek when he smiled. He'd thought he wasn't a cuddler until Dylan. Now Ryan couldn't get enough of cuddling him.

How could he make his parents and sister understand Dylan was the right match for him?

CHAPTER TWENTY

RYAN REACHED across the console for Dylan's hand. Tonight would be the first time they spent an evening with anyone as a couple. It was only dinner with his friends Jason and Joy, but for Ryan it was a big deal. He was more eager than nervous.

"Are you sure you're okay with this?" A thread of worry sounded in Dylan's voice.

"I trust Jason and Joy. They understand better than anyone that we aren't ready to go public yet."

"I still can't believe you're friends with Jason Anderson. I mean, he's performed at the Grammys. How did you meet him?"

"We met at a charity function the Seattle Emeralds hold every year."

"The Emeralds are soccer, right?"

Ryan nodded. "Yeah, Seattle is a big soccer town. Jason's brother Nick plays for the Emeralds, and Nick's wife, Holly, works at Children's hospital with Joy."

"One big happy family," Dylan said with a wistful smile.

"Do you have a lot of friends in LA? You've mentioned your friends Alexis and her husband. Who else do you hang out with?"

"A few other teachers and some regulars at the pool." Dylan shrugged. "I keep my circle pretty small."

Ryan shifted in his seat. "Does that go for boyfriends too?"

The corner of Dylan's mouth curled up. "Jealous?"

Ryan brushed his thumb over Dylan's knuckles. "Maybe a little bit. I'm not sure I've ever been jealous before, so I don't know if that's the feeling I have."

"Describe it to me?"

"Well, I get a knot in my stomach when I think about you seeing someone else. And I know it's selfish, but I want to be the only one who gets to see the sparkle in your eyes when you laugh and know how soft your lips are under mine."

Dylan's eyes widened, his smile growing bigger. "Oh yeah, I have a jealous boyfriend." He winced. "Sorry, I shouldn't have said that."

"Boyfriend? I'm glad you did. I like it. There's one problem, though." Dylan gave him a worried frown. "Hearing you call me your boyfriend makes me want to pull this car over and get you naked."

Dylan's breath quickened. "Maybe before we go back home?"

"Or maybe we can find someplace better," he said with a wink.

Ryan definitely had plans for Dylan after dinner. Something for the libido he'd wondered if he'd even had. Dylan had awoken something in him, and now every part of his body felt alive to the point where it was almost physically painful. The kisses and touches they'd shared weren't enough. The idea of being naked with Dylan, touching every inch of his body, was keeping Ryan awake at night and distracted during the day.

An hour later, Ryan watched Dylan talking to Joy about kayaking. They'd had dinner on their deck overlooking the lake. Ryan could see his house on the other side. Even from this distance and illuminated by lights, it still looked stark and imposing.

A couple of hours later, he watched Dylan laughing with Joy at one of Jason's stories from his last tour. He couldn't remember the last time he'd been able to sit and relax with friends like this.

"Are you up for a nightcap?" Ryan asked as they pulled away from Jason and Joy's house.

Dylan turned his face to him, a faint smile playing on his lips. "I'm up for anything with you."

Instead of heading for home, Ryan sped toward the glow of downtown Seattle's city lights. "I have somewhere special I want to take you."

Ryan pulled into a parking space in front of a brick building at the north end of the downtown core. The six floors of the vintage building were dark. Ryan had meant to rent them after the last tenant moved out, but Lindsay's death and Leo's illness put it low on his priority list.

"Trust me." Ryan smiled, seeing the wary look in Dylan's eyes as he entered a code into the keypad and opened the front door. "This was my first big purchase when Blackstone Financial took off," Ryan said, using a key card to send the elevator to the top floor. "This was our original corporate headquarters. I used the lower floors for office space and lived up here." The elevator doors opened to reveal an expansive loft space.

The double-height windows showcased a view of Puget Sound. A kitchen with a large island took up one corner, with a living room space in another. The loft was everything Ryan's home wasn't. An eclectic mix of vintage pieces melded with modern ones. Brown, warm shades of red, and gold blended with exposed brick. Instead of stark white, cream walls and maple cabinets made the space feel warm and cozy. On the other side of the room, a simple, modern black metal bed frame sat against the wall facing the windows and the view of the water. A small chest of drawers served as a nightstand, its polished wood gleaming in the soft lamplight. Ryan stood by and watched Dylan explore the space.

Ryan pointed to the only doorway in the room. "Bathroom and closet are through there."

"This is amazing. It's so different from your house," Dylan said.

"You didn't want to make love in the same bed I shared with Lindsay. You had every right to feel that way. I didn't listen to others when they told me to give up this place after getting married, and now I know why. I want to explore every inch of your body, to feel the warmth and texture of your skin, and to truly know what it's like to be with you in every way. So I brought you here. I thought this could be a place we could be together. Can we make this a special place that's just for us?"

DYLAN SEARCHED Ryan's face, looking for any sign of hesitation, and found only his own face reflected in the depths of Ryan's eyes. Yes, he wanted to spend the night but.… "Are you sure this is what you want?"

Ryan cupped his cheek, breathing in as he pressed his lips to Dylan's. Ryan's kisses had become his addiction.

"I've never been so sure of anything as I am of the way I feel about you." Ryan nuzzled Dylan's neck, kissing the pulse at the base of his throat before returning to his lips again.

When Ryan broke the kiss, Dylan was so dazed it took him a minute before he realized Ryan was asking him a question.

"What?"

Ryan brushed his thumb over Dylan's bottom lip. "I asked if this is what you want?"

"I—" His face heated. "I tried not to, but I can't stop the feelings I have. But I…. Our families will not accept this. Us. I don't want to ruin your life. This will change everything. This isn't only about us. It's about our families, Leo, your friends—"

"No." Ryan stopped him. "This is only us in this moment. What happens next"—he shrugged—"whatever it is, we'll face those changes together." Ryan wrapped his hand around the back of Dylan's neck, pulling him even closer until their faces were a breath apart. "You aren't going to ruin my life. I was only living a half-life until you came into it. The day I met you, something shifted. I felt a spark. It was the feeling I'd heard about but never felt. Each day I got to know you, that feeling grew. Leo showed me what it meant to love someone unconditionally, but you showed me what it felt like to desire someone, to want to be with someone so much that you ache. Making me feel this way isn't ruining my life—it's making my life whole and complete."

He was falling. Dylan swallowed, blinking back his tears. He was tumbling head over heels. It was too much. All he'd ever wanted was to have someone feel about him the way Ryan did. To say the words that he was saying to him. Now that it was happening, his own need to claim Ryan as his overwhelmed him. He looked down at his hands wrapped around Ryan's waist. He couldn't let go.

He kissed Ryan, pouring everything he was feeling into kissing him, his hands reaching for the hem of his shirt. Dylan reveled in the low hum in the back of Ryan's throat when his fingers dipped into the waistband of his pants.

Ryan walked them backward toward the bed until Dylan's legs hit the mattress. His fingers fumbled with the buttons on Dylan's shirt. "Every time I've watched you swim, I've wondered what it would be like to touch you, to feel these muscles under my hands."

Dylan shuddered as Ryan slipped his shirt off his shoulders, the palms of his hands caressing his skin. He unbuttoned the first button on Ryan's shirt and hesitated. "Can I?"

Ryan popped the rest of the buttons and wrenched the shirt off, throwing it toward the corner of the room. He grabbed Dylan's hands, placing them against the coarse hair on his chest as a low moan vibrated from his throat.

Ryan hesitated. "How do you want this to work?"

"What do you mean?"

"Some men like to top, and some—"

Dylan held up his hands. "Stop. I'll make this simple. I usually bottom, but I don't mind topping every once in a while. You've never done this before, so you might not know until you've...."

"You're right. I've never made love to a man before. All my life I've had people telling me what I think and what my feelings are. I don't want to put definitions on what we do or who we are supposed to be when we're in bed together. I want everything with you." Ryan laughed softly, burying his face in Dylan's neck. "This is the most intimate conversation I've ever had with a man or a woman."

"I'm glad you feel safe enough to have it with me."

Ryan looked up at Dylan with a sheepish smile. "Can we get naked now?"

Dylan responded by popping the button on Ryan's jeans and opening his fly. Ryan pushed his jeans down, toeing off his shoes simultaneously. Before Dylan could get his fingers into the waistband of Ryan's briefs, Ryan was on his knees, yanking Dylan's jeans and briefs down together.

"I haven't been able to stop thinking about wanting to do this," he said, pulling Dylan's cock into his mouth, caressing the underside of his shaft with his tongue as his fingers traced the line of hair from his belly button to the thatch of hair at his groin.

"Oh God," Dylan groaned. He meant to be gentle, but his fingers dug into Ryan's hair, holding him as his hips flexed.

It was too much. Spots danced in front of his eyes and his balls drew tight. He pulled back, and Ryan's mouth released him with a soft pop. Ryan stared up at him with a dazed, confused look.

Dylan brushed his thumb over Ryan's bottom lip. "You're going to make me come, and I want this to last."

He put his arms around Ryan's waist and pulled them both down onto the bed. A low moan escaped him feeling Ryan's weight on top of him. Dylan wrapped his legs around Ryan, aligning their cocks.

Ryan grunted and thrust against him. Dylan took it as a sign and was totally on board, wanting to feel Ryan inside of him. He wanted this to happen. He'd even prepped for tonight. He was prepared to sneak off to the movie room again, but this was a much better option.

"Do you have lube?" he asked.

Ryan opened the top drawer of the dresser and fumbled for a second before pulling out a bottle of lube.

Dylan leaned in. "Open me up," he whispered in Ryan's ear.

He closed his eyes, listening to the bottle open. A second later, he felt Ryan's slick finger teasing his entrance. Ryan traced a line of kisses down his neck and over Dylan's pecs, flicking his tongue over his nipples as he opened him up. Impatience and need hummed under his skin, and he reached between them for Ryan's cock, which slid through the palm of Dylan's hand, slick with precum.

Ryan hissed and thrust his hips. "Can I, can we do this bare?" he panted.

Dylan pulled his knees up. "Yes," he said in a low, strained voice. The first time they were together in the movie room, they'd discussed their status. Dylan had never been bare with anyone before, but he wanted this with Ryan. He wanted every minute, each touch, and the feel of Ryan's cock inside of him imprinted on his memory.

Ryan let out a low keening sound of pleasure as he pushed inside, filling Dylan.

Dylan reveled in every thrust. He pressed his hand to Ryan's chest, feeling his heart pounding and matching the rhythm of his own lunges around Ryan's cock with it.

Nothing would ever be the same after this. His heartbeat was now in sync with Ryan's and it couldn't be untethered.

"Oh fuck," Ryan shouted.

Ryan captured Dylan's cries with a searing kiss as they both reached their climax. He collapsed on top of Dylan, their bodies sliding against each other, slick with sweat and cum.

"That was…." Ryan sighed and kissed the shell of Dylan's ear.

"Everything," Dylan finished for him.

"Everything." Ryan kissed him.

Gentle kisses became urgent touches that led to the two of them jerking each other off. Eventually they ended up in the shower and then back in bed with Dylan lying against Ryan's side, his legs tangled with Ryan's and his head resting on his chest.

"Thank you," Ryan said, his voice thick with emotion.

"What are you thanking me for?"

Ryan turned on his side so they were face-to-face. "Thank you for letting me be me. For making my first time making love to a man perfect."

Dylan draped his arm over Ryan's waist and leaned forward, nuzzling his nose. "Nothing is ever perfect. We're just... us. We're a match. Against all odds, we found each other. It's wonderful and amazing. I don't want perfect. I want you."

Ryan smiled against his lips. "You've got me."

CHAPTER TWENTY-ONE

A SOFT KNOCK on his office door pulled Ryan away from the spreadsheet on his desktop screen. He'd been staring at it all morning. Normally, the neat orderly lines filled with numbers would provide the calming focus that he'd always found comforting. The weeks of stress and worry had caught up with him, and all he'd been able to do was stare at the screen, unable to make sense of it. Plus this time the numbers weren't adding up. He would need to check the servers. The number of licenses for one of his products didn't match the number of users.

His door opened, and Dylan poked his head in. "Do you have a minute?"

"For you, always. Is everything okay?"

"Everything's fine." Dylan pointed at his computer. "Is that anything that needs to be taken care of right away?"

Ryan frowned at the screen. "No, not really."

"Good. Then come with me."

Ryan got up from his desk. "Where are we going?"

Dylan smiled at him over his shoulder, his lips full and soft and tempting Ryan to push him against the wall and kiss them. The two days since they made love had passed in a blur of work, brief touches, and frantic kisses. They were going back to the apartment tonight, and Ryan's body already thrummed with anticipation.

"It's a surprise. But first you need to change." He stopped in front of Ryan's bedroom. "Clothes are on the bed."

Ryan looked through the doorway and saw board shorts and a T-shirt on the bed, along with a pair of sandals. He glanced at Dylan with surprise.

"I asked Mrs. Lieu about your size. Hopefully everything fits." Dylan gave him a gentle push inside his room. "Meet me downstairs when you're ready."

Ryan watched Dylan retreat down the hallway, inhaling the faint scent of coconut sunscreen that lingered in his wake. His hands trembled with anticipation as he changed into the dark green shorts, gray T-shirt, and sandals that matched the ones Dylan wore. There was something about the way Dylan ordered him around that Ryan found enticing. It wasn't the same as when his parents, his sister, or Lindsay made demands. His bossiness came with a tender smile and a warm look in his eye that made Ryan a willing disciple. Whatever Dylan had planned, he would happily go along with it.

Dylan was waiting for him in the front hall with a backpack slung over his shoulder. When Ryan hesitated, he said, "Mrs. Lieu is taking care of Leo for the rest of the day. Come on." He tilted his head toward the doorway.

Ryan followed him outside to the new SUV, which was parked out front with a two-person kayak strapped to the roof rack. He looked at Dylan in surprise.

"Just go with the flow," Dylan said, throwing the backpack into the back seat and getting behind the wheel. He reached across the passenger seat and opened the door for Ryan.

"Are you going to tell me where we're going?" he asked as Dylan pulled out of the driveway.

"Does it matter?"

Ryan leaned back against the headrest, watching the city retreat in the rearview mirror. "No, I guess not."

Dylan turned on the sound system and pressed a button on his phone, and the car filled with an upbeat indie rock song. The sunroof was open, and the breeze ruffled through Ryan's hair. He lifted his face to the sun and took a deep breath.

"Feels good, doesn't it?" Dylan smiled.

"It does."

They headed east into the mountains, the landscape becoming a thick carpet of green that stretched in front of them. Ryan eyed Dylan, his tan arms with a light dusting of hair stretched out, his hands grasping the steering wheel. He was a confident driver, maneuvering through the twists and curves with ease. The road extended in front of them, and the car grew warm from the sun. He blinked, feeling his eyes growing heavy with a languid tranquility.

"Ryan," Dylan called to him from the warm darkness. "Ryan, wake up. We're here."

His eyes opened to Dylan leaning toward him across the center console with his hand on his shoulder. "Where are we?" he murmured, looking out the window at dark blue water surrounded by a ring of trees.

"Cle Elum Lake." Dylan kissed his cheek. "I'll let you wake up while I get the kayak down."

Ryan yawned and got out. Stretching, he took in his surroundings. The clouds above reflected in the mirrorlike surface, undisturbed on a quiet midweek day. Dylan unstrapped the kayak, deftly lifted it from the roof rack, and set it on the ground.

"What can I do to help?"

"You can get the life vests out of the back, and I'll grab the backpack."

With Dylan at the front and Ryan at the back, they carried the kayak and their gear from the parking spot down to the water's edge.

"Where did you get all this?" Ryan asked, buckling his life jacket.

"There's a rental place close to the hospital." Dylan reached into the backpack and pulled out a bottle of sunscreen. He squeezed a dollop into his palm and held it out to Ryan. "Make sure you get the tops of your ears."

Ryan took it from him and applied a generous amount to his neck, face, and arms. Dylan stowed the backpack in a small cargo hold at the back of the kayak. "Ready?"

"Oh captain, my captain," he said with a mock salute.

They waded into the water and climbed in, taking a moment to steady themselves. Dylan dipped his paddle in the water, pulling them away from shore. They glided through the water, the only sound a soft splash as Dylan slipped his oar in and out. Ryan mimicked Dylan's movements, paddling in sync with him as they made their way toward the middle of the lake.

Dylan looked over his shoulder. "You'd never know you haven't kayaked before. You're a natural."

"This is beautiful," Ryan said in a hushed voice.

"You've never been here before?"

"No. I've wanted to do something like this for a while, but there always seemed to be a reason I couldn't."

"Did you do stuff like that when you were a kid?" Dylan asked.

"No. What about you?"

Dylan snorted a laugh. "I was a Boy Scout. For a long time, I hated camping and hiking. I had to unlearn the straight-boy bullshit they taught me nature was supposed to be." Ryan noted his frown when Dylan turned to look over the water. Dylan balanced his oar on his lap and dipped his hand into the water. "I've always loved the water. When I moved to LA, I started swimming laps, and then I discovered kayaking. It gave me a way to get back to nature in a way that felt authentic, without trying to conform to the idea of what my dad thought a man should be." He shuddered. "Nature doesn't exist only as a place to kill animals."

"Your dad made you go hunting, didn't he?"

Dylan bowed his head. "I hated it."

Ryan reached forward and put his hand on his neck. Dylan dropped his head back and sighed. His skin was soft and warm from the sun. Ryan flipped his hand over and brushed it across his neck. Dylan shuddered and turned to Ryan with one of his brilliant smiles.

"I'm sure you did," Ryan said. "It's not in your nature to hurt anyone or anything."

Dylan picked up his paddle, and they resumed their journey around the lake.

"It wasn't only the hunting, it was the whole macho bullshit attitude. The way some guys talked about girls they liked. If I was gay or not, it was still disgusting. I hated all of it, but I loved this." Dylan lifted his oar out of the water and turned around to face him. "So, you know I enjoy swimming, being outdoors, and watching old movies. But I don't know anything about what you like to do when you're not working."

Ryan admired the ring of emerald green trees that circled the lake and sighed. "I've been thinking about that a lot lately. I'd like to figure it out."

"You don't have any hobbies?"

"No, not really. I golf with my dad occasionally, but that's only when he insists on my presence when he's wooing a client."

"Books, movies, plays, anything?"

Ryan sat back with a sigh. "The sad truth is, most of my life involves running Blackstone and being Leo's dad."

"What about you and Lindsay?"

"What about us?"

"What did you have in common? What did you like to do together?"

Ryan's jaw ticked. "Nothing."

"Can I ask you a question?"

"You want to know why I married your sister?"

Dylan turned away and paddled again. "You don't have to answer."

Ryan matched his strokes, taking them farther across the lake. "Lindsay was so outgoing. She loved going to parties and playing hostess. I'm the opposite. Opposites are supposed to attract, right?"

"Not always," Dylan said quietly.

"Everyone kept telling me we were the perfect couple. That her outgoing nature would balance my introvert tendencies."

"How did you meet?"

"My sister introduced us. They were sorority sisters."

"You must have loved her. You asked her to marry you." When Ryan didn't answer, Dylan murmured, "I'm sorry."

Ryan didn't want to hold anything back. Dylan deserved to know everything. "I thought the love would come with time. That's what my parents and my sister kept telling me, and I believed it too. I thought if I tried hard enough…."

Dylan balanced his oar over his lap and reached behind him for Ryan's hand. "It's okay. You don't have to talk about this."

"No," he said in a hoarse voice. "I want to talk about it, and I want to talk about it with you. It was selfish and, I don't know, maybe… arrogant to think I could change myself and be someone different to make someone happy. I asked Lindsay one time why she married me, and she said she knew I'd be a good husband and provider. It was a long time after our conversation before I realized neither of us said we wanted to be together because we loved each other. Lindsay wanted a certain lifestyle, and I wanted a family. We were both selfish." Ryan shook his head. "I'm sorry."

Dylan paddled them toward a small cove along the shoreline. Ryan followed him getting out of the boat. As soon as Dylan pulled the kayak onto the shore, he wrapped Ryan in a tight embrace. "You're human, Ryan. Don't punish yourself."

Ryan shuddered and nodded. "I try, but sometimes I'm so angry with myself."

Dylan lifted Ryan's head and cupped his cheek. "Being perfect won't solve all your problems. You're trying so hard to be perfect all the time you're not living. Sometimes things are messy, and emotions aren't black and white. Give yourself some grace."

"Thank you for listening to me. I've never had someone I could talk to the way I talk to you."

Dylan frowned. "What about Stephanie?"

Ryan smirked. "I talk, she doesn't listen. No, that's not fair. Sometimes Stephanie hears only what she wants."

Dylan bit back the sharp words that sat on the tip of his tongue for Ryan's sister. "You can tell me anything, Ryan. I'll always listen."

Ryan's eyes darkened and his lips curled into a smile as he whispered in Dylan's ear. Whispers turned into touches and kisses that led to making love against a tree hidden away from anyone else on the lake in the little cove.

CHAPTER TWENTY-TWO

"YOU LOOK better."

Dylan looked up from the edge of the pool where he'd been sitting, catching his breath after his first swim in almost three weeks. He finally felt like he was physically back to normal. Emotionally, he was completely off-kilter. The times when he was alone with Ryan, when they could block out the world, he was happier than he'd ever been. The same was true when he was with Leo, and when it was the three of them, he felt whole and complete. His feelings were so big sometimes he thought his heart would burst.

"Thanks, I'm feeling much better."

Ryan's sister towered over him in her red-soled heels. Her hair was almost white under the summer sun, and her blue eyes glittered, but not with the same warmth as Ryan's.

Her lips curled into an unfriendly smile. "Good, then you can go."

"Ryan's asked me to stay for the summer."

"I know, but I don't think that's a good idea."

Dylan carefully got up, his legs slightly shaky from the exertion. He took his time, choosing his words carefully. "Stephanie, I know you still believe what my parents said about me. Have I done anything that proves what they've said about me was true since I've been here?"

"I think you faked some kind of relapse, probably to get drugs, so yeah, I think you're exactly what your parents said you were. You see how much money Ryan has and think you can worm your way into his life. Look at you, wearing that disgusting bathing suit, flaunting yourself, acting like you belong here."

"He does belong here," Ryan said quietly from the doorway.

Stephanie turned to Ryan. "Ryan, this has gone on long enough. I don't know why you're always so gullible, but I'm not going to let Dylan continue to take advantage of you."

Dylan pulled off his swim cap and goggles. He reached for a towel and started to wrap it around his waist. He stopped, putting it around his neck instead. There was nothing wrong with his Speedos. They were the same kind anyone who was on a rec swim team or a collegiate team wore. Stephanie's not-so-subtle homophobia disgusted him as much as his choice of swimwear disgusted her.

But it also scared him. Dylan's gaze darted between Ryan and his sister. He could see the troubled look in his eyes, along with uncertainty. Ryan wasn't ready to tell her about them yet. Dylan realized he might never be.

He spoke up before Ryan could say anything he might regret or, even worse, something that he wasn't really ready to say.

"The summer's almost over. I have a job back in California that I love. I have no intention of staying here." He paused, noticing Ryan wince slightly at his statement. "If it will make you feel better, I can stay somewhere else and just come to tutor Leo."

Ryan stiffened, his jaw ticked, and his eyes narrowed at Dylan's offer.

Stephanie lifted her chin. "If you won't leave, I think that would be best."

"That's not your decision to make."

There was a hardness in Ryan's voice Dylan had never heard before. He watched helplessly while Ryan and his sister stared at each other, locked in a battle of wills. He had the feeling this was the first time Ryan hadn't backed down.

"Ryan, you've taken on so much since Lindsay died. I'm only trying to help," Stephanie said in a placating tone that came across as more patronizing than anything else.

"But you're not helping. If you wanted to help, you'd be respectful of my decisions." He held up his hand to stop her when she started to speak again. "Do you think I'm incapable of making decisions for myself?"

"Well, no, but I—"

"That is the last time you will speak to me like I'm a child. Do you understand?"

"Ryan, I…." She pressed her lips together. "I understand," she finished quietly.

The glint of defiance in her eyes told Dylan that the only thing she understood was that her usual tactics weren't working.

"Are you here for any other reason than trying to intimidate Dylan?" Ryan asked.

"I wanted to check on Leo and let you know mom and dad are back from their trip and wanted us to meet them for dinner tonight."

"Leo's sleeping. As for dinner, I'm assuming it's the usual time at the club?"

"Yes."

"I'll be there. You can go now."

Dylan drew in a sharp breath at the same time Stephanie did. Ryan was making a point, but was he really prepared to take a stand and face the consequences?

"If you'll excuse me," Dylan murmured, walking back into the house, forcing himself not to rush so it wouldn't look like he was running away.

He didn't stop until he made it up to his room. After closing the door, he leaned against it, blowing out a shaky breath.

What had he been thinking? There was no way the summer was going to end without someone getting hurt. This wasn't fair to Ryan, Leo, any of them. Dylan pushed himself from the door, stripped out of his swim trunks, and made his way to the bathroom. He got into the shower, the steam releasing the chlorine smell from his skin. He leaned against the tiled wall, letting the hot water ease his tense muscles, blinking back tears.

He came out of the shower, resolved to set boundaries with Ryan, only to find him sitting on his bed when he exited the bathroom with a towel wrapped around his waist.

"I'm sorry." Ryan looked at him with a pained expression, his voice shaking. He held his hand out, and with one word, all of Dylan's resolve melted. "Please."

As soon as he was within reach, Ryan grabbed his hand, spread his legs, and pulled him in, wrapping his arms around him as he pressed his cheek to Dylan's stomach. Dylan could feel the wetness on his skin.

"I've never, ever been so angry with her." He gazed up at Dylan. "I wasn't very happy with you either. Why would you offer to leave like that?"

"I thought it might make things easier for you."

"Don't make sacrifices like that. You have more value than you allow yourself to believe."

Dylan stroked Ryan's jaw and kissed him.

"I don't know if I can go to dinner tonight and pretend like everything is normal. I used to be able to... to hide how I felt, and now it's like everything is bubbling up," Ryan said.

Dylan ran his fingers through Ryan's hair. "I wish I knew what to say, but I don't. This is your life, Ryan, your family. I know what it's like to lose your family, and I wouldn't wish it on anyone. But I can't tell you what you should do. Only you can decide what's best for you and for Leo. I'm here to support you, but I never want to do anything that would hurt you or Leo."

"Do you think I don't know that? I trust you, Dylan. Right now I trust you more than my sister or my parents to have Leo's and my best interests at heart." Ryan stood up and wrapped Dylan in an embrace. He kissed him gently before pulling back, his eyes searching Dylan's. "I wanted to ask. I've been thinking about changing my will. If anything ever happened to me, I think you should be Leo's guardian. Would that be all right with you?"

Dylan gasped, his lips trembling. "Are you sure?"

"You're the only thing that feels absolutely right in my life right now. You'll love and care for Leo the same way I do, unconditionally. You'll let him be his own person, whatever that looks like."

"Ryan, I'd be honored to be Leo's guardian. I love him so much."

"And he loves his uncle Dylan." Ryan kissed him again and then pressed his forehead against Dylan's. "Maybe the three of us can run away."

Dylan shook his head. "Leo's life is here. It wouldn't be fair to him, or Mrs. Lieu or Rebecca, and even though you're mad at her right now, it's not fair to your sister. She loves Leo too."

"She does, but the way she shows it.... I've changed, and I need Stephanie to respect that." Ryan ran his hands up and down Dylan's arms. "If we can't run away, what would you think about going away for the weekend, the two of us? I could rent a cabin somewhere, or we could go camping." He leaned in and nuzzled Dylan's neck.

"That would be nice," he said, his voice trembling.

Dylan groaned when Ryan nipped at his ear. He couldn't say no when Ryan touched him like that, whispering all the things he'd like to do to him when they were alone.

Hearing voices, Dylan twisted out of Ryan's arms and stepped away, needing to put distance between them so he could think straight.

He dressed quickly, his hands shaking as Ryan tracked his every move, watching him pull on a pair of shorts and a T-shirt. He backed up toward the door before Ryan could lure him into his arms again. "I'll see you later."

The corner of Ryan's mouth curled up into a knowing smile.

Dylan shook his finger at him and said, "Behave yourself," before he turned and left.

He blew out a shaky breath as he headed downstairs. He wasn't a prude, but he wasn't the kind of guy who was big on public displays of affection either. Ryan had a way of breaking through the protective walls he built around himself. It was reckless and dangerous. Every time he told himself to slow things down, all Ryan had to do was give him that half smile or look at him with a heated gaze and his resolve would melt away. Ryan said he came alive when he met Dylan, but he'd changed something in Dylan too. Dreams he'd never allowed himself to have before seemed within reach. He and Ryan and Leo, the three of them, could become a family. Maybe they could welcome another child through a surrogate or adoption. He'd never even thought about having a family. When he thought about it, he'd never really believed he'd even settle down with someone until now. Those were dangerous thoughts. Hope could be a wonderful thing, or it could be crushed in an instant.

Chapter Twenty-Three

WHY WERE country clubs still a thing? Ryan sat across from his parents in the large dining room with a view of a perfectly maintained golf course with a glimpse of Puget Sound beyond. Ryan thought country clubs were antiquated relics, but his parents still valued the social hierarchy they symbolized.

He'd taken part in this ritual his entire life, but this time he felt too tight in his skin.

"Sorry I'm late." His sister arrived at the table with a tall woman with glossy chestnut-brown hair and intense brown eyes. Her full lips didn't fit on her sharp, pale, angular face.

"Oh, Courtney." His mother beamed at the woman. "How nice that you could join us."

His dad jumped up and pulled out a chair next to Ryan for her while his sister sat down on the other side. If he hadn't been so caught up in his musings, he would have clued into the fifth place setting at the round table.

"Ryan, you remember Courtney, Senator Graham's daughter. You met a few years ago at a fundraising gala here at the club," his mother said.

He didn't remember Courtney, but he knew Senator Graham and his conservative leanings.

He played polite and shook her hand. The four of them launched into a conversation like old friends. He wanted to be back home, sitting around the table with Leo, Dylan, and Mrs. Lieu. His parents, Stephanie, and Courtney were talking about people he didn't know or didn't care about until his father said, "Ryan, Courtney's father is becoming the ranking member of the Senate Banking Committee," with a pointed look.

Ryan took a sip of his whiskey before he turned to Courtney and said, "Congratulations to your father."

Courtney leaned toward him with a pout. "It must be so hard being a single father."

"Ryan's been wonderful, so strong and caring for little Leo," Stephanie chimed in.

"You know, I'd love to meet him," Courtney said.

Ryan shook his head. "I'm sorry, but his immune system is still recovering. I'm sure you can understand that I can't allow anyone to visit on a whim."

Courtney's sympathetic pout disappeared, replaced with a confused glance in Stephanie's direction. "Oh, I thought you were looking for—"

"No, I'm not."

"What Ryan means is—" his mother started.

"Ryan is perfectly capable of speaking for himself," he interrupted. He turned to Courtney. "I'm sorry if they gave you the impression that I am interested in finding another mother for Leo or a wife for myself." He pushed his chair back and stood. "If you'll excuse me, I have to get back to my son."

He made it as far as the lobby before his father grabbed his arm.

"Damn it, Ryan, what the hell is wrong with you? Senator Graham is on the banking committee," he said between clenched teeth.

"So what does that mean—his daughter is for sale to the highest bidder? As long as I'm the head of Blackstone Financial, we will run the company ethically."

"And everyone else gets ahead? When are you ever going to learn to play ball? This is how things get done. The board is tiring of your refusal to put the best interests of the company first. We let you take time off to take care of Leo, but he's fine now. Blackstone Financial can dominate the industry if you'd—"

"Is that all that matters to you? Nice of you and mom to ask about Leo, by the way."

"We'd just sat down. We didn't get a chance before your sister and Courtney arrived," his father sputtered.

"And yet you told me all about your trip."

He pressed his mouth into a thin line. At least he had the decency to look a little embarrassed.

"When will it be enough? We have more money than we'll ever need in this lifetime, or ten lifetimes. What do you need more power for? What will it get you? I'd rather leave this world knowing I was a good father and husb—" His voice broke. "—husband than being wealthy and powerful. If you and the board want to run

Blackstone Financial with someone else at the helm, go ahead. But remember, I own all the tech." He pressed his fist to his chest. "Me."

"What's happened to you? You were always reasonable, easy to manage." Ryan sucked in his breath. His father stepped back. "Ryan, that's not what I meant."

"But it's what you said."

"Stephanie told us about the influence that boy has been having on you. Clearly that's what's caused this change in you."

Ryan's jaw ticked. "Dylan has nothing to do with this. I'm tired of trying to make everyone happy and ending up miserable. I'm not going to marry Courtney or anyone else you pick out for me. I did it once, and the only good thing that came out of it was Leo. I'm not doing it again. You can't manage or manipulate me to get what you want anymore. I will no longer go along with whatever you want because it's easier than standing up for myself, and you're going to have to get used to that. I'm done here. When you decide you want to have a real family dinner, you can come to the house and eat at the kitchen table with Leo and me."

Ryan left his father in the lobby with an angry frown on his face and didn't look back. He got into his car. Hands shaking, he gripped the steering wheel and took a few deep breaths. He made a call before pulling out of the parking lot, and instead of heading home, ended up at a small bar on the other side of the bridge.

Jason Anderson walked in a few minutes later and slid into a seat next to him at the bar. He tipped his chin and held up two fingers to the bartender, who answered with a nod.

"Thanks for coming. I figured you'd be on the road playing some sold-out arena somewhere."

"Next week. How's Leo? Is Dylan okay?"

"You know my parents didn't even ask about Leo tonight," he said with a half laugh.

The bartender came over with two beers. "You waiting to pick up Joy from the hospital?"

"Naw, just hanging with a friend. Ryan, this is Kip. He owns the Wedgwood Alehouse."

Kip shook his hand and said to let him know if they needed anything else.

"This place is popular with a lot of the staff at Children's Hospital. It's special to Joy and me. This is where I asked her to marry me."

Ryan raised an eyebrow. "In a bar?"

"It was a Christmas party. Trust me, it was perfect. But we're not here to talk about me. What's going on?"

Ryan told Jason what had happened at dinner. "I can't go back to the way things were. Dylan does this thing where he looks at me like I'm…." He sighed with a smile. "When he looks at me like that, it makes me feel like I'm the hero of the movie. It scares me too, because I want to live up to that."

Jason nodded. "When Joy gives me that look, I'd move heaven and earth to make her happy."

"Were you afraid you'd screw it up?"

"Terrified. And I did. We both did." He laughed softly. "And we'll probably do it again. It's what happens after you mess up that matters. If you try to be perfect for Dylan, I guarantee you'll screw it up. From what you told me about dinner, it sounds like you're going to have an uphill battle with your parents. We were lucky. Joy and I didn't have any issues with our families. That's not the case for a lot of people. Neither one of Joy's dads had an easy time with their families when they came out, and getting married didn't improve the dynamic. If anything, it got worse." Jason smiled, shaking his head with a sigh. "I love those guys, their patience and tenacity. They always lead with love."

"I'm in love with him," Ryan breathed.

"Joy and I kind of figured that when we spent time with the two of you. You're, I don't know… lighter with Dylan than you were with Lindsay."

"I am. Being with Dylan is easy."

"It's the rest of the stuff," Jason said.

"Yeah, the rest of the stuff."

"What are you going to do? What I mean is, what are you willing to do?"

"That's what I need to figure out. I don't want to let Dylan go, but I also know he has a life in LA. I can't ask him to move here and live in the house I shared with Lindsay."

"Ryan, you hate that house. Why don't you sell it?"

"That's the first thing I'm going to do."

Jason's mouth curled into a sly smile. "So now would be a good time to mention we have neighbors who might be moving? It's a nice house with a guesthouse that would be perfect for Mrs. Lieu. You'd still be on the water, just on the other side of the lake. And, you'd have awesome neighbors."

Ryan sat up straighter. "When can I see it?"

Jason laughed. "Hold on there, cowboy. I said might be moving. Let me do some recon and see what I can find out."

"It doesn't matter how much it costs, I'll—"

Jason put his hand on his arm. "Slow down. These are big decisions. You're about to make changes that will upend your entire life. Take it one step at a time. Joy and I are here to help if you need us."

THE NEXT day, Ryan was back at the corporate offices for the first time in weeks. He felt out of place sitting at the glass-and-chrome desk looking at the distant Seattle skyline through the window. In the past he'd come to work and immediately became engrossed with spreadsheets and analytics. Now he sat with his gaze unfocused and his mind on Leo and Dylan and the life he wanted to have with them.

Stephanie breezed into his office and ended his fantasies, announcing she'd invited his in-laws for a visit. Suddenly his dreams were shattered by the reality of his situation with Dylan.

"Did it occur to you that you should have asked me first?" he asked.

"It's Lindsay's parents. Leo's grandparents. Why should I have to ask?"

"Because you've created an uncomfortable situation for Dylan. Did it even occur to you he hasn't seen his parents since they kicked him out?"

Stephanie shrugged. "That's really not my problem. Leo's getting better now, and they wanted to see him."

"And you decided that was your decision to make?"

"I was only thinking about what would be best for Leo."

That wasn't what his sister was thinking at all. This was about Dylan. Did she suspect what was happening between them? Should he tell her?

"Also, I've asked HR to send a memo to your assistant."

"Lisa? What for?"

"Blue hair is not the best first impression, don't you think?"

Ryan glared at his sister while he picked up the phone and called the head of HR. "I understand my sister has asked you to draft a memo to

Lisa Blanchard. Cancel it." He hung up the phone and sat forward with his hands clasped tightly on his desk. "Let me ask you a question. Who is the head of Blackstone Financial Technologies?"

"Ryan, I—"

"I'm waiting," he said quietly, continuing to pin her with an angry glare.

"Obviously you are."

The note of dismissal in her tone only added fuel to his growing anger. "Sit down," he ordered.

She hesitated for a moment before taking the chair across from his desk, crossing her legs and arms.

"I let you take the lead here while I dealt with Lindsay's death and took care of Leo. But now you've overstepped. Don't do it again."

She glared at him for a moment before saying, "Noted," in a clipped tone.

He called his assistant in after his sister left.

"Lisa, I want to apologize if my sister made any inappropriate comments about your appearance."

She grimaced, fingering the blue streak in her pale blond short bob. "Thanks. I should have known better than to push the norm."

Ryan shook his head. "From now on, unless it's a request from me, you are free to ignore it."

Lisa eyed him skeptically. "Sure, okay."

"I mean it. Even if it's from my sister."

His assistant still looked uncomfortable. "Is there something else?" he asked.

"I wasn't sure if I should say anything, but when your sister called me into her office to talk about my hair I-I noticed something on her computer. I wasn't snooping—it was on her screen. She turned it off as soon as she saw me looking. It was a second, so quick I could be mistaken...."

"But you don't think you were, do you?"

Lisa slowly shook her head. "It was a sales agreement with ARW Group."

Ryan's jaw ticked. ARW was an investment corporation who'd tried to do business with Blackstone before. His parents and sister didn't find their questionable ethics as bothersome as Ryan did. He'd made it clear Blackstone wouldn't be doing business with them.

"Will you do me a favor and look into it? Quietly?"

"I'll keep my eyes open."

"Thanks, Lisa."

Ryan replayed their conversation after Lisa went back to her office. He needed to open his eyes. For too long he had chosen the easiest path without considering the consequences. Every time his sister reassured him that everything was in hand with his company, he'd taken her word for it without taking the time to look for himself.

It had been easier to follow along and let Stephanie take the lead with the company, just as it had been easier to pretend that everything was okay with Lindsay than face the fissures in his marriage.

Until that moment, he never really understood how much he'd taken for granted. True, he'd worked hard in college, and he'd worked hard to start his company, but he'd lived his life never having to really struggle. Even with Leo's cancer—yes, it was hard, but he'd been able to use his wealth and resources so that he didn't have to struggle the way other families did. He saw campers and RVs with license plates from the Pacific Northwest and even as far as Montana, Wyoming, and the Dakotas in the hospital parking lot. He'd never had to think about where he'd sleep or eat, or if he'd have a job to go back to after his child received lifesaving treatment.

"It's time to wake up, Ryan," he whispered to himself. He was ready to take on whatever struggles lay ahead. The opportunity to build a life with Dylan was worth it.

CHAPTER TWENTY-FOUR

"YOUR PARENTS are coming."

Dylan's eyes brightened. "Kevin and Carl? They didn't say anything."

Ryan shook his head sadly, hating the way the light in Dylan's eyes dimmed.

"Oh." Dylan's shoulders slumped.

"I didn't know. Stephanie invited them. I don't want them here, but what can I do?"

Dylan looked so small and forlorn. Ryan went over and put his arms around him. "It will be okay."

"I can't stay here with them. I… I can't. I should be brave. I know I have the right to be here, but…." He closed his eyes and shuddered.

Ryan kissed his temple. "It's okay. I figured you'd feel that way. I thought you could stay at the apartment."

Dylan nodded and sniffed. "I suppose so. Maybe I should go back to LA?"

Panic swept through him. Ryan grasped Dylan's shoulders. "No, no you can't. Leo needs you. Please, I need you to stay. I'm going to need to know you'll be here when they go. It's only a few days. We can make it work."

Dylan nodded mutely. Ryan lifted his chin with his finger and pressed a tender kiss to his lips. "Stay," he whispered.

They kissed and whispered promises they would stay for each other.

"When do they get here?" Dylan asked.

"Day after tomorrow. They get in Thursday morning and leave on Monday."

"What are we going to say to Leo?"

Ryan sighed. "I don't know."

"We… we could tell him I had to go back to LA for a few days."

"I hate making you hide away."

"I think it would be worse being here with them."

Dylan was right. Ryan knew in his gut his in-laws would do their best to make Dylan uncomfortable during their visit. And what would Arlene and Clay say if they knew their son-in-law was gay?

"Ryan, what's going on?"

Dylan was looking at him anxiously. He shook his head. "Nothing. I was trying to figure everything out."

"Is there something else you need me to do?"

Ryan snaked his arm around Dylan's waist and planted a brief, firm kiss on his lips. "You just did it."

"This is only a short-term solution, you know that, right? What happens when the summer's over?"

"We'll figure it out. I know you need to get back to your students, and I wouldn't ask you to leave them. I know how much you love your job. Leo and I could fly down on the weekends, or you could come up, and we can spend vacations and the holidays together. Maybe rent a cabin in the mountains for the holidays. We could invite Kevin and Carl." He nuzzled Dylan's temple, his voice dripping in a low, husky tone. "We could get cozy by the fire."

"Ryan," Dylan whispered his name.

"Let's watch a movie tonight."

Dylan smiled. "The last time we watched a movie, we didn't."

"Exactly," Ryan replied with a wink.

The brave face he put on for Dylan fell as soon as he was alone. Ryan felt nothing but dread at the thought of Arlene and Clay coming to visit. The last time he saw them was at Lindsay's funeral, where they tearfully accepted the condolences for the loss of another child. Only it was a lie. They weren't childless; they had a beautiful, warm, loving son who they'd rejected, who they'd rather pretend was dead than accept him for who he was. Ryan would never put conditions on his love for Leo. But wasn't that exactly what his parents had done to him? Marry the right woman, entertain clients, make more money, live in the right house, drive the right car. What was right? What did *right* really mean?

The one thing he knew with absolute certainty was how right he felt when he held Dylan in his arms.

They came together in the theater room with a frenzy that night, with sloppy kisses, their hands everywhere, touching every inch of each other's bodies. The next morning, Dylan told Leo that he had to go to LA for a few days, promising he'd come back as soon as he could. Ryan

watched Dylan say goodbye with tears in his eyes as he hugged Leo with
a heavy heart. Nothing about this felt right, but putting up a fight would
cause more trouble. This was the easiest solution that would cause the
least amount of inconvenience for everyone. Except for Dylan and him.

"What's wrong with you?" Stephanie whispered, elbowing him at
dinner.

They were eating in the dining room that had been unused since
Lindsay died. His parents insisted. How quickly he'd given in, slipping
into the habit of going along, thinking it was easier than fighting.

With his in-laws there, they had to say grace at dinner, and they'd
asked if Mrs. Lieu could prepare a traditional meal since they weren't
used to ethnic foods. He'd have to give Mrs. Lieu another raise for
maintaining her composure despite the anger he saw flash in her eyes.
Ryan didn't blame her. The one thing he'd put his foot down on was
when they tried to insist Leo sit at the table and use his "best manners."
He would not make his son sit through dinner being corrected on his
manners. Leo, Rebecca, and Mrs. Lieu ate at the kitchen island, and
Ryan wished he were with them.

"Ryan, Leo is looking so much better. I told you prayer works,"
Arlene said.

He'd been half listening to the conversation until then. He set the
glass of wine in his hand down. "I think your son has more to do with
Leo's recovery than prayer," he said in a steely tone.

His mother-in-law flinched, pressing her mouth into a thin line.

"Well, now that he's getting better, there's a Pee Wee football camp
that I thought would be good for the boy."

Ryan couldn't believe what his father-in-law was suggesting. "Leo
is recovering, but he's nowhere near being able to play Pee Wee football.
I'm pretty sure when you asked him what he liked to play, I heard him
tell you he'd like to play soccer."

"Leo's too young to know what he likes," his father-in-law said
with a dismissive wave of his hand. "He needs guidance."

Ryan looked around the table, seeing his parents and sister nodding
in agreement. Now that he knew Dylan, he had a new perspective on his
in-laws' behavior. His heart hurt picturing Dylan as a little boy being told
his choices weren't right.

"Yes, he does. I'm his father, so I think I should be the one who
provides that guidance. Wouldn't you agree?"

Ryan enjoyed watching his father-in-law squirm in his seat. They spent the rest of the dinner in an uncomfortable silence while his parents and Stephanie tried to fill in the gap with mindless small talk.

Thank God Arlene and Clay weren't night owls. They didn't stay up to visit late into the evening, usually in bed by nine. Still, it took all of Ryan's self-discipline to play nice during the time he had to entertain them. His in-laws had an opinion about everything, and they were always rooted in their southern faith-based values. How could Ryan live in a state that legalized marijuana? Wouldn't that be bad for Leo? Seattle had too many electric cars. When would Ryan join a church and enroll Leo in Sunday school? The list was endless and exhausting. The conversation about Leo's schooling triggered memories of one of the last arguments Ryan had with Lindsay. She wanted to enroll Leo in a private Christian school. It was one of the few times Ryan put his foot down and refused to budge. Reading about the school, he'd been disgusted by the conservative values listed in their code of conduct. They were anti-gay, anti-trans and preached traditional roles for male and female students. Lindsay's choice of school made sense now. Of course she wanted to reinforce stereotypes of what a man was supposed to be. He wondered what would have happened if Lindsay were alive when Leo's leukemia was diagnosed. Would she have told him about Dylan? Would she risk the life of her son the same way her parents put their grandson's life in danger?

Late that night he walked into the apartment and into Dylan's arms. It crushed him to hear Dylan ask about his parents, his voice shaking, the pain visible in his eyes.

It broke his heart to untangle himself from Dylan's arms later, knowing he'd wake up in bed alone. As he drove across the bridge, he saw a faint glimmer of light appear on the horizon. Ryan vowed to make it up to Dylan. He couldn't undo the pain Dylan's parents caused him, but he could do everything possible to make sure he never felt unwanted or unloved again.

CHAPTER TWENTY-FIVE

DYLAN LOOKED up from the book in his lap, his eyes darting toward the sound of the key turning in the lock. He wasn't expecting to see Ryan until later, and his heart leaped with anticipation at an unexpected visit.

The moment Stephanie and his parents stepped inside, his anticipation turned to alarm. He jumped up, his book slipping from his grasp and hitting the floor.

Seeing his parents in person for the first time in over ten years jolted him. The same fear Dylan had experienced the last time he saw them swept over him. His father retained his former linebacker physique. Even with shoulders that had become slightly stooped, he was still an imposing figure. The brown skin on his face was unlined, gray hair at his temples the only evidence of his age. In her navy slacks and white blouse with a Peter Pan collar, his mother had kept the same youthful look from her cheerleading days. Her neatly cut blond bob was a clever disguise, concealing her gray hair. It was hard to tell if the frown lines around her mouth were from age or disgust when she glared at him with blue eyes that were more faded than he remembered.

"Does Ryan know you're here?" Dylan asked warily.

"No, and he's not going to." Stephanie came forward. She set down the designer tote bag in her hand, pulled out a white envelope the size of a sheet of paper, and held it out to him.

Dylan took it from her, glancing at his parents again. There had been no hello, only looks of disappointment. He opened the envelope while Stephanie stood by with a smug smile. His jaw clenched when the contents registered.

"You can't do this," he said in a shaky whisper, looking at the court documents.

"We can and we will. Take the money," his mother said in the same bitter tone she'd used the last time they spoke.

He looked at Stephanie. "How could you do this to your brother?"

"You didn't leave me any choice after what you've done."

Dylan's father shook his head. "Maybe we shouldn't have sent you away. I should have spent more time with you. I could have toughened you up and made a man out of you. I gave up too easily. You needed a father figure."

"None of this is your fault, sweetheart." Dylan's mother patted his father's arm.

"I have a father figure. His name is Kevin."

"And you ruined his life the same way you're going to ruin Ryan's," his father said.

"What are you talking about? I didn't ruin Kevin's life. He saved mine."

"Sure, he kept you from ending up on the streets, but he sacrificed his career to do it. Did you really believe that he didn't pay a price for taking you in? I made sure he lost his job at the high school and couldn't get a job anywhere else in this state. Who wants a teacher who would groom kids?"

His father's cruelty shouldn't have surprised him, but it still had him shaking with anger. "You're a hateful man."

His father lifted his chin. "I'm a Christian. It was the right thing to do. And now I'm going to make sure to do what I have to do to protect my grandson."

Dylan's stomach twisted in disgust. He fisted his hands at his sides, anticipating what his parents considered the right thing for Leo.

"I've spent most of my life trying to keep Ryan from getting into trouble. I knew the minute you arrived that you'd be a problem," Stephanie spat out.

Dylan forced himself to speak calmly. "And it looks like you've decided you need to do something about it."

"No, you're going to clean up the mess you made. You'll go back to LA tonight. You won't come back to Seattle, and you will never contact Ryan or Leo again."

When he shook his head, his father said, "If you aren't on a plane by midnight, we will file for custody of Leo tomorrow. We'll do it in Tennessee. You'll remember we're very close friends with Judge Adkins."

"You won't win."

"Maybe, maybe not, but we will get temporary custody while it drags on through the courts."

Stephanie pointed to the sheaf of paper Dylan was holding. "We have a lawyer ready to file the paperwork."

"That should be enough for you to disappear and never come back again," his mother said.

"You hate me that much? Ten million dollars. That's how much you hate me?"

"Oh son, I don't hate you. I'm disappointed in you, and I'm so sad that your immortal soul will burn in hell," his mother said in a sympathetic tone tinged with malice.

"You're sick."

"No, you are."

"Get out," he shouted.

"Leave the keys on the table when you go," Stephanie said.

They filed out like soldiers, determined expressions, heads held high.

Dylan dropped the paper and sank down on the end of the bed with his head in his hands. He took a few shaky breaths and reached for his phone.

"Dad."

"Dylan, what's the matter?"

"You, you went to work every day after you took me in." He drew in a deep shuddering breath. "Where did you go?"

After a long pause, and with a tremor in his voice, he finally answered. "I found a job doing data entry for an insurance company."

"You loved being a teacher."

"I loved you more."

"I'm sorry. I'm so sorry," he sobbed.

"Oh, sweetheart, your dad and I aren't. We love you so much. Carl and I never planned on having children. You were a gift. Taking you in gave us the opportunity to be parents, and it's been one of the greatest joys of our lives. You filled a hole in our lives we didn't know was there. Never be sorry for how happy and proud you made us."

Dylan was too wracked with tears to answer.

"How did you find out?" Kevin asked.

Dylan sniffed, wiping his eyes with his sleeve. "My par—" They weren't his parents anymore. He'd never call them that again. "Arlene and Clay showed up. They…." He swallowed the bile in his throat. "I have to leave. They'll take Leo from Ryan if I don't."

"Ryan won't allow that to happen."

"I don't know. I can't take the risk."

"Son, take a breath. Have you talked to Ryan? What did he say?"

"I don't—I haven't talked to him." But at that moment the door opened again, and Ryan walked in. "Ryan's here. I've got to go."

"Tell him, Dylan. Loving someone means you trust them with the good and the bad."

"I… I'll call you later."

Dylan ended the call. He pressed his hand to his stomach, the weight of his emotions overwhelming him, and forced himself to take a deep breath, but another sob escaped. Ryan rushed over and tightly gripped his shoulders, his face filled with concern.

"What haven't you talked to me about?" Ryan asked.

"Your sister was here with my parents. Ryan, I have to go. If I stay, you'll lose Leo. I can't—" His voice broke. Dylan turned his head away, shut his eyes, and pressed his hands over his heart, trying to keep it from shattering.

Ryan took Dylan's face in his hands and gently turned it back. "Open your eyes, sweetheart, and tell me everything."

He opened his mouth and a sob came out. Ryan held him close as he cried, spilling out incoherent details of his parents' visit. When he'd cried himself out, Ryan led him over to the sofa and sat Dylan down while he got him a glass of water and made him a cup of tea. After he made sure Dylan was calm, he went over and took the envelope Dylan had thrown on the bed.

Ryan sat down next to Dylan and pulled out the contents. Dylan watched, feeling a knot tighten in his stomach as Ryan's body went rigid upon seeing the court documents. Ryan's face became mottled with fury, holding the cashier's check in his hand.

When he'd gone through everything, he put the papers down and shifted to face Dylan. Dylan steeled himself, knowing this was the end and Ryan would tell him he had to go.

"Dylan, look at me," Ryan said, his voice steady and unexpectedly composed.

Dylan took a shaky breath and looked at Ryan.

"You're not going anywhere."

"But they'll take Leo from you."

Ryan shook his head. "No, they won't. We need to make it look like you've left town for a few days while I take care of this, but you're not leaving." He took Dylan's hands in his and held them tightly. "You're mine, Dylan, and I'm not letting you go."

Dylan's lips trembled. "I thought you were going to say I had to leave."

"Why would you think that?"

"I-I wouldn't expect you to risk your family for me."

Ryan cupped his cheek and pulled him in for a gentle kiss. "Sweetheart, you are my family. You, Leo, and me—we're a family. You're all I need in this world."

Dylan's heart raced, thumping against his rib cage. It was everything he'd been longing for, filling him with hope and fear at the same time.

"I'm going to spend the rest of my life kissing all of the fears and doubts I can from your eyes," Ryan said, brushing away a tear that hovered at the corner of Dylan's eye and keeping any more from falling with more gentle kisses.

"I'm so fucking scared," Dylan confessed.

Ryan nodded and pressed his forehead against his. "I'm scared too. But I'm not afraid of your parents or my sister. I'm afraid of what my life would look like without you in it."

After a few tender kisses, Ryan pulled away with a heavy sigh. "There are calls I need to make."

"What can I do?"

Ryan kissed his temple. "Stay right here by my side."

That's exactly what Dylan did while Ryan made calls to his assistant and his friends Jason and Joy.

Ryan helped Dylan pack up his things. Dylan's bank had branches in Seattle, and they stopped to deposit the cashier's check into his account. It disgusted him to do it. Ryan stood by his side, his hand on Dylan's lower back as Dylan endorsed the check. The cashier looked at him with wide eyes when she looked at the check. She eyed him warily and took the check to the bank manager before depositing it. Depositing the check was the first part of Ryan's plan. As much as Dylan disliked doing it, he believed in Ryan. Once they finished at the bank, they headed over to Jason and Joy's, who welcomed them with warm hugs and unwavering support.

Joy came over, sat next to Dylan, and wrapped her arm around his shoulder. "It's going to be okay."

Dylan took a shaky breath, watching Ryan and Jason talking quietly in the kitchen. Both their faces were masks of grim determination. "I know."

Despite the fear that made him numb, Dylan did believe deep in his bones that somehow everything would be all right. Knowing he'd have Ryan by his side to fight life's battles, little ones or big ones, he felt strong.

"Thanks for letting me stay with you," he said to Joy.

"Of course. I'm glad Ryan knew he could reach out to us." Joy peered at him with a curious smile. "So does this mean you'll be staying in Seattle permanently?"

"I guess so. I'll miss my friends and students in LA, but I would miss Leo and Ryan more. I can't imagine my life without them. It's big, scary, and overwhelming, but it will be worth it."

"I felt the same way when I fell in love with Jason," Joy said with a knowing smile. "I wasn't expecting it, and bam, here I was, risking my heart, and I was so scared I kind of ran away. Thank goodness I had friends who helped me realize I'd lose more if I didn't trust… us. Both of us—Jason and me together—were better."

Ryan came over and held his hand out for Dylan. "Take a walk with me?"

It would always be the easiest thing in the world to put his hand in Ryan's. They exited out of a set of french doors that led to the backyard and followed a path to a dock on the lake.

"Same lake, and yet so different from the other side," Dylan said.

"It seems calmer over here," Ryan said.

"Maybe that's because all our problems are over there," Dylan said, pointing to the lights from Ryan's house across the water. "Are you sure you want to do this?" He rested his head on Ryan's shoulder. "I know how it feels to lose your family, even one who doesn't love you, and it still hurts. I don't want that for you."

Ryan wrapped his arm around Dylan's waist and pulled him close to his side. "I've lived with that fear. Thinking I couldn't make it on my own, that I needed the support of my family. Now I know what I thought was support, them loving me, wasn't that at all. You can't love someone by trying to control them. I'll hope that my sister and my parents will change, but I won't put my life on hold waiting for it, and I won't risk Leo's either." Ryan sighed. "I'm sorry about your parents. I wish I could say I have the same hope for them, but I can't. After this, I'll make sure none of them ever gets the chance to see Leo again."

"I'm glad. When the time is right, I'd like Kevin and Carl to meet Leo. Maybe… maybe they could be Leo's grandparents."

"They'll be wonderful grandparents, and I can't wait to meet them. As soon as I've taken care of everything, I'll fly them out."

"We." Dylan turned in Ryan's arms, pressing his hands against Ryan's chest. "We'll take care of everything together. We're a team, right?"

Ryan nodded and took a deep breath. "And that's why I love you. You're the partner I always dreamed of having, someone who didn't dictate but really talked to me, listened, and offered suggestions. I feel stronger knowing I can support you and you'll do the same for me. You didn't run away today, Dylan. You stayed."

Dylan dropped his head to Ryan's shoulder and shuddered. "I love you too. But I thought about running away. I was so scared, and I-I panicked and didn't know what to do. If you hadn't walked in when you did, I don't know what I would have done. I know I've let you down and—"

"Dylan, stop." Ryan held Dylan's face in his hands. "You didn't let me down. You panicked. I did too when I saw the court documents"—his voice shook—"when I saw what our families were capable of. Then I thought of how much I love you, how much I love Leo, and I'm ready to fight to hold on to what we have."

"I love you so much." Dylan wrapped his hands around Ryan's wrists and leaned in, fusing their mouths. It was a long, slow, languid kiss that cemented their love. In Ryan, Dylan found his home, a family to call his own, and the love he'd always wanted but never believed in his heart he'd find.

LEAVING DYLAN behind at Jason and Joy's was agony. It helped to have Dylan with friends instead of alone in some hotel room like they'd originally discussed. What helped ease Ryan's anxiety the most was knowing Dylan loved him. Knowing that gave Ryan the strength to do what he needed.

In the time it took to get Dylan settled with Jason and Joy, the sun set in a blaze of orange-and-pink hues. The same private investigator Ryan had used to get information about Dylan was already sending detailed reports. It was obvious Stephanie and his parents didn't think anyone would ever look into their business activities. They were careless and hadn't done much to cover their tracks. He'd trusted them, and they'd used that trust to their advantage. Ryan directed most of his anger toward himself for passively taking part in his own life.

He got in touch with Lisa on the way back.

"Ryan, is everything okay?" she asked when she answered his call.

The surprise in her voice wasn't unexpected. He rarely reached out outside office hours, wanting to be respectful of her time.

"No," he said in a clipped voice. "I'm going to ask you a question. Have you been working with my sister behind my back?"

"Absolutely not." Lisa's answer came swift and firm.

Ryan exhaled. "Deep down I knew that, but I had to ask. I'm sorry."

"What happened that you felt you needed to ask?"

Ryan gave Lisa a brief, emotionless summary.

Lisa muttered an oath before she asked, "What do you need me to do?"

"For now, pretend everything is normal. I hope you don't mind putting in some overtime. I have forty-eight hours to make sure Dylan and my son are safe." He told her about the discrepancy he'd found earlier.

"Let me do some digging, and I'll get back to you."

Ryan thanked Lisa and hung up. His jaw ached from clenching his teeth as he prepared to return home, where he'd have to face people he would never trust again and pretend everything was okay.

CHAPTER TWENTY-SIX

THE SUN was shining, framing the Olympic mountains against a clear blue sky across the Sound. Ryan stared at the scene without taking it in. Physically he stood in the living room of a house he hated. His heart was on the other side of the lake. Now that he'd told Dylan he loved him, he didn't want them to spend another night apart. He needed to end this quickly for both their sakes.

If there was a hell, it was coming home and having to smile and pretend everything was okay. Ryan read and reread the unsigned agreement his sister and in-laws wanted Dylan to sign. The agreement stated Dylan would stay away from Ryan and Leo if he took the money. The second document was far more menacing, paperwork filing for custody of Leo, signed by Lindsay's parents, his parents, and his sister. Stephanie was asking for custody. Their claim was that Ryan was leading a promiscuous lifestyle, that his relationship with Dylan exposed and groomed Leo. Filing for custody in Lindsay's parents' hometown was a smart and diabolical move. The McKenzies had a lot of influence, and the political and judicial climate was becoming unfriendly toward gay people. Although there was only a slim possibility of them winning, the court might grant them temporary custody of Leo during the ongoing legal battle.

His sister walked into the room, and he steeled himself. He wasn't an actor, but he'd have to put on the best performance of his life.

"Ryan, you seem down. What's the matter? Is it Leo?"

It wasn't hard to appear upset when he turned and looked at his sister, recognizing her sympathetic expression was completely fake.

"It's Dylan." He sighed. "He went back to LA. Just up and left. I can't believe he would abandon Leo this way."

Turns out his sister wasn't as good an actress as she thought. Or maybe Ryan was. He could see the insincerity in her eyes now that he knew the depths of her malevolence. But when she said, "That's what I was afraid of when you asked him to stay. I know what's best for you, Ryan," Stephanie's words rang hollow.

"You're right." The words tasted like a bitter lemon in his mouth. Despite the sense of disconnect, he summoned the strength to embrace his sister, mirroring the brotherly gesture that had always been a part of their bond, even though it now felt as though he was embracing a stranger.

"Of course, I'll always be here for you. Why don't you join us for dinner at the club tonight? Arlene and Clay leave the day after tomorrow, and they'd like to spend more time with you."

"I will." Ryan looked down at his watch. "I'm going into the office again. I need to get back to work regularly now that Leo's feeling better."

Stephanie nodded, smiling with approval. "Absolutely. Getting back to work will be good for you."

"Did you look over the list of candidates I gave you to fill the board position?"

"I did. They are all good suggestions, but I have another candidate, and mom and dad agree with me we should have Derrick Holloway join the board."

Derrick Holloway was an asshole. His slick smile had never fooled Ryan. Derrick had avoided a tax fraud charge and settled the sexual harassment lawsuit against him out of court. He'd been trying to do business with Ryan, wanting him to develop Bitcoin software at first, and then approached him about developing a program for non-fungible tokens, so-called NFTs. The guy was a scammer, and Ryan turned him down, making it clear he wouldn't do business with him under any circumstances. Now he was reading a report from the private investigator that said Derrick had been fucking Ryan's sister for the last six months.

"If you think that's what's best," he said, forcing a benevolent smile. "I'd like to get that position filled. Let's call a meeting for tomorrow and make it official."

Stephanie beamed, triumph glittering in her eyes. "Great. I'll take care of it."

He swallowed the bile rising in his throat, continuing to play nice until Stephanie left.

After spending the morning with Leo, he headed straight to Lisa's office at Blackstone Financial.

"Do we have everything we need?" he asked, shutting the door behind him.

"We do," she said, shuffling the papers on her desk. "Plus a bonus."

Ryan's eyebrows shot up.

"Remember I mentioned I saw something suspicious on your sister's computer about ARW?" Lisa smirked. "I did a little digging. Your sister has been selling your tech to them under the table. Guess who bought ARW six months ago?"

Ryan's eyebrows shot up. "Derrick Holloway. How did you find out?"

"You've never asked what my girlfriend does for a living," she said with a mischievous smile.

"What does Mattie do?"

"She's a cyber security expert."

Ryan barked a laugh.

Lisa tapped a flash drive on her desk. "With what I have on here, combined with what your private investigator has sent over, I think we have more than enough."

Ryan blew out a shaky breath and nodded. Despite the tight knot in his gut, he found reassurance in knowing he could do what needed to be done. Out of the corner of his eye, he watched his sister breeze into the office.

"It's your company, Ryan," Lisa said quietly, "and we've got enough to make sure it stays that way."

"As soon as my sister puts the board meeting on the schedule, let security know. Can you have someone available to change the lock on my sister's office as soon as the meeting starts?"

Lisa nodded, adding a note to her computer. "Anything else?"

"I feel like a fool," he said when they finished.

"No one thinks their family will betray them. And certainly not like this. I'm sorry, Ryan." Lisa flipped through her notes. "Your lawyer is sending over documents for you to review later this afternoon."

"Thanks."

Lisa nodded. "I'm on it."

He got up and held out his hand. "Thank you, Lisa. I'm going to make sure you and your girlfriend get that house you've been saving for."

She shook his hand. "Right now I'm more interested in revenge." She smirked. "I guess now is as good a time as any to show you my ruthless side."

"I'm counting on it," he said with a grim smile.

Ryan went home. He pulled into the garage, steeling himself before he went inside. He could hear his in-laws in the living room, along with his sister and parents. Before he went in, he sought Mrs. Lieu. He found her in her apartment.

She took one look at him and asked, "*Con*, what's wrong?"

"My sister and Dylan's parents tried to bribe him to leave."

Mrs. Lieu's eyes flashed with anger. "I've been respectful because they're your family, but those people"—she pointed a shaking finger toward the living room—"are not good." She lifted her chin. "I love you, *con*, but I will not continue to work for you if you don't put a stop to this."

Ryan put his arm around her. "I will." He exhaled. "I need you to pretend everything's okay for one more day."

"I can do that. Where's Dylan? Is he okay? My poor sweetheart."

"He's okay. He's with Jason and Joy. We had to make it look like he left town." Ryan kissed her cheek. "There's the family you're born into and the family that you love. I love you, Mrs. Lieu. After tomorrow, you might have to adopt me."

She sniffed and wiped her eyes. "I love you too, my *con*. I already think of you as my son."

Ryan left Mrs. Lieu's apartment and took a deep, fortifying breath as he walked into the living room with the biggest smile he could muster. He visited for a few minutes before he used wanting to spend time with Leo as an excuse to leave.

Ryan retreated upstairs before he let his composure slip. He found Leo in Rebecca's lap. He sat down next to them. "What are you reading?" he asked as Leo scrambled out of Rebecca's lap into his with his book.

Leo held up the book. "*The Lotterys Plus One*."

"What's it about?"

"It's about two families, one with two dads and one with two moms, and they live in a big house with all different kinds of kids and a grumpy grandpa." Leo wrinkled his little nose. "I don't like him, though. He reminds me of Grandpa Clay."

Ryan exchanged a look with Rebecca over Leo's head. She gave him a pinched smile. He looked around, noticing the bookshelves that Dylan had filled now seemed half empty.

"What happened to all the books?" he asked Rebecca.

She shifted uncomfortably, biting her lip.

"Leo, can you make me a picture while I talk to Rebecca for a minute?"

Leo climbed off his lap and over to his play table. "I'm going to use lots of blue because that's your favorite."

"I can't wait to see it."

He got up and motioned for Rebecca to follow him into her room next to Leo's, leaving the connecting door open so they could keep an eye on him. "What happened to the books?" he asked again.

"Leo's grandma came in and went through his bookshelves. She took all the 'unsuitable'"—Rebecca made air quotes—"ones and threw them away." She grabbed Ryan's arm when he started for the door. "It's okay. Mrs. Lieu and I salvaged them. They're in the garage. I had the *Lotterys* book in here, so it escaped Mrs. McKenzie's self-righteous wrath." She sighed. "I don't mean to be rude, but that woman is a menace."

"You're not rude at all." He glanced toward the play table where Leo was standing over a piece of paper, his little tongue sticking out while he worked on his picture. He looked back at Rebecca. "You won't have to worry about the McKenzies after tomorrow."

Rebecca nodded solemnly. "You should know your mother-in-law doesn't think very highly of your parenting. She mentioned several times today that Leo needs a mother."

Ryan clenched his fists at his sides. "Thanks for telling me."

"I got your back." Rebecca patted his shoulder.

"Daddy, come look at my picture."

Ryan went over and knelt down next to Leo's play table. He bit back a sob when he saw Leo's picture. Three stick figures in shades of blue were holding hands. Leo was the little stick figure in the middle. The figure on the right was clearly Dylan, with his curly black hair, while Ryan was on the left with blond spiky hair. In the background was a tent. "Grandpa Clay said Uncle Dylan isn't coming back." Leo looked at Ryan, his large round eyes filling with tears. "But I love Uncle Dylan."

"So do I, sweetheart. I love your uncle Dylan, and he'll be back soon, I promise. How about we call him and you can show him your picture?"

Ryan fought back tears when Dylan's face filled the screen. They'd been texting throughout the day, but seeing Dylan and the haggard look on his face made Ryan want to reach through the screen and hug him. They kept the call short, not wanting anyone to overhear and realize Dylan hadn't really left town.

With a heavy heart, Ryan went back downstairs, his emotions raw after hearing what his mother-in-law did and talking to Dylan.

His sister met him halfway up the stairs. "I was just coming to find you. We're getting ready to go to the club for dinner."

He made a show of rubbing his temple. "I'll have to pass tonight. I have a headache."

"I know you're disappointed in how Dylan used us, but you have to put it behind you. Trust me, the right woman is out there, but you won't meet her unless you go out more."

"What about you? Where's the right guy for you?" Ryan asked.

Stephanie's gaze shifted away. "I'm focused on my career right now. I still have time."

He didn't miss the slight twitch of her eye.

Ryan raised an eyebrow. "And I don't?"

"It's different for you. You have Leo to think about."

That was the only thing she'd said he could agree with. "You're right, I do. But I'm not going to dinner. I wasn't making an excuse. I do have a headache."

Stephanie eyed him skeptically before she sighed. "All right. Dad and Clay are going golfing after the board meeting tomorrow. Why don't you join them?"

"Sure, I can do that." The lie fell easily from his lips. "Why don't we have Clay and Arlene come to the board meeting, and we can all leave from there? They don't have seats on the board, but I did gift them ten shares when Lindsay and I got married. It might be fun for them."

"I'm sure they'd love it."

As soon as everyone left for dinner, he called Dylan again.

"Hey, baby, how are you holding up?"

Dylan sniffed. "I lost it when I saw the picture Leo drew. I miss him so much."

"We're going to take care of everything tomorrow. A car will pick you up early, and I'll be at the office waiting for you."

"I don't have a suit."

"That doesn't matter."

"I know. I want to look… like I'm worthy of being there."

"Sweetheart, you are more than worthy, and I'll be so proud to have you standing by my side."

"All hell's going to break loose," Dylan said in a shaky voice.

"Probably. But it's for the best." At first Ryan didn't want to tell Dylan about Leo's books. But they'd promised each other their love united them as a team, and there would be no secrets between them. Taking a deep breath, he shared what had happened. Dylan's anger was palpable through the phone.

"I don't want them near Leo," Dylan seethed.

"I know, neither do I, and after tomorrow, they won't be. Once we get through this, let's take Leo camping for real. He's doing well, and we could find a quiet place, for only the three of us."

"I'd like that," Dylan said with a sigh.

"I love you," Ryan whispered. "I should be worried about what's about to happen, but I'm not because I know you'll be by my side."

"I love you so much. I'd be lying if I said I wasn't scared, but I would walk through fire before letting my parents' ugliness influence Leo. Once I can see you and hold your hand, I'll be okay."

"I feel the same way."

They whispered quiet hopes and promises until they reluctantly said good night. After they hung up, Ryan went back to Leo's room. He picked Leo up, feeling the soft fuzz of new hair growing on Leo's head under his chin. Ryan settled back on the bed with Leo tucked by his side, the covers over him. Ryan watched his son sleep.

CHAPTER TWENTY-SEVEN

Ryan waited anxiously for Dylan to arrive. As soon as the black SUV pulled into the loading zone of the parking garage, he yanked open the back door and pulled Dylan out and into his arms. Dylan shuddered, burying his face in Ryan's neck.

"I missed you," Dylan said, pressing a soft kiss along Ryan's jawline before his lips grazed his mouth.

Ryan groaned, kissing him deeply. Tonight he'd have Dylan back in his arms. He pulled away and cupped Dylan's cheek. "Are you ready?"

Dylan nodded. Ryan took him up in the freight elevator, and Lisa was waiting for them when the doors opened.

"Coast clear?" Ryan asked.

Lisa nodded and rushed them into Ryan's office.

"It's nice to meet you, Dylan. I'm sorry it's under these circumstances," she said, closing the blinds to Ryan's office once they were inside. It was early, and the office was empty, but people would start showing up any minute now.

"Is everything set up in the conference room?" Ryan asked.

"Coffee, tea, and mimosas. I also have pastries. I'll say you wanted to do a little something special since the McKenzies are here. I'll let them know you're wrapping up a call and you'll be in momentarily. As soon as everyone is here, I'll text you to come in."

"What if someone comes looking for you in here?" Dylan asked.

Ryan dipped his head toward the door against one wall. "I have a private bathroom. You can duck in there."

Dylan nodded, glancing around nervously. Ryan took Dylan's hand and led him over to a small loveseat by the large glass window that took up an entire wall in his office.

"Can I get you anything?" Lisa asked.

"No." Dylan shook his head. "Thank you. I think if I try to put anything into my stomach, it won't stay down."

Ryan clasped Dylan's hand, rubbing his thumb over his knuckles.

Lisa checked her watch. "I should get out there. Hang tight. I'll text you when it's time."

"Thanks, Lisa."

"This is going to be fun." She bounced on her toes with a gleam in her eye.

Dylan leaned over and whispered to Ryan, "I like her."

"She's getting a huge bonus and a promotion when this is over."

Dylan nodded. "I approve." He got up and paced, rubbing his hands together. Suddenly he stopped. "Is this okay?" he asked, gesturing to the dark gray trousers and powder-blue shirt he wore. He tugged at his collar. "I don't have a tie."

"Sweetheart, look at me. I'm not wearing a tie either." Ryan stopped Dylan's pacing, cupping the back of his neck.

Dylan reached up and fingered the collar of Ryan's pale gray dress shirt. "You look nice," he said in a shaky voice.

Ryan kissed his forehead. "So do you. Now come and sit down with me."

"This will work," Dylan said quietly, not asking but trying to reassure himself.

"You'll be back home with us today."

Dylan nodded, chewing on his lip. But Ryan could see the unease in his eyes. Dylan may have been nervous, but Ryan felt a strange sense of calm. He wouldn't regret what he was about to do.

"Sweetheart, there are things about your dad in the report from the PI that might upset you. Do you want me to tell you now?"

"Does it matter? Is it going to lower my opinion any more than it already is?"

"No." Ryan shook his head. "It won't."

"Then it doesn't matter, and I don't care."

Ryan tried to keep them distracted, making plans for their camping trip, telling Dylan about different spots around the state. There were so many places he wanted to explore with Dylan and Leo. Not quite a year ago he was scared to death he might lose his son, and now he was planning a future with adventures together as a family with Dylan.

Dylan stiffened at his side when Ryan's phone buzzed.

Ryan stood up and held his hand out for Dylan. "Are you ready?"

Dylan got up and put his hand in Ryan's, pressing a quick, firm kiss against his lips. "Let's go."

No matter how things turned out, they would walk hand in hand toward their future.

The conversation and laughter around the conference table came to an abrupt end when Ryan walked into the conference room with Dylan at his side.

He watched his sister's face morph from shock to suspicion and then anger.

"What is he doing here?" Dylan's mother asked, her mouth turned down into an angry scowl.

Ryan nodded to Lisa, who started handing out the stack of folders she'd been holding.

"Thank you all for coming," he began, looking around the room at the confused, angry faces. Except for one. Derrick Holloway sat across from him at the head of the table, with Ryan's sister at his right. He was so arrogant he didn't read the room, not picking up on the change in the atmosphere. Derrick's appearance matched his scumbag personality— slicked back hair, an expensive suit, and matching gold cufflinks and watch. He had a thin narrow face with a fake tan and sharp dark brown eyes. Derrick looked at Ryan with a smug smile.

"Let's get this vote over with," a gray-haired, stodgy older man his parents insisted should be on the board said, looking at his watch. "I have a golf date in an hour."

"Ryan, what is going on?" his sister asked with a nervous glance at Derrick.

"We will not be voting Derrick Holloway onto the board today," Ryan announced, watching Derrick's confident smile fall. There were gasps and murmurs around the table.

His sister's face paled. "What are you talking about?"

"If you look in your folders, you'll understand," Ryan continued, ignoring his sister.

He turned to his parents. "I have removed your names from all of my personal bank accounts and have cancelled the credit cards and lines of credit that I have covered for the three of you. I have also had my will revised, excluding all three of you from making any claim to my estate or Leo's trust fund."

His father jumped out of his chair. "You can't do this."

"I can and I have. Look in your folder," Ryan said once more, his voice deadly calm. "I've sold Dylan McKenzie the majority of my stock." Following a pointed look at his sister and the McKenzies, Ryan turned to the red-faced man. "You didn't pay attention to the bylaws of the company, did you? I have the authority to appoint anyone I want to the board. This is a privately held company, and I may sell or gift shares to anyone I wish. Dylan McKenzie is now the principal owner of Blackstone Financial."

Dylan grabbed Ryan's hand. "And I've appointed Ryan Blackstone as President and CEO." He swallowed and looked up at Ryan, his gaze full of love and trust. He kept his eyes on Ryan as he spoke. "It doesn't really matter anyway since we'll be getting married and this is a community property state. What's mine is his."

Ryan took Dylan's other hand. Holding both of them he leaned close. "And what's his is mine."

There was no other vow and no officiant needed to validate their commitment. Their bond was unbreakable.

Chaos broke out in the room as people found evidence of corruption and illegal activities in their folders, perpetrated by Stephanie, the McKenzies, and Derrick Holloway. Ryan forcefully brought his hand down on the table. He stared Dylan's parents and his sister down. "Let me make this clear. You will never get your hands on Leo. I've provided all of you with the same evidence I gave to the prosecutor's office. The evidence of your bribery of my employees and Dylan, as well as the judge in Kentucky." He looked at Derrick and his sister. "I made a separate report for corporate espionage for the two of you. Selling my tech when I specifically said no wasn't a very smart move, Stephanie. Corporate espionage is a crime." Ryan glanced around the table. "Effective immediately, I'm removing all of you from the board."

Stephanie stared at him, her face pale. "I'm your sister. How could you do this to me?"

"I can ask you the same question. How could you do this to me? How could you threaten to take my son away from me?"

"Because of him." She pointed a shaking finger at Dylan. "I've spent my entire life keeping you on the right path. We all knew what you were. I made sure to stop you from ruining your life, and then he comes along and seduces you."

Dylan tightened his hold on Ryan's hand but stayed silent.

"Dylan didn't seduce me. I chose him."

"You're disgracing our daughter's memory." Arlene pursed her lips, glaring at Dylan.

"You're a disgrace," Ryan started, and then stopped when Dylan squeezed his hand with a slight shake of his head.

"Don't," Dylan whispered. "There's nothing you can say that will change their minds."

"We're your family," Ryan's mother said, her lips quivering.

"No, not anymore. Leo and Dylan are my family."

Dylan's mom looked away, her face a mask of disgust. Ryan turned back to them.

"Arlene, Clay, if you ever try a stunt like this again, I will destroy you. I will end Clay's coaching career the same way you ended Kevin Cooper's teaching career."

"I'd like to see you try," Clay blustered.

"Look in your file." Ryan pointed to the folder sitting in front of him, still unopened. Clay opened the folder, and then his eyes flew to Ryan, his face gray. Arlene gasped, her hand going to her heart.

"I don't think folks in town want a man around their kids who got one of the high school cheerleaders pregnant and made her get an abortion, do you?" Ryan said.

Dylan swayed slightly, sucking in his breath.

His mother got up and came toward him, her hands clasped in front of her. "Ryan, you don't know what you're doing. This boy has blinded you. We're your family. We only want what's best for you."

He backed away when she reached for him. "No. Family doesn't take out a life insurance policy on an innocent child with cancer. Family doesn't lie."

His mother clamped her mouth shut, bright spots appearing on her cheeks.

"We can work this out, Ryan," Stephanie said, getting up from her seat to walk toward him.

Ryan pulled Dylan closer to his side, moving slightly in front of him in a protective stance. Stephanie stopped, her gaze dropping to where Ryan had his arm wrapped around Dylan's waist.

"Would you really choose him over me?" she asked with a slight tremor in her voice.

"Yes," Ryan said without hesitation. Stephanie shook her head as her eyes filled with tears. "There's nothing to work out. You lied and manipulated, and you hurt the two people I love most in this world." He turned to the table. "Security is waiting to escort you from the building."

Lisa opened the door and waved the security team in. Everyone seated at the table looked from the security team to Ryan in shock.

"Get. Out," he said with deadly calm.

With their fingers intertwined, Ryan and Dylan left behind their former families and the past, ready for a new future.

There was a huddle of employees waiting by his office. "I expect you have all heard what happened. There are going to be quite a few changes. To start with, Lisa Blanchard is being promoted to vice president of operations. Some of you—" Ryan glanced around the room, noting the employees who were avoiding his gaze. "—will be let go. I have zero tolerance for unethical behavior."

Dylan jumped as security started pulling his protesting parents out of the boardroom.

Ryan turned to Lisa. "Can you take care of the rest?"

Lisa nodded, and Ryan took Dylan back to his office and pulled him into a hug.

"Are you all right?"

Dylan took a deep breath and nodded. He looked up at Ryan. "They won't try to fight you, will they?"

Ryan shook his head. "My parents' worst nightmare is losing their social status. This won't ruin my parents financially. They had enough money before I founded Blackstone Financial. But they'll be social outcasts once people learn they had a life insurance policy on Leo and assisted Stephanie in selling my tech without my consent. I gave an interview to the *Seattle Business Journal* this morning. I gave them copies of the files I gave my parents and Stephanie. If your parents try anything, I'll send the report I have on your father to their local paper."

Dylan closed his eyes and nodded. "I'm going to hope we never have to do that, but it's a relief to know we have something to fight them with."

"I like hearing you say 'we,'" Ryan said, leaning close to nuzzle Dylan's neck. "We're going to be all right."

Lisa interrupted their kiss, poking her head in the door. "Sorry to interrupt. I wanted you to know security has escorted everyone from the building. Your sister tried to go back to her office and was pretty upset when she learned we had changed the locks. I made sure security took everyone's key cards and had their credentials removed from the system."

"Thank you, Lisa. You can start house shopping, because I'm giving you a bonus and adding stock options to your employment package. I couldn't have done this without your support."

"Thanks," she said with a wide smile.

Dylan gasped, putting his hand over his mouth. "Leo. They'll go back to your house and try to take Leo," he said in a panicked voice.

"Sweetheart, it's okay." Ryan rubbed Dylan's arms. "There's security at the house, and I had Mrs. Lieu pack Arlene and Clay's bags."

Lisa mentioned that security had given them their bags when they were escorted out of the building.

Ryan wrapped his arm around Dylan's shoulder. "Let's go home."

CHAPTER TWENTY-EIGHT

"I STILL CAN'T believe it," Dylan said, adrenaline continuing to surge through his veins as they drove away from Blackstone Financial Technologies.

"I'm sure there will be more fallout, but I know we can handle anything that comes our way."

Dylan frowned when they turned onto the bridge instead of taking the last off-ramp toward Ryan's home. "Where are we going?"

"I want to show you something."

Dylan reached across the center console and brushed his fingers along the hair at the nape of Ryan's neck. Since he'd arrived at Ryan's office that morning, there hadn't been a moment where they weren't touching each other. There were several times while they were in the conference room when Dylan thought his knees would buckle, his heart was pounding so hard. But he had Ryan at his side, with his arm around him. He'd felt helpless during the meeting, not knowing what to say. Looking at his parents, though, Dylan realized he didn't have to say anything. He didn't need their validation or love. Ryan believed in him. Ryan didn't just love him, he respected him and saw him as his equal. That's what it meant to truly love someone. It's what Dylan admired about Kevin and Carl's relationship and always hoped he'd find one day.

Ryan pulled off the bridge, heading toward Jason and Joy's house. Dylan stared at Ryan with a raised eyebrow when they pulled onto Jason and Joy's street. Instead of going to their house, however, Ryan turned into the driveway of a house two doors down. He parked and got out, jogging around to Dylan's side to open the door for him.

"What's going on?" Dylan asked, peering up at the large Craftsman-style home. It was a new build but had all the charm of a vintage home, with light gray shingles, white trim and black shutters. Similar to Jason and Joy's, the house had a sweeping lawn leading down to the lake. Ryan clasped Dylan's hand and pulled him toward the front door, which was painted a pale sage green. Dylan watched as Ryan removed a key from his pocket and unlocked the front door.

Light hardwood floors and soft white walls reflected the light from a wall of windows on the other side of a massive open-concept floor plan. Instead of a grand staircase, a more modest one along one wall led upstairs.

Ryan gently guided him into a spacious kitchen with white upper cabinets, dark green lower cabinets, and a large island with white countertops. The lower level had its own small kitchen, a bathroom, a den, and a guest room with an en suite. Upstairs, Ryan showed him two more bedrooms, each with their own bathroom.

At the last door, Ryan took a deep breath before he opened it. Dylan walked into the only furnished room in the house. The enormous primary suite was placed at the opposite end of the house from the other bedrooms, so there were windows on three sides of the room. A black metal modern four-poster bed with silver-gray sheets and a blue-and-gray paisley duvet graced the bedroom, which also boasted a walk-in closet. The en suite held a freestanding tub big enough for two and an even bigger shower. The room was already equipped with white fluffy towels.

"Did you rent this for us?" Dylan asked.

Ryan shook his head. "Do you like it?"

"I love it. It's beautiful."

Ryan held the key toward him, a slow smile spreading over his face. "That's a relief because I bought it."

Dylan's mouth dropped open. "You did what?"

"Jason mentioned a few days ago that the owners were thinking about selling."

"But you can't buy a house in a few days." Dylan sputtered, his mind still spinning.

"It's not officially ours yet. But the owners were okay with moving out now and giving me the keys."

"You gave them a lot of money, didn't you?"

Ryan gave him a sheepish smile. "I may have sent them on an all-expense-paid trip to Tahiti."

Dylan threw his arms around Ryan's neck. "I love it."

"I want both of our names on the deed."

"I can't afford to put—"

Ryan silenced him with a kiss. "You have shares in Blackstone Technologies, and it doesn't matter. The money isn't what's important— what we build here together is. I don't want to spend another minute living a half-life. I want a whole life with you, Dylan. I want us to raise Leo here. Maybe we can even give him a sibling one day. I want us to wake up in this bed together every morning and fall asleep together every night. I love you, Dylan, and I want to spend the rest of my life loving you. That's all that matters to me."

Dylan nodded. The lump in his throat was so big he could barely speak. Ryan was offering him all he'd ever wanted and so much more. "I love you, Ryan. You're my strength and my happiness. You taught me I'm not a burden. Knowing you love me, you make me feel invincible. I thought I was the match, but you're my match, Ryan."

Ryan reached for him and wrapped his arms around him. They held on to each other for a long time. Dylan realized they both needed a chance to finally breathe and live their lives without fear. If that meant their hugs needed to last a little longer while they reassured each other everything would be all right, Dylan was okay with it. Ryan pulled out of the embrace only enough so he could hold Dylan's face in his hands and kiss him. All the fear and longing they had faced over the last few days was released in a flurry of desperate kisses, their bodies craving each other's touch.

"Yes," Ryan moaned when Dylan wrapped his hand around his cock. Ryan lifted his head and nipped at Dylan's shoulder. "Need you now," he said, his voice strained with urgency.

Their bodies writhed together, trying to get closer, touching everywhere. They didn't make it from the floor to the bed. Dylan joined their cocks together in his hand, slick with precum, and they both cried out their release. They lay panting on the floor, exchanging soft kisses and murmured words of love. Gentle kisses soon became heated again, and they moved to the bed, where Ryan's dick pressed against him as he peppered Dylan' s face with kisses before moving down his body, tasting every inch while he told Dylan how beautiful he was and how much Ryan wanted him. By the time Ryan pushed into him, Dylan was moaning and begging.

"Open your eyes, baby," Ryan whispered.

Dylan obeyed his command and looked at Ryan, his eyes dark with desire, beads of sweat on his forehead.

"There you are," Ryan smiled, easing himself the rest of the way in.

Dylan groaned. Nothing would ever feel as good as this, and it wasn't just the physical closeness. An invisible thread tied them together, connecting his heart to Ryan's.

After round two, Dylan lay in the tub, his back against Ryan's chest, surrounded by tendrils of steam. Dylan sighed, his body finally sated. Ryan kissed the shell of his ear, his fingers gently running up and down Dylan's chest.

"I think we're off to a good start making memories in this house," Dylan said.

Ryan chuckled, the sound vibrating in his chest and going straight to Dylan's heart.

"I know I should have waited, and if you want, we can look for something together. When Jason told me about this house and we walked down to see it, I knew I wanted us to live here as soon as I saw it. I could picture us here as a family."

Dylan turned his neck and kissed Ryan's jaw. "It's perfect. It's exactly the type of home I pictured for us."

"But?" Ryan said, sensing Dylan's unease.

"I miss Leo. Can we go back and get him? We could bring the tent and have a campout in the living room."

"I love that idea. Let's go get our son."

Dylan turned so quickly water sloshed over the side of the tub. "What did you say?"

Ryan cupped his cheek, brushing away the drops of water from his face with his thumb. "I said 'our son.'"

Dylan's breath hitched. Ryan said out loud what he'd secretly wished for but thought was too selfish to hope for.

"Thank you," he said, pressing a kiss to Ryan's lips. "I already think of Leo as more than a nephew, but let's let Leo decide who he wants me to be in his life."

"Uncle Dylan or Daddy Dylan, he's ours."

They got out of the bath, dressed quickly, and went back to the stark white mansion.

"Would it be okay if I never came back here?" Dylan asked when they pulled up to the house.

Ryan reached for his hand and pressed a kiss to the back of it. "I was thinking the same thing. Let's pack up both cars and go home."

Mrs. Lieu welcomed them with a big smile and hugs. Leo came running into the kitchen a minute later, flinging himself into Dylan's arms. "Uncle Dylan, I missed you," he said, wrapping his arms and legs around him when Dylan picked him up.

"I missed you too," Dylan said, kissing the top of Leo's head.

They sat down at the kitchen table and shared their plan with Mrs. Lieu and Rebecca. Mrs. Lieu was eager to move into the guesthouse that came with the house, and Ryan offered the apartment over the garage to Rebecca, who had decided to stay in Seattle. Rebecca had applied for a job at Seattle Children's and was thrilled to move closer to the hospital.

Dylan reached across the table for Ryan's hand, and their eyes met, silently communicating their happiness.

When they told Leo they were going camping at their new house, he ran upstairs and started filling his backpack with his favorite books and toys. With Rebecca's help, they packed more practical items. They'd have his bed delivered the next day.

Dylan found Ryan in his room, packing a bag. "Is there anything else you want to bring? Have you decided what furniture you want to keep?"

"I don't want any of it," Ryan said, shaking his head. "I'm keeping my desk and that's it. I want to start over with you and have rooms filled with color."

They packed clothes, toiletries, the tent, sleeping bags, and pillows in their cars, along with enough food from Mrs. Lieu to feed them for a week.

Dylan noticed Ryan standing by his car, looking up at the house. He went over and put his hand on Ryan's shoulder. "Are you okay?"

Ryan gave him a wistful smile. "Just saying goodbye."

"We can come back if you need to."

"No, I don't need to come back. I was never really here. I lived in this house, but I wasn't really living. Not until you came." Ryan pressed his shoulder against Dylan's. "Home is with you and Leo. That's where I'll always feel alive."

"Love you," Dylan said, kissing Ryan's cheek.

"Love you too. Let's take our family home."

They both had tears in their eyes watching Leo explore his new home. They spent their first night in their tent set up in the living room, taking turns reading books to Leo. When Leo fell asleep, Dylan held Ryan's hand across Leo's sleeping form, smiling in the darkness.

EPILOGUE

One year later…

LAUGHTER ECHOED through the backyard as Leo ran across the lawn, followed by his best friend, Jamie Prescott. Jamie's parents, Dane and Maya, had become close friends of Ryan and Dylan over the past year, and the boys were thick as thieves. Ryan remembered what Noelle said to him almost a year before about mixed kids recognizing each other. That was certainly the case with Jamie and Leo. From their first day of school together, the two were inseparable.

Along with Jamie's parents, Rebecca and her boyfriend were there, chatting with Lisa and her wife. Dylan's parents, now known as Grandpa Kevin and Pop Pop, were sitting on the dock with Mrs. Lieu and Mr. Croft, their neighbor from across the street, who'd become a frequent visitor and spent a lot of time in Mrs. Lieu's kitchen—and, as Ryan and Dylan had recently discovered, nights in Mrs. Lieu's cottage. Jason brought his guitar over and was strumming his latest song while Joy, Thanh, and Thanh's husband, Milo, sang along.

Jason and Joy's neighbor on the other side, Stellan, joined them as well. They were still getting to know the quiet, serious young man. Dylan instantly recognized a kindred spirit, understanding Stellan was also an outcast in his family. Ryan was happy they'd been able to convince him to join the celebration. It seemed like Stellan was always at his stepmother's beck and call and didn't have a lot of time for fun.

They'd all gathered together to celebrate Leo's one-year anniversary being cancer free. Ryan couldn't think about the day he'd sat in the doctor's office, Dylan's hand gripped in his as the doctor confirmed the engraftment of Dylan's bone marrow was a success, without tearing up.

Dylan came over and wrapped his arm around Ryan's waist. "Are we ready for cake?"

"I think so." Ryan snagged Dylan's wrist when he moved away. "Stay for another minute."

Dylan returned to his side, their fingers laced together as they watched their friends and family enjoy the celebration.

Ryan had gone from living a cold, colorless life in an equally cold and colorless mansion to a new life in a house filled with color and an eclectic mix of vintage furniture and brightly upholstered pieces. There was laughter and sometimes tears, because life wasn't perfect.

The tears came in therapy where Ryan unpacked years of suppressing his feelings. Anger, hurt, and shame—he was still processing his feelings about his parents and sister. They were strangers to him now. He hadn't interacted with them directly since that day in the boardroom. Dylan had been by his side when the news came out about the indictments against his parents and Stephanie. It turned out what they'd attempted to do to them was the least of their crimes. Bribing a senator and insider trading were much bigger crimes. It was Mrs. Lieu who walked Ryan down the aisle at his wedding, as it should be. Over the last year, Ryan learned that his ties to his found family were stronger than those to the people he shared DNA with.

Dylan also went back to therapy, dealing with a bout of survivor guilt. Ryan was so proud watching Dylan learn to accept that he was worthy of the love and affection from the people around him. Arlene and Clay didn't take Ryan's threat seriously. It was Dylan who came to him and said they had no choice but to follow through with exposing them when they tried to file for custody of Leo. But before they could take appropriate steps, another former student came forward with a claim against Clay that unlocked the floodgates, and at last count there were five women who'd brought sexual assault claims against the venerated football coach. Arlene and Clay packed up and fled to a small town in Arkansas as the wheels of justice slowly ground. They wouldn't interfere with Dylan's happiness ever again.

Blackstone Technologies was a different company now, focusing on money management software for small companies and nonprofits. Long days at the office were a thing of the past. Now Ryan kept a strict schedule, his workday ending at 5:00 p.m. He'd instituted a four-day workweek during the summer months so his employees could take advantage of long summer days. Dylan balanced his time teaching and working as the director of the Blackstone Foundation, identifying small organizations to receive grants. His dads happily accepted board positions for the foundation, and Ryan loved watching the three of them work together.

The foundation's first major grant was given to the Be the Match Registry, to help the organization sign up more potential donors. They also set up a fund at Children's Hospital to provide additional resources for families traveling from out of town for stem cell treatment. Ryan abandoned the sleek glass building and moved his company back to the brick building where he founded it. He sold the house he'd shared with Lindsay, and now when Ryan looked at its twinkling lights from across the lake, he felt like his time there was a distant bittersweet memory. It was the house that he and Lindsay brought newborn Leo home from the hospital to. The home where his marriage started and where the police showed up on his doorstep to tell him about the accident that brought his marriage to an abrupt end. It was also where Dylan came to them and made him whole, knowing what it meant to be fully loved for who he was.

Those stressful and chaotic first months after the boardroom confrontation passed, and six months ago, standing in the same spot on the dock, Ryan and Dylan joined hands with Leo and exchanged vows, surrounded by family and friends.

Ryan was finally free to be the person he'd hidden away, fearing rejection. He was loved and accepted for who he was.

The man who'd opened Ryan's heart to his true self kissed his neck and leaned in to whisper in his ear. "The longer we wait to cut the cake, the longer it will be before we can celebrate in private."

Ryan cupped Dylan's cheek. "Every day with you is a celebration." His lips caressed Dylan's ear, making his husband shiver. "But naked celebrations are my favorite," he said in a low, sexy growl.

Dylan laughed, a sound that never failed to make Ryan's heart skip a beat.

DYLAN TRACKED Ryan walking toward him as he stood on the dock. The echo of children's shouts and laughter had faded to the gentle lapping of the water along the shoreline. Grandpa Kevin and Pop Pop were reading Leo bedtime stories. Mrs. Lieu was across the street at their neighbor's. She'd hurried over with a basket of leftovers packed with so much food Dylan suspected they wouldn't see her again until after the weekend.

"Hello," Ryan said when he reached him. He nuzzled Dylan's nose. "Good day?"

Dylan cupped Ryan's cheek, brushing his thumb over the silky strands of his beard. Ryan's starched dress shirts and khakis were gone, and the last time he'd worn a suit was at their wedding. He'd let his hair grow a little longer and grew a beard. Most days found him in a pair of worn jeans and a T-shirt, just like today. His bare feet brushed against Dylan's when he moved closer, wrapping his arms around Dylan.

"A beautiful day." Dylan sighed, resting his head on Ryan's shoulder.

He inhaled, taking in the smell of sunshine and the faint scent of coconut from Ryan's sunscreen. This was what home felt like. Kevin and Carl had given him a refuge, a safe place to heal and grow. Ryan had given his heart a home. For the first time in his life, he was rooted. He'd gone through another bout of grieving for his family, only this time he didn't feel the sting of their rejection, just a sorrow for the narrow-minded, hypocritical lives they'd chosen to live. Reaching that point of acceptance freed him to trust that his chosen family wouldn't reject him, and he was finally able to dismantle the protective walls he'd built around his heart.

Now he had a house filled with family and friends, laughter and joy, beyond anything he could have imagined. Sometimes it scared him just how amazing his life had become. Tomorrow they'd pack up the SUV and head to the ten-acre property Ryan had found only ninety minutes east of Seattle, an idyllic wooded spot with a small lake that became their private campground. They'd added an outdoor kitchen and a shower and bathroom complex, but that was the only structure on the property. Often Jamie would join them, the boys in one tent, allowing Ryan and Dylan to have a tent to themselves. Their days were spent kayaking on the lake, making s'mores, and reading stories by the campfire. It was by that campfire, on Dylan's birthday, that Leo climbed onto his lap and handed him his birthday card. He'd gasped when he opened the card and found adoption papers inside. His gaze flew to Ryan, who was down on one knee holding out a ring. Somehow Dylan had managed to stop bawling long enough to say yes to both of them.

The reality of life with Ryan was better than any romance he'd read. Of course, it wasn't perfect. Perfect was boring and didn't allow for shower sex after they'd gotten into a paint fight putting fresh color on the walls of their bedroom. Perfect didn't allow for those times when either of them felt vulnerable and needed their partner to listen without judgment and offer support.

Ryan sighed contentedly when Dylan wrapped his arms around his waist as they swayed to the rhythm of the waves. It was a sound he'd never grow tired of hearing. In Ryan's arms, he'd found a best friend, a confidant, a partner, and a lover. Dylan had found his home. His perfectly imperfect match.

Continue Reading for an Excerpt from
Port in a Storm,
Book 9 in the Sinners Series,
by Rhys Ford!

ONE

THE KID'S eyes were the color of fiery anguish poured into crystal blue waters, a shimmering shift of pain and fear clouded by tears and thick lashes stuck together by grime. Standing in the middle of a cloud of dissipating tear gas, he—maybe she—shook when Lt. Connor Morgan's light beam swept through the trash-filled room.

Not something Connor expected when he strapped his body armor on that afternoon. Sure as hell not where he ever thought his life would lead him to… standing in front of a frightened little kid who smelled of piss and fear.

Back at the station the raid scoped out like any other—breaking down doors and rousting whoever they found in the hopes of finding someone to connect the SFPD to a well-known and even more well-hidden drug dealer. On paper everything looked routine, but Connor and his team had rapped open enough doors to know the job was never routine, and this one was no exception.

This one sure as hell kicked them all in the balls.

The house wasn't much to talk about from the curb, unless of course it was one of the neighbors who bemoaned the abandoned rusting car parked in the weeds growing up through missing fenders and floorboards or complained to the city about the overturned trash bins spilling out used syringes and rotting food onto the broken cement driveway. At one point, the tiny cottage had boasted a bright blue coat of paint and cream gingerbread trim, but that was before time, neglect, and harsh weather had a chance to pick away at its frame. Half of its roof was missing shingles, leaving black tar paper flapping about when the wind picked up, and its few screens hung off-kilter on mostly broken windows.

Even with his face mask in place, Connor smelled the rot and mold as soon as they hit the porch, his team ducking down to avoid catching their equipment on the sagging overhang above their heads. A battering ram made quick work of a frail front door, the blasting boom of the leads coordinated with the second team's breach of the back entrance.

They'd gone in quietly, as swiftly as shadows moving across a grassy lawn on a hot midsummer day. Briefed on their target, each team member had memorized the sneering face they'd been presented with, but there were other unknowns to consider, especially since the house was a known buy-and-use spot. Bullets weren't the only thing they had to worry about—a stray needle prick brought its own horrific troubles, and every cop going through the doors that evening was well aware of the consequences of one wrong step. Steel or lead could bring them down, either quickly or slowly, but death was a grim certainty if something got through their heavy combat boots and body armor.

That wasn't the way Connor wanted to go out. And it sure as hell wasn't going to be how he'd ever lose a team member. He'd told his squad time and time again that retiring out was the only acceptable way to hang up their SWAT designation, yet at every briefing, he studied his team's faces, knowing it could very well be the last time.

Every time Connor went through the door, he reminded his team to stay safe. Everyone had people waiting for them to come home, and he was no exception. He saw the worry in Forest's soulful eyes every time they kissed each other before Connor left for work. The same look his mother often had when his father and any of her children who also wore an SFPD star walked out of the front door. There was always a slight chance the next cop on the stoop would be wearing a dress uniform, hat in hand and words of deep sympathy on their tongues. He never wanted to wear another piece of black tape on his star ever again, and he sure as hell didn't want one worn for him.

He'd gone in hot, weapon raised and leading the charge with a couple of other senior cops, ducking around the ram to burst into the cramped front hall. A rolling canister of gas hit the stained carpet clumped up over the living room floor, and from there, they began their assault.

"Left cleared!"

The rattle of thin floorboards being hammered by heavy boots partially muted the screaming coming from somewhere in the back of the house. Smoke from shield grenades shifted the air from dank to milky, the swirling ghostly fronds grabbing at the illumination spots on the ends of the team's weapons. Connor's team cut through the choking gases, their faces obscured by masks and goggles, but he knew them well enough to ID who moved around him, skulking through the decrepit, abandoned house to clear the way for the retention team that followed them in.

Broken furniture and rusted appliances gathered at the edges of the main room, much like seafoam and flotsam brought in by an erratic tide.

Several stained mattresses lay on the floor, cheap fleece throws bunched up between them. The acrid scent of cooking drugs was probably being drowned out by the tear gas they'd used after breaching the front door, but Connor could only smell the faint metallic tang of the filtered air he was pulling into his lungs. A bout of coughing alerted them to their first suspect—a skinny, scab-encrusted young man with wild eyes. Hansen grabbed him before he could bolt, the junior member of the team working the protesting teen's hands into a pair of crisscrossed zip ties to immobilize him.

"Leave him for the perimeter guys," Connor ordered. "Let's get the house clear."

It was a textbook takedown, scattering the squatters in the front of the house like cockroaches under a bright light. Connor's team followed the screaming as they hunted through the shadows for any of the faces they'd been briefed on. At first glance, the dilapidated property's cramped rooms didn't look large enough to hold more than five people at a time, but every single SWAT member knew appearances could be deceiving. There were bolt holes in the walls, drywall barriers set up along spaces that should have been hallways. The blueprints they'd studied before going in were wildly inaccurate—giant holes punched through old plaster in some places and a tangle of barbed wire and steel plates blocking what should have been open doorways.

Connor slowed his team down, pulling back slightly in order to give everyone time to adjust to the reconfigured layout. On his right side, Yamamoto gave the all-clear to enter through the door ahead of them, throwing up a hand signal and motioning the backup team forward. To Connor's left was a gaping maw where a wall should have been, and he covered the opening as the two-man crew hustled past. Someone shouted—probably Yamamoto—and another gas canister rolled down the hallway, obscuring progress of the advancing teams.

Even as hastily put together as the operation was, they knew who they were looking for. The DA and their captain kept their division hot on the trail of a drug dealer named Robinson, and a few hours ago, someone's informant gave good intel about the slippery criminal's intentions of shaking loose the squatters so he could use the property to cook up meth to supply his pipeline. Concentrating on breaking his supply chain, Connor and the other SWAT leaders coordinated their strikes, pulling in as many resources as they could to support the multipronged offensive. It'd been a long month, and this was his team's third pop-up raid in two weeks, with little time between them to plan.

The aggressive tactics orchestrated by the district attorney and the San Francisco Police Department appeared to be working, because Robinson seemed to be scrambling, working his way outward to locations far beyond his normal stomping grounds and into territories already held by other crime factions. It seemed lately the best way for someone to get rid of their competitor was simply a phone call to the cops, choosing to let the SFPD take them out rather than enter into a bloody war.

Whoever it was that dropped that dime would have his own reckoning sometime soon, but for today, he was safe in the shadows. As Yamamoto often said, they had bigger roaches to pin down.

"Morgan, I've got a runner in the back," a voice Connor recognized as another SWAT team leader rumbled through his earpiece. "Might be Robinson. My team's going to follow for backup."

"Typical Grady, always hogging the spotlight," Yamamoto teased over the mic. "Alpha C, continue to sweep."

"Watch your backs," Connor warned his team members over the line. "We don't know who Robinson brought with him and what they're carrying. Yama, cover me. I'm going to take the first room."

"Got your back." Yamamoto stepped in tight against the opening. Putting his weapon up and his back against the wall, the cop nodded at Connor. "On your go."

Turning toward the small bedroom visible only through the hole in the wall, Connor pulled up as soon as he spotted the kid.

Those damned eyes held him, trapping Con in midstep. Shocked wide but filled with pain and resignation, the child couldn't have been much more than five, but it was as hard to tell as trying to figure out its gender. Scrawny to the point of bony, he trembled when Connor ducked his head down to enter the room. Keeping the kid in view as he swept the room wasn't hard. The area was little more than a closet, walled off from the rest of a larger space by a few braced drywall sheets and heavy dinged-up bookcases.

None of them ever expected to find a kid, but no one was surprised either. Or at least Con wasn't. Not now. Not after finding so many tiny bodies nested in the filth shored up around society's edges. And here the boy was. Or at least, up close, the kid looked more like a boy. Only time would tell.

"Morgan—" Yamamoto's shout was cut off, staggered bits of sound sliced in between rapid pops of gunfire.

Something hot and hard struck Connor's shoulder, pushing him farther into the room. The kid peeled his mouth open, chipped front teeth cutting at his upper lip when he let loose a terrified yowl. Like Yamamoto's warning, the shrill fear-driven siren murmured beneath the louder screams of a hail of smoking bullets tearing into the hall's walls, and Connor leaped forward, hooked one arm around the boy's skinny torso, and pulled him down.

The bite of fear grabbed at Connor's throat, and he tamped away the flickering embers before they could catch hold. Facedown in a scatter of debris, he held the boy against him, chin to his chest, hoping his SWAT armor would be enough to stop anything from piercing the kid's body. The punch of bullets through the wall stretched out, elongating seconds, and Con sucked in some air, tasting the filth of the room even through his mask.

It wasn't until he moved his head to the right that he saw the dead woman lying half hidden under a pile of grimy blankets, her white, glazed eyes fixedly staring at some point in the universe only she could see, her slack lips speckled with blood and dried fly shit. Long knotted chunks of hair obscured a good part of her face, bits of blue dye faded to a dull aquamarine at the ends. Buried beneath the trash, he hadn't seen her when he'd come into the room, but lying on the ground, protecting the kid from gunfire gave Connor a very clear view of where she'd taken her last breath.

It was hard to tell how long she'd been dead. Her flesh stretched tight across her cheekbones and pointy chin, but the smeared mascara around her dulled dun-colored eyes could have hidden a number of sins and years. Her face, savaged by addiction and split-open sores, was as gray as the thin mattress she lay on. Her left hand poked out from under a crumpled blue tarp that covered the rest of her body. She'd been caught in the throes of a seizure, or maybe she'd been reaching for something or even someone, like the kid, but death grabbed her before she could grasp what she wanted. Her broken nails were as filthy as the boy's face, and her skeletal fingers were clenched at the empty air, cheap silver rings rattling around her bony knuckles.

Another booming blast shook the house.

"Keep your head down, kid," Connor growled when the boy began to squirm. If anything, the fray and shouting in the rest of the house seemed to intensify. "Yama, give me a status."

"Pinned down at the end of the hall, sir," the man's voice crackled over the headset. "You okay? Who ya' talking to?"

"Got a little boy—I think—here. Anywhere clear to get him out?" Pain flared in Connor's shoulder when he moved. The child's weight pulled down on his muscles, straining the tender spots blooming on his back. He'd either landed in something wet or the hits he'd taken were more serious than he thought.

"Negative, but I can give you cover," Yamamoto said over the comm. "Working back down the hall. Can you hold?"

"Holding." Connor wrapped his arms around the boy's torso, trying to cover as much as possible. "Get your arms down, kiddo, and grab anything you can on my vest."

The child was rigid, legs stick straight and stiff. His tiny hands were dotted with bruises and dried blood, his knuckles bleached white when his fingers tightened around the straps on Connor's armor. He buried his face into Connor's chest, breathing hard and heavy when another round of gunfire opened up in the hall.

A pair of large dark shadows fell across the opening in the wall, and then Yamamoto angled his back against one side of the broken drywall. He gave Connor a hand signal, then counted down from three to a closed fist and began a heavy barrage of sprayed shots. Gun drawn, Connor ducked out to the right, keeping the boy against his chest. He moved quickly, pausing at openings and long stretches of the hallway, alert to any movement.

When his boots hit the living room floor, Yamamoto gave the all-clear to move the fight to the back of the house again, leaving Connor with an easier egress. The young man they'd left for the other team was gone, hopefully safe and sound away from the raid. The pain along Connor's shoulders was turning from a dull throb to a raging fire, and as he tried to clear the mound of debris, he stumbled and caught the tip of his boot on something hard. The kid let out a short yelp of terror when Connor's grasp loosened. Then he sobbed brokenly as Connor tightened his grip.

"I'm not going to drop you," he reassured the little boy. "I've got you. You're safe."

The front door seemed miles away, the small house telescoping outward with each report of gunfire. Keeping down, Connor shouted his egress to the team members waiting outside. The canister smoke thickened as he ran, making the little boy cough with each breath. He burst through the off-kilter screen door, breaking the hinges with the force of his shoulder against the wobbly metal frame. The air outside wasn't any clearer, but Connor shoved his gun into its holster then removed his mask while he ran toward the SWAT vehicles parked along the opposite curb. Pressing the plastic cup over the boy's face, he picked up speed, trying to get them clear of the house and the raging gunfight.

Promises weighed heavy on Connor's shoulders—promises to come home, promises he'd keep someone safe. He felt every word he'd turned into a vow piercing his soul with each pounding stride he took and the boy's scared, rigid body trembling against his chest.

The comm chatter was a distraction, giving Connor a good idea of what was behind him. Children out first. That was how they operated, what the team swore to do on each raid. Another promise he'd made, despite the fear he was leaving his people behind to die. Yamamoto was good. Hell, the other team was nearly as good as his own. He should have had nothing to worry about, but dread crept in, wiggling past his defenses and eating away at the idea that everyone who answered to him would walk out of that door on their own.

The strobing blue-and-red lights flashed over the rain-damp asphalt, and a pair of medics broke from their cover behind a line of armored trucks and angled cop cars. Connor recognized one of them—an older woman named Darcy who'd done more than her fair share of stitching his team up after a brutal raid. This time her attention was focused on the little boy he held close, her hands automatically reaching for Connor's charge.

As soon as she touched him, the boy screamed, a piercing cry sharp enough to cut past the racket of the raid. His fear punched into Connor's guts, flashing memories of the squalor Connor had found the boy in and the dead woman lying on the floor. Their shuffle to safety was a clumsy affair, dodging cop cars to reach the relative cover of the thicker-walled transports. Uniformed officers covered them, weapons trained on the ramshackle house.

"Shit, tell him to let go." The female paramedic swore. "Is he hurt?"

"I don't think so. Kid, she's here to take care of you," Connor said, moving forward to herd them all to cover. The other paramedic hustled beside them, trying to dislodge the boy from the other side. "I've got to get back in there. My team—"

"Morgan, we're clear," Yamamoto's voice echoed in Connor's headset. "Moving to the back of the house now. Team is all good. We've got this."

"And you're bleeding, Morgan," Darcy cut him off, holding her hand up so he could see the blood smeared over her palm. "Shut up and let me do my job. You die on me and I'll end up shoveling horse shit out of the cop stables for the rest of my life."

"Not going to die on you," he growled back. "Just probably a crease or something. Happens sometimes. Him first. Then we worry about me."

As soon as they got behind the SWAT vehicles, Connor was surrounded by people, some trying to dislodge the boy while Darcy attempted to undo his vest. She pushed at him to sit down on a lowered gurney and his world tilted slightly, his stomach grumbling at the vertigo hitting him square between the eyes. The boy's screams grew louder, more frantic, and Connor closed his arms over the child, rocking slightly despite the nerve-churning dizziness clawing at the back of his head.

"Hey, give him some time, okay," Connor ordered, cutting through everyone's chatter. He was beginning to feel the spots of pain along his back and arm as adrenaline bled out of his system. The blood on Darcy's hand hadn't been a lot, but something had gotten through somewhere, and he needed triage. "See if we can't get my vest off, and then we can work on getting him calmed down. He's scared. He just needs a little more time to feel safe before he can let go."

"He's going to have to let go of you at some point, Morgan," Darcy shot back. "Because no matter what he wants, you can't carry him forever. CPS is on their way, and then he'll be their problem."

SCAN THE QR CODE
BELOW TO ORDER!

ELIANA WEST, the recipient of the 2022 Nancy Pearl Award for genre fiction, is committed to embracing diversity in her writing. That means she doesn't limit herself to a single genre. Instead, Eliana welcomes every story that comes her way with open arms. She aims to create characters that reflect the diversity of her community, with a range of social backgrounds, ethnicities, genders, and sexual orientations. Eliana loves to weave in historical elements whenever she can and fearlessly engage in challenging dialogues. Eliana believes everyone deserves a happy ending.

From small towns to close-knit communities, Eliana loves stories that bring people from different backgrounds together through the common language of unconditional love and acceptance. Eliana is a passionate advocate for diversity within the writing community. She is the founder of Writers for Diversity and teaches classes and workshops, encouraging writers to create diverse characters and worlds with an empathetic approach.

When Eliana isn't plotting her characters' happy endings, she can be found embarking on adventures with her husband, traversing winding country roads in their beloved vintage Volkswagen Westfalia, affectionately named Bianca. Weather it's traveling abroad or exploring locally, Eliana and her husband are always willing to get lost and see where the adventure takes them

Eliana loves connecting with readers through her website: www.elianawest.com

Follow me on BookBub

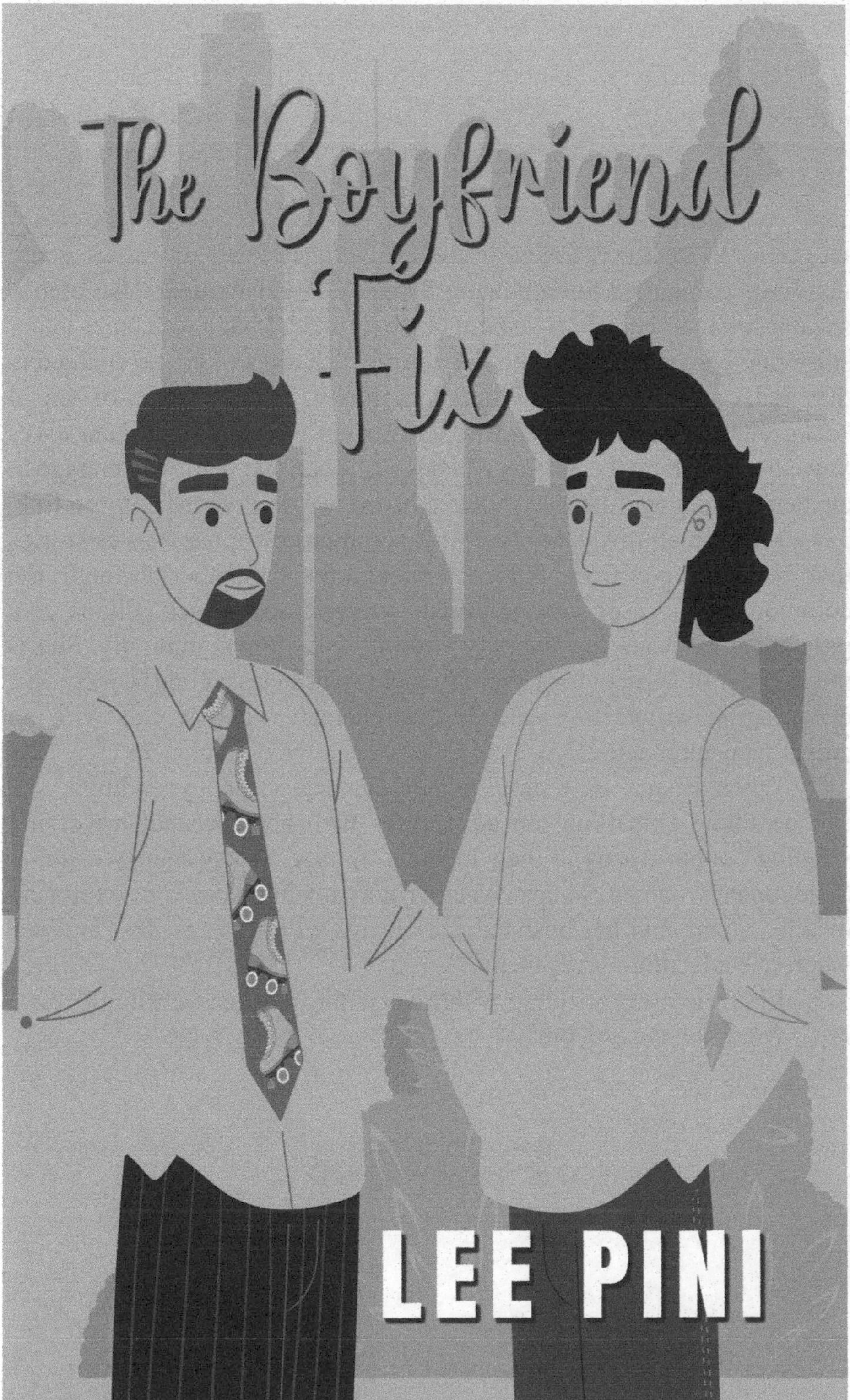
The Boyfriend Fix
LEE PINI

Renowned surgeon Ben McNatt is up for the job of his dreams, and when he gets it, he'll be the youngest chief of neurosurgery in his hospital's history. His success rate is flawless, but his perceived lack of compassion is hurting his chances. He's always viewed relationships as a distraction, but a loving partner might change his colleagues' ideas about his heartlessness. He'll do whatever it takes for this promotion—even pretend to date. The natural choice for his fake boyfriend is the cute guy at the coffee shop.

Jamie Anderson is in student loan debt up to his eyeballs. He has three roommates, and not in a quirky found-family way. He works sixty hours a week as a barista, and his boss won't stop hitting on him. He's even given up on love. He makes do with fantasies about the hot doctor that comes in for coffee every day like clockwork.

A fake relationship might solve Jamie's handsy boss problem too. And there's no way it will lead to real feelings when that's the last thing either of them wants.

So why are they having so much trouble convincing themselves they aren't falling for each other?

Scan the QR Code
Below to Order!

Bridging Hope

Raising kids and finding love is impossible, isn't it?

GREYSON McCOY

When workaholic Pierce Simms's sister passes, he suddenly finds himself unemployed, back in the hometown he fled, and raising his niece and nephew. Despite that, he's confident he has things under control—at least until his sister's high-school sweetheart shows up.

With his teaching grant ended, Dalton O'Dell is at loose ends and tight purse strings. Just as the world crashes down on him, he learns his ex-girlfriend has passed and named him guardian of her two young children. Chaos ensues when he and her brother, Pierce, are forced together to raise the toddlers in Pierce's family farmhouse.

Nestled in the enchanting beauty of the farm, Pierce and Dalton bond over the challenges of co-parenting and their shared grief as unexpected love blossoms. Love might not be enough, however, if they can't learn to bridge the gap between their different worlds and overcome the trauma of their pasts.

SCAN THE QR CODE
BELOW TO ORDER!

In a last-ditch effort to finish a manuscript, Thomas Kovacs packs up his teenage daughter, Alexis, and relocates to a small town in northern England. Things have been strained between them for months, but the closer Thomas gets to the end of his book, the more distant Alexis becomes.

Krishna Singh came to Corbridge to open a bookstore and start a family. After two years, his business is thriving. His family? Well, he hasn't gotten around to that yet. Actually, he hasn't even dated. The closest he gets is bonding over books and music with an American teenager who comes into his shop.

When it turns out the teenager's dad is none other than Krishna's favorite author, he wastes no time in getting to know Thomas. But attempts at something more go about as well as Thomas's writing, or his relationship with Alexis. Can Krishna convince Thomas that they all deserve a happy-ever-after?

SCAN THE QR CODE BELOW TO ORDER!

Treading Water

WHAT HAPPENS WHEN LOVE IS SINK OR SWIM?

ALEX WINTERS

Actor Tucker Crawford is having the worst summer ever. Thanks to a viral video of him trying to swim, he's the laughingstock of Hollywood and his role in a hit TV series is in jeopardy. The only bright spot is Tucker's sexy new swim coach, Reed Oliver, but even that has its problems—because Tucker is deep in the closet and has never been with a guy.

Reed Oliver is having the best summer ever. He's just scored a high-paying freelance gig teaching a Hollywood actor how to swim. The two of them have the run of a deserted summer camp, complete with an Olympic-size swimming pool. But when cocky playboy Reed meets shy, virgin Tucker, sparks fly and Reed's walk-in-the-park coaching job becomes a minefield of temptation. Once they kiss for the first time, there's no way to overcome their mutual passion and no looking back. But after two weeks of secluded intimacy, can they keep their romance alive in the real world?

SCAN THE QR CODE
BELOW TO ORDER!

DESTINED

JAMIE FESSENDEN

When Jay and Wallace first meet at an LGBTQ group, they have no idea they'll be dating six years later. In fact, they quickly forget each other's names. But although fate continues to throw them together, the timing is never quite right. Finally they're both single and realize they want to be together… but now they can't find each other!

With determination and the help of mutual friends, Jay and Wallace can finally pursue the relationship they've both wanted for so long. It's only the beginning of the battles they'll face to build a life together. From disapproving family members all the way to the state legislature, Jay and Wallace's road to happily ever after is littered with obstacles. But they've come too far to give up the fight.

SCAN THE QR CODE
BELOW TO ORDER!